rs

The World's Most Evil Gangsters

James Banting

Magpie, London

Constable & Robinson Ltd
3 The Lanchesters
162 Fulham Palace Road
London W6 9ER

This edition published by Magpie Books,
an imprint of Constable & Robinson Ltd 2006
www.constablerobinson.com

A copy of the British Library Cataloguing in Publication Data
is available from the British Library.

ISBN-10: 1-84529-457-2
ISBN-13: 978-1-84529-457-1

Printed and bound in the European Union

3 5 7 9 10 8 6 4 2

Contents

Introduction

It is perhaps easy to visualize gangsters or organized criminal gangs in a somehow romantic or glamorous light. For years, feature films have successfully idolized their lawless lives and activities, songs have been sung about their exploits and long-running television series have tracked often highly mysterious goings-on. The felonious reality, however, is somewhat different. Any look at the most evil gangsters in the world must start by looking at who or what fits that description or definition – what is a gangster? Gangs setting out to break the law by robbing, injuring and/or killing have been around for centuries but we tend to associate the rise of gangsters with the 1920s in America, when the term came into widespread public use. For the first time, organized gangs with the aid of motor vehicles had great mobility – this allowed them not only to escape a crime scene but also regularly to meet fellow conspirators, plan bigger jobs and vastly increase the scale of their operations. While this would not have been the aim that drove inventors and engineers to mass-produce cars, it was certainly one unwanted consequence. Modern weapons, telephones and general prosperity all came together to provide gangsters with the means to develop on a previously unseen scale. The forces of law and order were being challenged to an unprecedented degree with mobs effectively ruling many towns, cities and businesses and controlling the supply of key goods. Vast areas of America's major cities became 'no go' areas for the police and for anyone else who valued his or her life, and certain business deals could only be carried out by making payments to hugely powerful gangs.

A dictionary defines a gangster as 'a member of an organized gang of criminals'. Although a reasonable starting point, this definition is really just the tip of the iceberg and doesn't do full justice to organized criminals. Gangsters are truly professional – crime is their occupation – and they set out to increase their power base and wealth from an often vast array of illegal methods, no matter who or how many people get in their way. The Serious Organized Crime Agency (SOCA) of the National Criminal Intelligence Service (NCIS) in the United Kingdom defines an organized crime group as one which satisfies all of the following criteria: it must contain at least three people; its criminal activity must be prolonged or of indefinite duration; its members are motivated by profit or power; the group is responsible for serious criminal offences.

The NCIS believe this definition is consistent with the characteristics used by the Home Office in the United Kingdom, the European Union, the FBI and by other agencies elsewhere in the world. It does add some interesting new elements to the definition of a gangster, such as longevity, thereby excluding one-off capers, and incidents which are not serious offences. This is as much to do with the policing of gangsters as to the specific nature of acts carried out. The true origins of 'gangsterism' date back to Roman and Greek times, when pirates would gather in large groups to pillage prosperous cities and corruption was rife in many places. The slave trade was a highly sophisticated, international network which transformed whole continents and set a new benchmark in organized crime. It was not wholly different from present-day human trafficking or, for that matter, some present-day drug-related activities. As many of these immoral and clandestine deeds were carried out centuries ago, information on gang members, their networks and activities, and even their exact whereabouts can be sketchy and not always completely verifiable. This is also true of many modern gangsters and criminals as well. Gangsters exist in a dark underworld and it is impossible to know at times exactly when or where criminal activity begins and ends or who is ultimately responsible for what. Often the true nature of many gangster activities will never be fully known or understood as these are carried out, for obvious reasons, beneath a cloak of obscurity. It is possible to piece together certain facts, analyze events that have taken place and search for clues as to the motivations which drive some of the most notorious and lawless people ever to form or join a gang and start a life of crime.

We know that the various activities of gangsters and individual gang members are affected by many things but most are influenced to a large extent by their surroundings, in particular the demand for certain goods and services. Many of the recent, high-profile American gangs deal in the supply of drugs and prostitutes, both of which are in huge demand in the major cities of the USA. Many Far Eastern organizations are involved in extortion and human trafficking. The Russian Mafia can count arms dealing as a primary source of revenue and uses bribery to influence people in positions of power. The scope of activities and the ambitions of gangsters have also changed – some operate within small patches or areas but many seek to operate on a truly international scale with networks of interrelated organizations and covert enterprises running twenty-four hours a day, three hundred and sixty-five days of the year. Some gangs have formed relatively recently while others have a long history – the American Mafia can trace its roots back to Sicily and is, of course, now far larger and more powerful in the USA than in its original homeland. There are many stories and anecdotes about how the Mafia got its name. One of these is that the word Mafia is derived from a similar Arabic word meaning 'place of refuge'. Another dates back to the thirteenth century when Sicily was occupied by French forces and the story goes that a young Italian girl was being raped by a French soldier and her mother ran down the street shouting '*Ma fia! Ma fia!*' ('My daughter! My daughter!') The incident supposedly served to incite the people to rise up in a rebellion which expelled the French from Sicily.

In an examination of organized, gang-related crime, we should exclude certain areas of unlawful and villainous activity. The term gangster should not include groups who are fighting a religious or political war, freedom fighters, self-proclaimed anarchists or terrorists. Although many such bands often use similar methods to achieve their goals, their motivations are very different. History has shown us that violent, organized criminals can come from many different social backgrounds. Although it is true that periods of extreme poverty and areas of significant social deprivation have helped to produce more than their fair share of crooks and gangs over the years, gangsters come from every class and background, and both men and women are represented as well as just about every creed and colour. Many are lured by the enormous perceived rewards of success, but the penalties for failure are often harsh and uncompromising. The Great Depression in America spawned the beginnings of organized crime rings on a new scale in virtually every major city across the USA and put the term 'gangster' on the front page of every newspaper in every country in the world. Prohibition, which outlawed alcohol, was arguably the single most significant factor in fuelling criminal gangs. It drove rival groups to work together and acted as a spur to different ethnic organizations to collaborate in order to reap the immense rewards associated with the manufacture, distribution and sale of illegal alcohol.

As well as the supply of alcohol, often referred to at the time as 'bootlegging', large gangs were coming together to benefit from other illegal activities such as gambling, prostitution and abortion. Once a sizeable gang or network came together, often to take advantage of the demand for booze, they found themselves exploring other avenues of criminal activity –

another curious result of legislation which was trying to curb illegal social behaviour. While individual criminals operated independently of the increasing number of powerful groups, they did rely on them for the tools of their trade – firearms, bullet-proof vests, armoured cars and the like. Protection money and informal arrangements on which patch to operate were agreed so that everyone could get a slice of the pie. However, with the end of prohibition in America and the tightening of law and order came a new phase for the gangster. Violent fighting and feuds between rival gangs, which still capture headlines today, became a real issue not just for certain key individuals but for everyone who was openly part of any of the major groups. Many of these rows were extremely violent, as gangs struggled to gain control of illegal activities and the provision of illegitimate services in the rapidly growing American cities. No single event typified this era more than events which took place in a small garage on the northern side of Chicago on 14 February, 1929. A number of unknown men wearing police uniforms lined up seven members of a rival gang, opened fire and shot them all in cold blood. This well-planned and effectively executed hit made headlines all round the world and shocked America. The St Valentine's Day Massacre, as it came to be known, was the beginning of a new era. America was streets ahead of the rest of the world in the size and impact of its gangs.

Organized crime would never be the same again, either in America or in the rest of the world. Gang bosses had to invest in protection for themselves, spend time developing a greater level of operational organization and use all the tricks at their disposal to fight for control. This often included collaborating with and bribing police officers, politicians, newspaper owners and other influential people. The tentacles of organized crime reached further into the heart of society than ever before. Gangs with highly organized structures were certainly nothing new – the Italian crime mobs had been past masters for years – but the scale was now something different. The crime scene in America was greatly affected towards the end of the nineteenth century by a wave of Italian and, in particular, Sicilian immigrants which swept across the Atlantic in search of a new life. Many were honest and hard-working men and women, but included in this wave of immigration were some who were less desirable and from the beginning anti-immigration feeling ran high. This reached a crescendo when in January 1897, the US Congress passed a bill aimed at immigrant Italian families, prohibiting the entry of illiterates into America. It is difficult to know whether some of the senators on Capitol Hill knew that members of the Mafia had already made the long sea voyage from the warm Mediterranean waters but as feelings towards Italians hardened, there was a noticeable closing of the ranks. Decades before the Mafia was deemed to be operating in America, it was known that certain significant members had arrived, pushed by the regular purges of the Italian authorities and pulled by the scale of opportunities that lay across the ocean.

By the 1920s, the Mafia organization within America was in full swing, although it was far from being a single organization or one with any form of centralized control at that time. There was some communication between East and West Coast gangs, but even the large crime families in the same cities often operated very separate enterprises. Competition broke out at times but generally different elements worked their own patches and they were happy to let others do the same. However, fearing the end of Prohibition, Mafia leaders called a landmark meeting in May 1929. The location was Atlantic City, New Jersey, and what came out of the three-day conference was an agreement that there would be greater co-operation between families, a decision to diversify their activities within racketeering and to develop legitimate businesses which could be used as fronts. This vision proved hugely successful and the power of the Mafia grew exponentially in the following years into a body that would be feared by law enforcement agencies, politicians and ordinary citizens. From the times of the earliest Sicilian settlers, many Mafia groups had made money from illegal gambling. Often this was simply getting barber shops or convenience stores to sell lottery-type tickets (known as 'running numbers') at affordable prices. There was obviously no process for validating these tickets and they continued to spread across urban areas throughout America. With little in the way of overheads, running costs or tax, for that matter, the cash generated was substantial. Many gangsters used their ill-gotten gains to buy smart suits, fast cars and big houses and generally live the high life. This made many leading figures, notably Al Capone, and their antics highly newsworthy – where they ate and so on became headline stories. Other gangsters around the world were beginning to follow this lead, especially in London where organized crime was beginning to flourish.

Crime on a large and international scale was nothing new in Great Britain. Smuggling, piracy and arguably many of the activities of colonialism helped promote criminal enterprises and networks. At the turn of the twentieth century, however, a mix of foreigners and home-grown gangsters ran lucrative prostitution rings, protection rackets in London's West End, illegal gambling and drug-trafficking rings. Drugs are certainly not just a modern-day phenomenon – the drug trade between London and other European cities, especially Amsterdam, Paris and Berlin, was rife in the 1920s and 1930s. However, compared to the gains to be had from other areas of criminal activity, drugs were certainly second best. The same routes pioneered by the drug-runners provided potential openings for other goods and services. Precious stones, especially pearls from Spain, gold from South Africa and human cargo from Eastern Europe were beginning to flow through the same illegal channels. The first of the British gangs at this time to have any significant international connections were the Sabini brothers, who had a reputation for hiring overseas henchmen to do their dirty work. They carried out a number of armed robberies, bought and sold illegal goods from around the world and controlled a sizeable slice of London's club protection business. They were still small-scale hoodlums compared with the Mafia gangs of New York, Chicago and the other large American cities but with enviable opportunites for expansion.

Broadly speaking, gangsters can be grouped in two main categories: the first being those who operate in a clearly defined territory, usually know as their 'turf'; the second group are those whose illegal activities stretch further afield, often straddling national borders or even different continents. Often the local gangs have been smaller, less well funded and have restricted themselves to a limited number of specialist activities. The international gangs, on the other hand, have built networks and partnerships right across the globe. The demand for many of their products and services remains remarkably consistent in many developed countries – drugs and prostitution being the best examples. Once a pipeline and trusted alliances have been formed, the door opens to increased diversity and scale of operations. Usually trade is in US dollars, a currency very close to the hearts of gangsters and other lawbreakers. In the fight against organized crime, governments and their police forces have had to look outside their usual jurisdiction or patch to make real inroads into the larger criminal operations. One of the first major steps forward in America occurred in 1908 when the US Attorney General Charles J. Bonaparte met with President Theodore Roosevelt. The two men discussed the need for a federal investigative service, a highly controversial move at the time and one which cut across many of the traditional methods of law enforcement at that time. This meeting led to the birth of the Federal Bureau of Investigation (FBI). Roosevelt personified 'progressivism' in all things and convinced the people of America that a force of well-disciplined, highly trained experts was needed to fight crime on a national level. Both Attorney General Bonaparte and President Roosevelt completed their terms in office in March 1909, recommending that the force of thirty-four Special Agents become a permanent fixture within the Justice Department. Bonaparte's successor, George Wickersham, named the force the Bureau of Investigation later that year.

The FBI has a global remit but its direction is usually driven by events originating within the USA or actions believed likely to affect the American people. Interpol, on the other hand, has a very different remit. It was created in 1923 and is the world's largest international police organization with 184 member countries. It runs a global police communications system called I-24/7, which provides a platform for sharing information about criminals and criminal activity on a truly international scale. Its database has detailed records on most international gangs and those who operate in crime networks. It holds fingerprints, DNA profiles, tracking data and an evaluation of what these criminals are up to. Although this body sounds like the sort of organization required, the reality is that it is only as good as the information it gets from individual territories plus the extent to which timely communication can be of assistance in preventing crimes or bringing people to justice. Many feel that the international gangsters seem to be able to keep one step ahead of Interpol and that a radical revamp is required to make real inroads in today's major crime areas. The problems associated with the movement, supply and use of drugs continue to grow in most parts of the world and represent one of the main focal points of virtually every law enforcement agency in the world. The global drug problem is greater than the remit of any individual law enforcement agency, so great efforts are made by the various forces to collaborate effectively. There are a number of reasons why drugs have become public enemy number one, but the emergence of a more affluent class of drug user with a higher income to spend on so-called 'recreational' drugs is high on the list. The immoral chain that drives the drug trade – involving growers, producers, couriers, suppliers, dealers and users – has benefited from the meteoric rise in demand for all types of controlled substances. A growing proportion of organized criminal activity is now firmly established on the international stage, something which is proving much harder to restrict and police.

How one defines the most evil gangs or tries to compare different forms of immoral behaviour is always going to be highly subjective. Evaluating criminals who have lived a hundred years apart also brings its own issues and complications, although the desire to carry out harmful, destructive and often brutal acts has remained constant. Gangsters have developed in just about every major country and territory on earth, suggesting that no one nationality has a monopoly on gangsterism. On the other hand, although there may be greater similarities in how contemporary gangsters go about their work due to improved communication and co-operation, nevertheless, there remain significant differences in the way that organized criminal gangs go about their business in different parts of the world. Gangsters believe that they can operate above the law, whether they are acting locally, nationally or on the international stage they think that they can stay one step ahead of bumbling police officials. Al Capone, probably the world's best-known gangster, once famously stated, 'The income tax law is a lot of bunk. The government can't collect legal taxes from illegal money.' This statement, like many others made by Capone, inflated his already significant public persona – however, it is also, perhaps, a comment that he wished he had not made. Many of Capone's activities were followed with avid interest by the public, but the exploits of Bonnie and Clyde captured the attention of the whole nation like nothing before or even, perhaps, since. Bonnie and Clyde's tale had an added dimension compared with other gangster stories – theirs was also a remarkable love affair, although a very unlikely one.

Clyde Barrow and Bonnie Parker met in January 1930 in a quiet Texas backwater. The people who knew Bonnie said she was a quiet nineteen-year-old at the time and was already married when she met her true love. Clyde was twenty-one. Soon after, he was arrested and sent to jail for burglary but managed to escape with the aid of Bonnie. However, he was recaptured and send back to prison, before being paroled in 1932. When the two lovers were reunited, an amazingly violent crime spree began which included murder, bank robbery, kidnapping, abduction and burglary of numerous small stores and other targets in states across America's Midwest and beyond. In 1932 Bonnie and Clyde started travelling with Raymond Hamilton, a notorious gunman. It has never been known exactly what went on but the three did not get along and Raymond was soon replaced by William Jones later the same year. Clyde's brother, Ivan Barrow, and his wife, Blanche, joined in early 1933 and a gang of five was complete. A series of bold, high-profile robberies hit the headlines and, time and again, the gang escaped capture. In the summer of 1933, Ivan was fatally shot and Blanche was captured by Iowa State Police. Jones succumbed to the same fate four months later. The group had shrunk to just two as the real-life, cult status 'Romeo and Juliet' story continued to rumble from town to town.

Although the Great Depression had a profound effect in every developed economy, not only in America, gangs in different parts of the world nevertheless remained at different stages of development. Few had the same kinds of sophisticated weapons, powerful cars or vaulting ambitions, but even so gang-related violence was on the rise in most parts of the world. China was one such place and the secretive Triad gangs or networks were beginning to increase their grip on parts of the Far East. It is generally thought that the Triads came into being in China as far back as the seventeenth century, making them one of the oldest criminal gangs. The objective for setting up a gang under this banner seems to have been to topple the Man Chi Ch'ing dynasty, a task which took over 200 years (it was finally brought down in 1911). This ferocious band of criminals built a fearsome reputation, all under the cloak of secrecy. Their activities extended to protection, drug smuggling (opium being the primary commodity), prostitution and human trafficking. The Triad name comes from a triangular emblem representing man, earth and heaven. The Triad activities grew in diversity in the 1920s and 1930s along with overall prosperity in the region, but the control of many workers' unions made this enterprise unique in the world of gangsterism. In 1947, the Triad societies reorganized themselves and a national group was formed from the previous fourteen associations. With China turning itself into a Communist state, many of the leading Triads fled to Hong Kong, while managing to retain much of their original strength. They showed themselves to be adaptable and resourceful in the face of challenges from law enforcement and even in response to extreme political change, something that would help them to prosper in the years after the Second World War.

Drug smuggling is often associated with parts of the Far East, although many countries have some local production as well as distribution infrastructure. The history of drug smuggling dates back to at least the eighth century when opium was brought to India by Arab traders and then exported by British traders to China and other parts of the world. Opium has been put to many good uses by humanity – in particular in the field of medicine. An example is the creation of morphine, which had a dramatic positive impact in helping to alleviate suffering in all wars from the 1930s onwards. It is perhaps slightly ironic that the heroin problem spread right across the USA following their involvement in the Vietnam War – a place where the drug was easily available to the troops. Heroin received its name in a very strange way. Alder Wright, a British chemist, working at St Mary's Hospital in Paddington, London, in the 1870s, heated morphine and acetic anhydride with great success. Later marketed by a German company, they called it 'heroish' which means 'having supernatural powers'. It was freely available in chemists and pharmacies for some time before it was banned. Similarly, for many years cocaine was thought not to have addictive properties and was promoted during the 1880s as a drug which could 'make a coward brave and free the victims of alcohol'. This also shows that smooth-talking marketers are not a recent invention either! Few would have foretold at the time the profound impact that drugs such as heroin and cocaine would have on today's societies, and on the gangs around the world who supply the drugs.

A short distance across the East China Sea from China lies a much smaller country but one which has developed a notorious underworld of its own. The Japanese Yakuza is one of the largest and most traditional organized crime groups in the world. In Paul Lunde's book *Organized Crime*, he estimates that there are no less than 2,500 gangs in Japan with between 100,000 and 150,000 members collectively making up the Yakuza.

The name Yakuza derives from the losing number set 8-9-3 (which is spoken as ya-ku-za) of the game oicho-kabu, a form of blackjack; the inference is that Yakuza are outcasts from society. The Yakuza, through its extensive network of members, are very active in gambling, drugs, prostitution, the supply of weapons, money-laundering and extortion. Recently it has also moved into human trafficking as this has become big business in the Far East, and although its power base is certainly in the islands that make up Japan, it has outposts in many other Asian countries, the USA, Canada and parts of Europe. For many years there has been relative stability among the rival factions within the Yakuza network, but in 2001 there was a series of incidents, most notably a shooting at a funeral in Toyko, which started an alarming chain of events. Pretending to be mourners, hitmen Yoshio Murakami and Kazumi Yoshikawa opened fire on the crowd and assassinated Sumiyoshi-kai boss Ikuo Kumagawa and another man, Takshi Endo. The whole assault took place right in front of the police authorities who had surrounded the crematorium anticipating trouble. The two gunmen eventually gave themselves up and admitted that this was a turf war. The two Yakuza groups involved, Sumiyakoshi-kai and Inagawa-kai, made a kind of peace, but individual personal feuds and power struggles persist to this day, resulting in many more casualties.

In 2002, after a series of attacks on Omaeda Ikka targets, a senior member of the organization, Takashi Ishizuka, was shot dead. Many believe the murderers, Masao Tatsuriki and Kumio Arai, were working on the orders of Osamu Yano, the leading figure behind the Yamo Mutsaumi-kai. A reprisal attack less than a year later saw the shooting of three innocent civilians and a single Yakuza member. This was known as the Maebashi Bar Massacre and was carried out by men wearing white face helmets. This incident sent profound shock waves through Japanese society, which had hoped that it had seen the end of daytime shootings and violent attacks of this sort. Although the Yakuza have tremendous influence in Japan and in other Pacific Rim countries, they are unable to exert the same kind of power as the Russian Mafia, the Organizatsiya. These ruthless gangsters own a huge proportion of Russia itself, including banks, businesses and property and are even able to build their own weapons in specialist factories. The leading Russian gangs have spread out since the fall of the Soviet Union and have now established bases in America, Canada, the Middle East and across Europe. They enjoy particularly strong links with the Colombian drug cartels, trading large amounts of weapons of all kinds, usually in exchange for drugs.

When the Soviet Union fell, a series of gangsters were ready and willing to pick up the pieces. Sergei Mikhailov is one of the most powerful mobsters in Russia and the boss of the Solsnetskaya Organization who are reputed to have more than 5,000 members worldwide. This enterprise controls everything from casinos and hotels to car dealerships and brothels, while running an international criminal network able to rival national states in terms of power and influence. One particularly popular location for Russia's leading gangsters was Israel, due to the fact that any Jew may return there even if they are on the run. Some non-Jewish Russians also carry a fake Jewish passport for just this purpose – one of the most famous being Mikhailov himself. In the mid-1990s Mikhailov, in an attempt to make his dealings more respectable, moved himself and his family to Switzerland. According to Swiss court documents, the Russian laundered an estimated $60 billion through Swiss banks alone, living the high life on his castle estate and driving his Rolls-Royce. He was, however, not the sort of person that the socially conscious Swiss wanted to have in their country and was a serious thorn in the side of the authorities. The government were keen to extradite him from Switzerland and Mikhailov was arrested and charged with being the head of a criminal organization, using false documents and breaking local laws. He spent two years in jail waiting for his case to come to court and was eventually acquitted after key evidence from the Russian government was not forthcoming. He was a free man again and able to run his organization exactly as he wished. He even won a court battle to get compensation from the Swiss authorities for holding him without bail.

The meteoric rise in power and influence of the Russian Mafia has been incredible but compared to the Colombian drug cartels they have been in the slow lane. Before the explosion in demand for recreational drugs, Latin America generally, and Colombia specifically, were nowhere to be seen on the league table of international crime. There were, of course, organized criminal activities, but they were on a small scale, parochial and generated only a relatively small amount of cash for the participants, especially when compared to the activities of other crime syndicates around the world at that time. Colombia shares borders with Brazil, Peru, Ecuador, Venezuela and Panama, which has helped to facilitate trade on many fronts – some of it legal, but the most lucrative, highly illegal. Its mountainous terrain provides a perfect environment for clandestine operations and its climate is perfect for growing the raw materials for drugs. Added to which years of political instability meant that Colombia was poised to become a drug superpower. The two largest and most significant cartels to develop were the

Medellín and Cali. The Medellín consisted of four main men but Pablo Escobar Gavira, known was El Padrino, was the most influential. A former car thief and contract killer in the mid-1970s, he saw the opportunity in cocaine production and distribution and set about building a chain from grower to distributor. His timing was good as Chile, which had had a strong lead on them in the drugs business, was going through a major regime change. When Pinochet came to power he deported or jailed many of the leading drug-runners in Chile, many of whom needed vast amounts of cocaine and heroin for their networks supplying North America, Europe and the Far East.

Escobar set up a network of 'mules' who transported cocaine to Panama and from there to other parts of the world. Many were women forced to work for him under fear of death or made to work as prostitutes. His protection rackets, swindles (fake lottery tickets being a favourite) and kid-napping dwindled in the face of the seemingly endless demand for various forms of cocaine. This latter sideline caused Escobar some unwanted attention when, in 1971, he was suspected of holding a leading businessman, Diego Echavarria, to ransom. It was alleged that $50,000 was paid before he was found murdered and the large amount of unwanted publicity helped investigators to track down other aspects of his empire. The Colombian authorities have tried to fight against the cartels and their violent exploits but with rumours of leading politicians being paid by a number of gangs and widespread distrust of the military, it is an uphill struggle. However, after American funding and aid, there were a number of high-profile successes, with some leading figures being put behind bars. The Medellín and Cali cartels and others believed that a show of force was called for and in 1984 a team of hired hitmen assassinated the country's Justice Minister and an estimated 3,000 others, including leading judges, government officials and policemen. Fuelled by the amazing amounts of cash from drug trafficking, the cartels were able to arm and equip themselves to a better standard than even the government, able to import the very latest and most sophisticated technology to assist them. They continued to import outside mercenaries whenever 'work' needed to be done, leaving little evidence that could be pinned on the cartel bosses. More recently, the Colombian government have been helped by cash and personnel from several countries in an effort to make inroads into the power base of the cartels. Towards the end of the 1980s, a new twist appeared. After a massive car bomb exploded in a Medellín suburb, Escobar blamed the Cali cartel bosses for the hit and went on the offensive. He had reason to believe that the Cali cartel was working with the government to erode his position and in the space of just nine months over eighty people had been killed. The cash from drugs created wealth for some well beyond their dreams but was leaving a trail of dead bodies that was proving difficult to keep track of.

Notoriety can be a help to gangsters at times but it can also be a hindrance. Virtually all gang members, and especially those higher up in criminal organizations, like the power and esteem that comes with criminal success. It is perhaps a part of human nature that is present to a greater or lesser extent in most people, but the true adrenaline of the underworld fuels egoism, self-adulation and narcissistic behaviour. This often makes for very colourful characters but can lead to violent reactions and unpredictable behaviour. Leading gangsters often exhibit strong leadership skills in getting others to follow them and excellent organizational skills in running their often massive enterprises, however many gangsters have brought about their own downfall by allowing their egos and their vanity to take the upper hand. Understanding the actions of a gangster often involves understanding their state of mind rather than any motives they might have or what business opportunity they are pursuing.

There are many well-known British gangsters, but none more notorious that the Kray Twins. Ronnie Kray famously stated, 'They were the best years of our lives. They called them the Swinging Sixties. The Beatles and the Rolling

Stones were the rulers of pop music, Carnaby Street ruled the fashion world . . . and me and my brother ruled London. We were fucking untouchable.'

Ronnie and Reggie Kray were born in 1933 in an impoverished part of London's East End and seemed to egg each other on to perpetrate ever more violent acts. They first appeared at the Old Bailey in 1950 on assault charges, and it would not be the last time that they appeared before the highest court in the United Kingdom. In 1952 they began a period of National Service which, rather than straightening them out, almost seemed to fuel their aggressive tendencies. Soon after leaving the army, Ronnie was back in trouble, being jailed for three years for assaulting Terence Martin in a classic gang-related incident. While serving his time in Wandsworth prison, he was diagnosed as having paranoid schizophrenia, which many close friends thought was the cause of his violent tendencies. On his release from prison, Ronnie and Reggie were reunited again and it was as if they were making up for lost time. A plethora of protection rackets, contract killings, extortion and even assisting jail breaks hit the headlines throughout the 1950s and 1960s. Efforts by police and a new force called the Special Squad to put them behind bars seemed destined to fail as witnesses were blatantly intimidated and nothing could be pinned on the brothers. In 1965 a very public feud broke out at the Astor Club in London's fashionable West End between the Krays and the Richardsons, other leading gangsters of the time, when Ronnie was referred to as a 'fat poof'. His sexuality had been in some doubt for several years and he had reportedly had a string of gay relationships. A gang war broke out and the Krays, driven by revenge and fury, were getting more careless with their actions believing they were above the law.

The Krays did not by any means have the largest gang in UK but their reputation spread across the length and breadth of the land. They had trouble trusting others and they got involved in deals and illegal activities close to their patch. It was the way most gangsters worked in the UK and Europe at that time – small gangs working their 'turf', distrustful of other groups and having relatively small scope for their operations. Most crimes were unsophisticated in nature, poorly planned and no real organized networks existed. However, the face of organized crime changed considerably from the 1970s onwards; a far larger group was beginning to form. 'Yardie' has become a term for Caribbean immigrants into Britain, coined by themselves and derived from the expression 'back yard', meaning back home. The build up of the West Indian gangs goes back to the 1950s and 1960s when the British government encouraged immigration to help fill jobs which were created by a strong period of economic growth. Mostly unskilled, many Caribbean immigrants sought cheap places to live in run-down urban areas close to city centres. Ghettos were formed on a massive scale, initially in London but then right across the country and violence began to build. Rather than earn relatively small incomes from low-skilled occupations, many immigrants turned to crime. The development and infrastructures of these criminal organizations, which have spread across the land, are fuelled by drug money. The long-established use of marijuana gave rise to harder drugs in the form of cocaine, heroin and crack. This business often followed the production and distribution model found in so many American cities, with heavily armed distribution centres feeding street dealers and then on to the end user – use of firearms is rife by the gangs to protect their very valuable interests. The rise of the drug culture and widespread demand has meant that the traditional gangster has had to evolve to take full advantage of this development – Great Britain, like many other prosperous countries, now has networks of highly organized gangs who use the same distribution methods and contacts to secure banned substances in large quantities.

A 2003 report from London's Metropolitan Police suggested Jamaican Yardies had invaded Britain at an 'alarming rate' and their control of the crack cocaine trade had gradually spread north, reaching as far as the major cities in Scotland. Of the forty-three police forces in England and Wales, thirty-six reported serious problems with Yardies. Despite their use at times of extreme brutality, the Yardies have not always fared well against home-grown rivals. Many believe this is due to their complete preoccupation with drug trafficking, but this could well change as the spoils from drug dealing grow at an exponential rate. The UK and USA have followed many similar cultural and ideological paths over the years and this has been true in business as well – and is now for crime. The street gangs in Great Britain have developed similar networks to those in America but on a smaller scale up till now both in terms of the number of people involved and the amount of money changing hands. Until law enforcement agencies can make greater inroads into the supply chain of the large drug traffickers, both recreational and more serious use of these banned 'Class A' substances will continue to grow.

The spotlight of fame and notoriety in the arena of America's drug-related street crime is probably shared between two gangs: the Crips and the Bloods. The Crips were founded by two men, Stanley 'Tookie' Williams and Raymond Lee Washington, in 1971. Williams was just fifteen years old but soon the gang was linked to a string of murders, robberies and a labyrinth of West Coast drug dealing. Much of the development of the gang from its Los Angeles origins has been on a 'franchise' basis, creating a loose network of people whose product and method of doing business are often identical. The Crips wanted people to do business their way or not at all and they were becoming ever more powerful. Several existing gangs sought independence and started to come together to strengthen their position in order to fight for their own patch on which to sell. Many of these smaller groups formed a similar network called the Bloods and became bitter rivals to the Crips. The 1970s saw an outbreak of hostilities across a number of cities in southern California with many innocent bystanders being caught in the crossfire. This feud went on for many years but worsened in the early 1980s as a new, extremely lucrative, product became available. A quicker and cheaper process for extracting the stimulant from the coca plant created overnight a deadly alternative to cocaine. It was called crack and would expand the drug market in a way that had been unimaginable previously. Lower-income groups, kids and many ordinary people could suddenly now afford to experiment and the potential gains for these gangs were incredible. The Crips and the Bloods had the means to access this new drug and their infrastructures expanded at an alarming rate. With this increase in scale came greater profitability and the ability to take the war to the authorities. Machine guns, explosives, rocket-launchers and grenades were now no longer the exclusive preserve of the American military!

The nature of gangs and gangsters has changed enormously since the turn of the century. Their transition in the USA and the UK from simply spending their time fighting turf wars, to being highly organized and sophisticated criminal organizations has been mirrored all over the world. The American street gangs have even developed their own form of communication and language, which continues to evolve to keep ahead of the law enforcement agencies. Their networks are specialized and well developed and what binds these criminals together are the rich pickings from drug-related activities as well as other crimes. It is true that prostitution, human trafficking, extortion, robbery, blackmail and countless other illegal and black-market operations continue and show no sign of shrinking but the drug business is the locomotive. Crime, along with sports like football, baseball, boxing, tennis and others, has always provided a way to prosper and make a better life. Many criminals start by believing they will leave the life of crime once they have made some money, the reality is that few actually can. Robbing trains or banks has for the most part been left for directors of feature films rather than our criminal classes, but as long as there is the slightest chance of making money illegally from certain activities, some individuals will use all their efforts to exploit it. It is perhaps a great irony that if these people put the same amount of effort and application into a lawful occupation they could also be highly successful.

Al Capone

'Don't you get the idea I'm one of those goddam radicals. Don't get the idea I'm knocking the American system.'

Al Capone

Alphonse Gabriel Capone was a famous man, perhaps the most famous gangster that has ever lived – this is not entirely due to his criminal behaviour but also to the way he lived his life in the full glare of publicity. He liked entertaining people and often made quips and comments to waiting newspaper men, police officials and, in fact, just about anyone who was around at the time. He was born on 17 January 1899 in Brooklyn, New York, and grew up in a tough, uncompromising urban neighbourhood. These were slums by any other name and even at a young age Al would be leading a small gang of kids, trying to earn respect and put money in his pocket. Al's father, Gabriel was a barber from Castellammare di Stabia, a small village south of Naples and his mother, Teresina (often called Teresa), was from Angri, in the region of Salerno. She was a seamstress by profession and both made the long boat journey to America in 1894 and like many Italian families settling in New York at that time, they had lots of kids and not much money. The couple had seven sons and two daughters with Alphonse being the fourth. In order of age, the siblings were Vincenzo, Raffaele, Salvatore, Alphonse, Ermonio, Umberto, Amedeo, Rose and Mafalda. The children would spread themselves on either side of the law with Vincenzo being a highly successful law enforcement officer and later becoming a US Marshall in Nebraska. Salvatore, on the other hand, was killed by Chicago police in 1924 while working for his brother, and several others worked, in one way or another, for Al. Gabriel died in 1920 and Teresa at the ripe age of 85 in 1952.

Gabriel, Teresa and their small children were known as quiet, reserved and conventional. People who lived close to them would testify that they never saw either Al or his brothers being mistreated in any way. The family was Roman Catholic, like most immigrant Italians living in New York, and records seem to suggest that they were neither dishonest nor violent. In his biography *Capone: The Man and the Era*, Laurence Bergreen says, 'The mother kept to herself. The husband, Gabriel, made more of an impression, since he was, in the words of one family friend, both tall and handsome, very good-looking. Like his wife, he was subdued, even when it came to discipline. He never hit the kids. He used to talk to them. He used to preach to them and they listened to their father.' In the same book, Bergreen goes on to describe the Capone family life: 'nothing about the Capone family was inherently disturbed, violent or dishonest. The children and the parents were close; there was no apparent mental disability, no traumatic event that sent the boys hurtling into a life of crime. They did not display sociopathic or psychotic personalities; they were not crazy. Nor did they inherit a predilection for a criminal career or belong to a criminal society . . . They were a law-abiding, unremarkable Italian-American family with conventional patterns of behaviour and frustrations.' Many books have tried to look into the backgrounds of gangsters and criminals to see what turned them into such people and very few similar traits seem to emerge. It is something within some people and not others, something that burns inside them and drives them to achieve either money or power, or perhaps both, at all costs and seemingly in spite of the risks.

Though quite a bright and capable student, Alphonse got expelled from school at the age of fourteen for assaulting a teacher and never went back. It was clear from a very young age that he had a hot temper, something that would get him into trouble but also at times keep enemies at bay. From leaving school, he would focus all his attention on a life of crime, initially with the Five Point gang, whose principal activities were organizing small-scale gambling dens, pimping, prostitution, extortion and running protection rackets. It would be quite an education. Most kids of that age in Brooklyn would join one local group or another; it was the way of the streets, but many spent their time trying to find jobs and hanging out on days off. Being involved with the Five Point crowd was a statement of serious intent for the ambitious youg man. At the age of sixteen, Al Capone got into a fight at a local meeting place called the Harvard Inn because he was seen chatting to another gangster's girlfriend. The short but violent exchange resulted in Al receiving three slashes to his face and his infamous nickname: Scarface. In 1918, Al met and married Mae Coughlin, a young Irish woman, who gave birth to their son, Albert Francis 'Sonny' Capone, that year. A stable family life didn't have much of a calming effect on the new father and a move to the quieter Amityville, Long Island, was only made so they could be closer to the gang's smuggling operation. Capone's first formal arrest was in New York on a disorderly conduct charge while working for the Brooklyn-based gangster and club owner, Frankie Yale. He was also questioned by police in connection with the murder of two men, known to be rivals of Yale. Even though there were allegedly many witnesses to the killing, no one was willing to come forward and help the police with their inquiries. This was gangland New York and a strong etiquette existed, even among these hardened killers. These were the rules of the street and anyone who broke them would be turned upon not just by rival gangs but their own side as well.

The following year, Al heard about a small-time Irish

gangster who was going around insulting Italians and when he caught up with him, he beat him with his bare hands almost to death. The local Irish gangs were furious and the family decided to move to Chicago until things quietened down a little. This proved to be a decision of meteoric proportions and the Capones moved to a small, unassuming house at 7244 South Prairie Avenue in the suburb of Cicero, not far from the centre of Chicago. Al was given the contact of Johnny Torrio to look up and was offered a job working for the Colosimo mob. 'Big Jim' Colosimo was the head of the Chicago underworld and had created a powerful empire from the proceeds of illegal brewing, distilling and distribution of beer and alcohol. Torrio was a trusted second in command for Big Jim, which gave the hard-working Capone a chance to get an overview of the whole operation. Capone and Torrio got on well and decided to develop a string of legitimate business activities to act as a front for their growing bootlegging, extortion and racketeering business. This had the added benefit of helping the men to increase their influence with large labour unions and employee associations, something which proved very helpful down the line.

It would be wrong to think that serious gang-related crime in Chicago was something new that started only in the 1920s and 1930s. In 1903, three local gangsters calling themselves the 'Automatic Trio', terrorised the streets. In one four-month period, they reportedly carried out eight separate robberies, killing eight men, including two police officers, and wounding five others. One of these men, Gustave Marx, was caught by the police after having fatally shot another officer and made a full confession implicating the whole gang. The other gang members heard about the confession and quickly took themselves off to Indiana, but they were spotted in a country store buying provisions. After another violent shoot-out and the hijacking of a train, the whole gang were eventually captured and charged. The original trio were sent to their deaths by means of the electric chair, while the fourth member of the group, who joined later, was sentenced to life in prison. Chicago had seen its share of violence but the current gangsters were well organized and ruthless. Torrio seemed content to wait his chance within the Colosimo mob but eventually became head of the gang when 'Big Jim' was brutally murdered. Police launched a full investigation and one of the main leads was none other than Frankie Yale, who had travelled up to Chicago a few days before. It was suspected that Torrio had planned the execution and employed the New York-based Yale to do his dirty work. A waiter at the time of the shooting had seen the gunman and was sent to New York to identity Yale. When arriving in Brooklyn, the waiter was unable to confirm that Yale was the man and presumably saved his own skin in the process. The murder would go unpunished.

Capone also saw his chance and became the second in command taking full responsibility for a burgeoning array of activities, which now included a protection racket covering many districts in downtown Chicago, gambling, drugs and prostitution. Al knew the gang needed political power to be able to expand their operation and the elections in 1924 saw a puppet-mayor win by a landslide majority. This might have had something to do with the presence of armed thugs at polling stations but nothing could be proved. However, the mayor, once in office, publicly turned against Capone and promised to run him out of town. Al was not amused and caught up with the mayor on the steps leading to the town hall and in full view of the city's police, public and journalists, Capone personally knocked the mayor down every step. This became a defining moment for him and, in many ways, for the strength of the Torrio-Capone team. It was very public show of power and what was possible. Capone was famously quoted as saying, 'You can get much farther with a kind word and a gun than you can with a kind word alone.'

Torrio was something of an enigma in the Chicago underworld. He was dapper, which certainly didn't make him unique, but he was a non-smoker, non-drinker and non-drug taker and didn't womanize. Although he resorted to violence – and when he did it was with devastating effect – his first instinct was to be non-confrontational. When the turf wars between various Chicago gangsters were at their height, he did manage to organize a meeting which virtually every leading protagonist attended. Thanks to Torrio, the city was carved up peacefully and many of the disputes between gangs were resolved. In 1925 John Torrio was gunned down outside his house, an assassination attempt which he only narrowly escaped. After talking with Al and other members of the Chicago mob, he decided to retire to Italy and hand the reins over to his number two. Capone believed things had to change. With the forces of law and order trying to curb the Mafia power, he accelerated the process of combining small gangs into his operation and rubbing out competitive ones. Much of this was done by assassinating leaders of rival gangs in quick succession, before quickly moving his people in to mop up the business – a simple but highly effective plan which saw Capone gain full control of gangland Chicago in the space of a few years. The business interests, both legal and illegal, grew under Capone at an amazing pace. He was said to have had a tremendous ability to organize highly complex enterprises and motivate people around him. Some of this was certainly down to fear as everyone on his payroll knew the consequences if things didn't work out. Under his single control were bookmakers, gambling houses, prostitution rings and whole brothels, horse and race tracks, nightclubs, large bars and the traditional brewing interests. He had a substantial interest in the largest dyeing and cleaning chain in Chicago plus strings of distribution and packing firms. Between 1926 and 1930, it was estimated his activities generated income exceeding $100 million a year.

Virtually all the leading mob figures in Chicago, as well as in the other major crime centres in America, had attempts made on their life. Capone was no exception. He owed his life to a sizeable slice of good fortune on many occasions but also to the extensive spy network that he had built up –

everyone from lowly aspiring newspaper reporters to policemen, politicians and members of rival gangs was on his payroll. No one, however close to him, knew the identity of this special group – it was Capone's secret. He also believed in killing potential enemies before they could get to him. His usual method was to rent an apartment or building across the road from their headquarters and then simply have them gunned down at an appropriate time, usually under the cover of darkness. A time was chosen when Capone always had a good alibi, often when he was attending a public function or event. Also Capone set up a series of suburban head offices right across Chicago – access to appropriate buildings or properties would be extremely difficult for virtually anyone else in the city but if Capone wanted something, he would soon get it, usually through a mix of intimidation and threats or from the fruits of bribery of police and public officials. Each commercial building at that time needed by law to state the occupation of occupant and Capone would pose as a doctor, art dealer or various other things to provide a legitimate front. He was arrested in 1926 for the killing of three men but again witnesses were unwilling to come forward and he spent just one night behind bars. He did go to jail for ten months, having a privileged cell in the Eastern State Penitentiary, in 1929 under the charge of carrying an unlicensed, concealed firearm. Nothing major ever seemed to stick and Capone proved that he could run his empire from within the prison – much to the annoyance of the police authorities.

One chapter that showed the kind of power that Capone had at his fingertips was the murder of Bill McSwiggins. This highly successful and famed local prosecutor tried to make major inroads into 'bootlegging' as he knew it was one of the major revenue-generating areas of the Chicago gangs, and for Capone, in particular. After the killing, 'Big Al' went into hiding fearing that he could be linked with the violent death of McSwiggins, but after three months he came out to face the music. He negotiated his surrender to the police and a very public court battle swiftly followed. As with so many previous attempts, a lack of substantial evidence saw Capone walk free once more. It was quoted in a local paper that Capone had more power than the mayor of Chicago himself – this was probably true. The man was now tremendously rich and enjoyed fame right across the America. He was a politician when he wanted to be and was seen doing good deeds such as opening soup kitchens for the poor. He seemed to be quoted in the *Chicago Tribune* and other newspapers every week, and many of his quotations have passed into folklore. When asked by one waiting reporter whether his influence would stretch all the way to Canada, he said, 'I don't even know what street Canada is on.' In another quip, he stated, 'I am going to St Petersburg, Florida, tomorrow. Let the worthy citizens of Chicago get their own liquor the best they can. I'm sick of the job – it's a thankless one and full of grief. I've been spending the best years of my life as a public benefactor.' He was undoubtedly a man with a great comic touch and capable of delivering lines of which the likes of Groucho Marx and Bob Hope would have been proud. By 1927 Capone had reached something akin to national celebrity status – seen almost as a romantic, Robin Hood-type figure. He was invited to big social occasions, the sort of events at which prominent criminals would not normally be present. Figures estimating his annual earnings vary enormously but his power was unquestionable. However, on 23 April 1930, the Chigaco Crime Commission issued its first public enemies list – there were twenty-eight names on it and Al Capone was the first, the authorities were not able to look the other way and knew they had to nail him if the streets of Chicago were to be made safe.

Capone had many hideouts away from the city as well – his instinct for trouble was legendary and at critical times he would head for a quiet place, pool all his information and intelligence and plan the next move – often a bold strike. The hideouts were far and wide, Dubuque in Iowa, Hot Sprint in Arkansas, Lansing in Michigan and Johnson City,

Tennessee. He purchased another retreat on Palm Island, Florida, in 1928 and it was there that he orchestrated the infamous Valentine's Day attack. Again, he had a perfect alibi. He was trying to remove a rival by the name of Bugs Moran who operated, among other things, a growing racketeering business on the north side of Chicago. On the day of the planned attack, he was fortunately late for the meeting, something that undoubtedly saved his life. It was widely understood that this audacious hit was carried out by Jack 'Machine Gun' McGurn, someone who had been employed by Capone for many years. No one was ever charged or prosecuted for the murder of the seven men. But this incident did harden public resolve against Capone and additional resources were made available to local law enforcement officials from the FBI and Treasury as a result of the hit.

Most of the attempts on Capone's life were unlike the Valentine's Day massacre, which was meticulously planned. Strikes were usually amateur by comparison and poorly executed. He was once shot in a restaurant but the injury was minor. His car was riddled with bullets on several occasions but he was never seriously wounded. It is difficult to know how he managed to live for so long – it was far from the norm for such a public figure with so many enemies to be in the same top job for more than a few years. Many assassination attempts were co-ordinated by people inside powerful gangs, men looking to take the next step up the ladder, but Capone paid his men well and managed to command great loyalty. He was decisive in his actions. If he felt a problem was looming, he would step in and deal with it before anything could materialize. This was harsh street justice, but he never saw anything wrong in removing people who seemed to have done very little to him. His position as 'Public Enemy Number One' was fully justified. After just a few days in office, Herbert Hoover put pressure on Andrew Mellon, the US Secretary of the Treasury, to spearhead a massive investigation against Capone. The approach had two elements, each run by different teams of investigators. The first was to collect all necessary evidence to prove income tax evasion, and the second related to violations of Prohibition. Legislation was not then as comprehensive or watertight as it is today and both these areas of the American legal system are now in much better shape to convict offenders. Much of the work was done undercover and it took the department five years to be certain of their case. One of the main problems was the very clever way Capone went about his business. He always used front men and had no accounting records. He owned no properties or vehicles, shares or assets of any description. Even the mansion that he and his family had lived in for many years was in his wife's name. The investigation had started on a small scale in the mid-1920s and while little real progress was made, some new laws passed by the federal government allowed investigators to delve deeper into his affairs.

Capone's influence, authority and control ran not only to local police and government personnel but right to central government as well. Many investigators and people close to the team were removed from the case after suspicions were aroused. It was when Treasury Special Agent, Eliot Ness insisted on hand-picking an incorruptible team of US Treasury officials, called 'The Untouchables' that real, uninterrupted progress was made. Ness was greatly helped by IRS agents Elmer Irey and Frank Wilson, who were able to locate paperwork linking Capone to illegal gambling income and therefore an evasion of taxes on that revenue stream could be proven. The task force secretly held concerns about their ability to prosecute on the prohibition charges and were much more confident on tax evasion. In the background, President Herbert Hoover was becoming impatient and was reported to have asked Mellon, 'Have you got this fellow Capone yet? I want that man in jail.'

Capone was fully aware of the work being done by Eliot Ness and that he could well be called before the grand jury in Chicago, but didn't seem to fully understand the seriousness of the charges that might be brought. He believed that he was above the law and that tax evasion charges could never stick because nothing was ever held in his name. It was also felt that he had been distracted for many months by rumours that several members of his organization were plotting against him.

At a banquet hosted by Capone, supposedly in honour of the three ringleaders, the eating and drinking carried on till long past midnight with Capone at his most charming, all smiles and constantly proposing toasts to the three 'guests of honour'. Abruptly, however, the mood changed. As Capone stood, the banqueting hall fell silent. Only the three plotters were still smiling, but even their smiles faded as they took in the continued silence. Then Capone spoke: did they imagine he didn't know? Did they think that they would get away with the single most unforgivable offence, disloyalty? The old Sicilian custom of hospitality before execution had been observed; the three victims were unarmed and defenceless. Swiftly Capone's bodyguards bound them to their chairs with wire and gagged them. With a baseball bat, Capone beat each man in turn, breaking just about every bone in their arms and torsos before delivering the *coup de grâce* with a bullet to the back of the head with a gun brought by one of his bodyguards.

Nothing on the scale of Ness's investigation had ever been attempted in the American judicial system or, for that matter, anywhere in the world up till then. The investigating team compiled hundreds of interviews each year, had multiple bugs and phone taps running simultaneously and tracked key suspected for months on end. Bank records, copies of leases and accounts were all meticulously sorted and evaluated. Ness was undoubtedly the right man for the job, he had a master's degree in criminology and managed to turn a very ordinary Cleveland police department into an efficient and respected force within a couple of years. Crime in the city dropped 38 per cent. Ness went on after the Capone affair for another decade and continued his policy of not sitting behind a desk for too long – he believed in taking to the streets and getting to the roots of crime. He would build up a network of trusted confidants from which information would flow and like Capone himself, he would act swiftly and decisively. It is perhaps sad that Ness never saw the nationwide success of the book he wrote, as he died from a heart attack, just months before its release. He would have been pleased with the reviews and coverage, as it was a valuable boost for the police authorities right across America.

Convicting Capone was never going to be easy and 'The Untouchables' had setbacks time and time again. Jake Lingle was the publisher of the *Chicago Tribune* and a long-time friend of Capone. Acting as a double agent, he agreed to inform against Capone with the help of the federal government. He was due to be appointed on 10 June 1930, but was shot in the back of the head a day before he was to take up his post. Capone stated, 'Newspapers and newspapermen should be suppressing rackets and not supporting them. It does not become me of all people to say that, but I believe it.' Ness had several men working undercover, slowly beginning to infiltrate Capone's empire. In an informal discussion, one of Capone's employees let slip that real evidence had already been found by the investigators, two book-keeping ledgers taken during a raid on the Hawthorne Hotel. These records were checked but were useless unless they found the book-keepers themselves. In a further discussion, the employee mentioned the names of the two accountants concerned, being Leslie Shumway and Fred Reis. Both men were eventually tracked down and agreed to co-operate. This was a major stroke of good fortune and was a big break in the case as records like this were the link between the activity that could be observed and the cash proceeds.

Ness, of course, wanted Capone behind bars but he also needed to remove the most lucrative part of his empire – the liquor business. The team of investigators, swollen by local members of the Chicago police department, became increasingly successful at finding and destroying distilleries and distribution centres. They captured millions of dollars of valuable equipment and vats of beers and spirits, endangering Capone's ongoing business. Ness also made inroads into Capone's extortion racket, and through informants managed to reduce the number of policemen and local officials who were on the take from Capone. The net, as Ness believed, was beginning to tighten. On 13 March 1931 a federal grand jury met to evaluate the claim that Al Capone owed taxes to the tune of $32,488.81 on his 1924 income. The jury indicted Capone but this was held over in secret until the investigation was complete for the five years covering 1925 to 1929 inclusive. Less than three months later the grand jury met again and indicted Capone on twenty-two separate counts of tax evasion. Capone and many members of his gang were charged with over 5,000 violations on a charge sheet that was very lengthy indeed.

The extent of the charges and mountain of evidence profoundly affected Capone, and all his advisers felt he would be convicted on some, if not all, counts. Capone, facing many years in jail if the federal government won its case, presented the American Attorney Johnson with a compromise. After discussing the proposal with the new US Treasury Secretary, Odgen Mills, Johnson agreed the very optimistic deal proposed by Capone's lawyers of a prison sentence of two to five years. Apparently there was a feeling that some of the evidence might have been getting close to the time limit for admissibility and if key witnesses failed to show, especially Shumway and Reis, that the case might begin to fall apart. Capone went to the Supreme Court in characteristically high spirits and he was already entertaining offers from Hollywood for a film deal of his life and times. In the official record of the court, Judge James Wilkerson heard the evidence of the proposed deal and replied, 'The parties to a criminal case may not stipulate as to the judgement to be entered. It is time for somebody to impress upon the defendant that it is utterly impossible to bargain with a federal court.' Capone was allowed to withdraw his guilty plea and the trial was scheduled for October. Capone was not about to go down without a fight. He managed to get a list of prospective jurors from a leading official and began getting to them by just about every means possible – mostly bribery and threatening them with physical violence. Judge Wilkerson got to hear of this and seemed unconcerned. On the day of the trial, fourteen heavily armed detectives escorted Capone to the federal court via a tunnel and freight elevator. It was a media circus, every major newspaper and radio station across the country had representatives camped outside the courthouse waiting for every shred of information or the faintest whiff of a story. Capone, believing that he had managed to turn the jury, was again in a good mood, smiling and dressed in a smart suit and tie.

As the judge entered the court, he announced that he wanted to meet privately with the entire jury. They were all told that some of them had been compromised and they were all summarily removed. A short while later a new jury was brought in, made up mostly of rural white men who had been gathered secretly at night so there was little chance that they could have been compromised. It was a tremendously smart move and one which had been done with the help of a very small, select band of officials. It took the court just eleven days to hear the evidence from both sides before the judge's final summing up: 'I have been a little bewildered in this case at the manner in which the defence has attempted to weave a halo of mystery and romance around the head of this man. Who is he? Who is this man who during the years that we have considered here has so lavishly expended what he claims to be almost half a million dollars? Is he the little boy out of the Second Reader, who succeeded in finding a pot of gold at the end of the rainbow, that he has been spending so lavishly, or maybe, as his counsel says, is he Robin Hood? But was it Robin Hood in this case who bought $8,000 worth of diamond belt buckles to give to the unemployed? No. Was it Robin Hood in this case who paid a meat bill of $6,500? Did that go to the unemployed? No, it went to the house on Palm Island. Did he buy these $27 shirts to protect the shivering men who sleep under Wacker Drive at night? No. At any time, at any place, has this defendant ever appeared in a reputable business? Has there appeared a single instance of contact with a reputable business? What a picture we have in this case: no income, but diamond belt buckles, $27 shirts, furnishings for his home – $116,000 that is not deductible from his income. And yet counsel comes here and argues to you that the man has no income!'

It was late in the evening of 17 October 1932 and after nearly nine hours of discussion that the jury found Capone guilty of nearly all counts. Judge Wilkerson passed a sentence of eleven years on Capone and required him to pay $80,000 in fines and court fees. He was sent first to an Atlanta prison but seemed able to direct most of his business from there, mostly through bribery. In 1934, he was moved to the most infamous prison in America, on the island of Alcatraz, in San Francisco Bay. Here, prisoner AZ85 was strictly guarded and was allowed only very restricted contact with the outside world. He was unable to influence guards or friends and was put in solitary confinement when he did. In an attempted to reduce his sentence, he became a model prisoner and did not take part in a number of prison strikes. Warden James Johnston remembered the intense public interest in Al Capone; he was always being asked about 'Big Al'. Each day he would be peppered by enquiries from journalists about everything from how Capone was enjoying the weather to what work he was doing in prison.

Capone was becoming sick and was eventually diagnosed with syphilitic dementia and spent the last years of his prison sentence in the Baltimore State Mental Hospital. He was finally released on 16 November 1939 and spent a short time in hospital having his condition fully analyzed. Capone returned to his home in Palm Island where he lived until 25 January 1947 when, after continued poor health, he died of a cardiac arrest. He was buried in Mount Olive Cemetery on the southern end of Chicago between his father and brother. In 1950 the remains of all three were moved to Mount Carmel Cemetery, Hillside, just west of Chicago.

The life of Capone has been immortalized on the big screen many times, and has featured in countless books and filled many column inches for years across the globe. He was, in many ways, the archetypal American gangster, having worked his way up from having virtually nothing and living in the slums of a major city, to being a rich and powerful enigma. He has been portrayed in film by many actors including Wallace Beery, Paul Muni, Neville Brand, William Devane, Robert De Niro, Ben Gazzara and, magnificently, by Rod Steiger. Many of his exploits make for fascinating viewing and the film *The Untouchables*, released in 1959, was one of the best. It was remade under the same name by Brian De Palma in 1987 starring Sean Connery and Kevin Costner. The name itself came from the runaway international bestselling book published in 1957 by Eliot Ness. This latter big screen version will probably be the one that current and future generations will most remember, although it hardly scratches the surface of the incredible life and times of Alphonse Gabriel Capone.

The Krays

The East End of London in the period immediately after the Second World War was a rough place to live and gangs roamed the streets almost unchallenged by the forces of law and order. Many parts were no-go areas after dark and criminals carrying guns, knives and other weapons were commonplace. Most of the local work was manual and the whole area was in need of massive redevelopment – in areas such as this, crime is not just part of the social fabric it is endemic – growing at an alarming rate. Most gangs operated out of small patches and were content with relatively minor jobs, such as robbery, protection, smuggling, pornography, fencing stolen goods, prostitution and drugs. However, greater prosperity in the 1950s and 1960s also brought an increased demand for many illegal goods and services – the opportunities for gangs were suddenly larger and battles between rival gangs made headline news. In was in this dark underworld that probably the most notorious criminals of that era would emerge – the Kray twins.

The twins Ronald and Reginald Kray were born in the early morning on 24 October 1933, separated by just ten minutes. Their early lives were spent in London's Shoreditch area before moving to 178 Vallance Road, Bethnal Green, in 1939. The centre of the family unit was their mother, Violet, a strong and single-minded mother who had given birth to the twins' elder brother, Charlie, fully six years before. The father, also called Charlie, was rarely to be seen and spent much of his time as a travelling salesman and trader, avoiding the law, the tax inspector and most other forms of authority. Bethnal Green was at that time a tough and uncompromising place – an area known for hardened drinkers, poor quality, cramped slum housing, seedy back-street pubs, illicit gambling dens, brothels and a love of boxing. The twins' paternal grandfather, 'Mad' Jimmy Kray, was a stallholder for many years in Petticoat Lane market and renowned for fighting and drinking. The maternal grandfather was Jimmy Lee also known as the 'Southpaw Cannonball', who had been a bare-knuckle boxer and music hall entertainer. This was no ordinary family. The Krays, from the outside, looked much like many other East End families – highly self-sufficient, devoted and tight-knit, but inside they were hard, street types who never walked away from a fight.

For as long as people could remember the large area north of the Thames docks was dirty and smelly. The warehouses contained slaughterhouses, glue-making factories, rendering plants, engineering works and many breweries. This latter trade filled the air with the pungent odour of fermenting yeast, barley and hops, which wasn't pretty at the best of times. The reason for many of these activities being located here was access to the open waterways of the Thames estuary but also because the prevailing south-westerly winds would take the smell of poverty and hard graft away from the much wealthier west side of London. The area was also a stopping-off point for immigrants, both legal and illegal. People from all over the world came through the London docks and many from Poland, Russia, Romania and elsewhere would find employment and stay. The governing rule was the law of the streets and the Krays immersed themselves in this rough and ready world. Violet was completely devoted to her sons and was rarely seen to be critical of anything they did. She taught them that the family came first and to treat people who had less than they did with respect. However, she had her hands full controlling the almost identical twins from very early on. They were tough, learning to box from their elder brother, and became virtually inseparable. Although Reggie liked the company of others, Ronnie was more of a loner, happy to spend long periods with his Alsatian dog, Freda, roaming the bomb craters, derelict buildings and general war devastation. At the age of twelve, they both attended Daniel Street School, where the only thing that really excited them was the next boxing lesson or fight in the fenced-in, concrete playground. At fifteen they both left school for a working life in Billingsgate fish market – this was to be the longest period of legitimate work they would ever do. Even from this early age, trouble seemed to follow the twins around and usually catch up with them with a bump. Differences between rival gangs were normally settled with fist fights, knives or other weapons but however things were sorted out, the Krays would usually come out on top. In 1948 the boys were persuaded to box in the local Hackney championships and Reggie won the event before becoming the London champion. The heritage of the Kray family was to be able to look after yourself, and both the boys could certainly do this.

Their first appearance at the Old Bailey was in 1950, when they were accused of assaulting a boy outside a local dance hall. The boy had been badly beaten, but as a foretaste of what was to come, someone managed to 'get' to the witnesses and the case was dropped for lack of evidence. Just under two years later they were both called for National Service, which was mandatory for all young men at that time. They were expected to serve two full years as all fit and able men had to do and they reported, as instructed, to the Waterloo Barracks where they were told they would be joining the Royal Fusiliers. Discipline was not the twins' strong suit and early on they had a run-in with a training sergeant who, after a serious row, they beat severely. The twins jumped the wall and headed back home, only to be picked up by the police the following day and returned for punishment. They spent most of the next two years on the run from the military or serving time behind bars where they met a whole new group of criminal types, all sharing the same view of discipline. Eventually they were dishonourably discharged and ended up back on the East End streets of their childhood. Once out of the clutches of the military authorities and with a loan from their older brother, the boys converted an old cinema into a snooker and billiard hall. It was their first business venture and having a solid base helped facilitate other deals and partnerships. Ronnie loved being 'king of the castle' and started taking on the mantle of a true gangster, in actions, dress code and ambitions. The twins continued to get into arguments, fights and brawls and, although seldom the tallest or heaviest, they always seemed to fare well. They both showed speed, agility and a true killer instinct. Ronnie was the team strategist and understood the need for information, employing a gang of inexpensive young spies to report back on what was going on at street level. Their premises soon became a haven and distribution centre for stolen goods and the Krays ensured that they always got a good slice of the cake.

The Krays were still seen at this time as small-time criminals by other London gangs and the various police authorities. However, opportunities were soon to present themselves. They were invited for a drink at a well-known hangout on the Mile End Road one Sunday lunchtime by three brothers who ruled the local area. The twins walked in just after noon and closed the door behind them – the aim was to discuss turf, but before long a massive brawl ensued, leaving a sea of broken glass and blood on the bar, the old-fashioned leather seats and running all over the floor. Two of the hoods were out cold and Ronnie had to be dragged from the third before he killed him with his bare hands. It was a statement of intent and the word soon went out that these guys should be taken seriously. Although the twins looked very similar, in many ways they were very different. While Reggie liked the high life, chased girls and was seen at many events and functions, Ronnie led a remarkably simple life. He continued to live with his mother in Vallance Road, he didn't drive, he did very little betting or gambling and was by nature much more cautious, unless provoked. He did have one yearning and that for was young boys, but this was an era when being openly homosexual could cause a lot of problems so he kept this secret hidden away. Reggie, on the other hand, seemed to want a wife, children and the rest of what he called 'the good life'. He could be violent when required, but often it was Ronnie who provoked confrontations. Their reputation was such that other gangs, nightclub owners, gambling outfits, bars and many other places were happy to pay for their 'protection'. They continued to grow their fencing business and rapidly became the first port of call for good quality stolen goods like jewellery, cars and precious metals. Business was going well even when they were only in their early twenties but they remained hungry for more, much more.

The year 1956 was a defining period for the Krays. Two of their associates, Jack Spot and Billy Hill, retired because they thought things were getting too hot: violence and killings in London's underworld were sharply on the rise. They had both been beaten up on several occasions and the stakes were getting higher. A group of Italian gangsters started to move in on the void that the 'retirement' of these two gangsters had left behind and Ronnie was up for a fight. One night, the Krays and a group of their closest allies paid a visit to the newcomers. Ronnie walked straight in to their opponents' club alone and pulled out a Mauser pistol, firing three rounds into the drinks cabinet behind the bar. No one was killed but he wanted this group to know who they were up against and put down a marker. It worked and the rival gang closed several of their premises – the Krays took up the new work and their empire was beginning to look like big business. Both the twins realized they needed to plan more and take things more seriously – less brawling and more co-ordinated action. They brought into the gang heavy hitters and people with better knowledge of how different organized crime rackets worked. They had to share some of the proceeds but they were very much lords of their manor and kept overall control. By the end of the year, they were making real money and had become known as the most dangerous gangsters in London. Ronnie got a call one day from a car dealer who used them for protection. A hard local docker had purchased a car and was not satisfied with it, wanting his money back. The car dealer explained this was impossible but the irate man said he would be back the following day to settle things. The following day, Ronnie turned up in time to see a heated argument in full swing and after several warnings the docker would still not leave. Ronnie pulled out his gun and shot the man in the leg. It was, in fact, the first man that Ronnie had shot. Ronnie was charged by the police but produced a cast-iron alibi and swore that it was his brother. The red-faced police officers had not been thorough in their investigation and were forced to let him go. The victim received a small payment from the Krays for his pain and was told to go quietly.

As we have seen before, fame can help certain deals and areas of business but can also bring unwanted trouble for gangsters. As the Krays became more notorious and well-known, so their egos swelled as individuals and other gangs brought them new opportunities. People wanted to be associated with the twins and in the summer of 1956, they were asked to be business partners with Billie Jones and Bobby Ramsey. These two shady characters owned a club called The Stranglers in London's Soho district and were having trouble with the police because of the amount of brawling and disturbances that were being created. Ronnie and Reggie were happy to expand their empire and having a toe-hold in Soho was seen as a positive move. However, soon after they got involved, Jones and Ramsey had a bust-up with the Watney Streeters, a hard group, many of whom had worked in the London docks. The gang had made most of their money from trading goods which they had 'liberated' from ships or the dock-side. Both the pub owners were badly beaten and it was time for the Krays to step in. Ronnie planned the hit, using his network of boys to track the rival gangs' whereabouts. Their strength was assessed and Ronnie assembled over a dozen of his men for a briefing in Vallance Road. The plan was not overly complicated. Ronnie and Reggie went in through the front door of the Britannia pub in the East End, but the opposition had found out about their plans and left by the back door. The only one left in the pub was the barman Terry Martin, who was suspected of being part of the gang. He was dragged outside and beaten. Much of what went on between rival gangs was rarely reported to the authorities – it was sorted on the streets, but this was an exception. There were witnesses and Ronnie was arrested and charged with assault. In November that year he was taken to the notorious Wandsworth prison in west London to commence a three-year sentence. Many inmates had a tough time in this institution but not Ronnie – just about all the inmates and guards alike had heard of the Krays – they knew he had people on the outside who would be looking after him. This would make Ronnie's time in prison much less arduous.

Ronnie was transferred to a prison on the Isle of Wight, off the south coast of Great Britain, and for the first time he was beginning to show reclusive tendencies and was becoming obsessed with the notion that someone was out to kill him. He was later moved on the recommendation of the head warden of the prison, to Winchester jail because they had a specialist psychiatric ward. He was diagnosed as having mental problems and in February 1958 was certified by the governor as being insane. He was moved to a lunatic asylum for examination and was further diagnosed as being schizophrenic but what the doctors had failed to see was that he was in fact suffering from paranoid schizophrenia, a much more serious condition. Drugs looked as though they had helped although the penal system wanted to keep him under this type of supervision. It was not the place Ronnie wanted to be – he had no real sway over the governor or staff and asylum life was not how he was used to living his life. He would prefer to be back in prison and the company of 'honest' criminals – people with whom he empathized. Reggie hatched a plan for his escape and, not for the first time, the twins fooled officers of the law by impersonating each other. During one of his Sunday morning visits, Reggie, wearing the same clothes as Ronnie under his raincoat, switched places with his brother. Soon Ronnie was out and in the waiting car, being driven off to a secure, pre-arranged hiding place. If he could stay 'at large' for six weeks, he would have to be recertified on recapture. Ronnie spent much of this time outside London living on a farm run by a close friend. Reggie was hopeful that being away from people and in beautiful, peaceful countryside would help Ronnie's state of mind. The reality was quite the reverse; if anything, it made him worse and he had greater mood swings along with homicidal tendencies. He was sent to see a trusted Harley Street specialist who confirmed that he was homicidal and showed all the signs of advanced paranoid schizophrenia. He had tried to kill himself on one occasion, which was the last straw for Reggie who went to the authorities to turn his brother in to the police. Ronnie was picked up and served the remainder of his sentence back in Wandsworth, as he had wanted.

While Ronnie was 'away', Reggie was outside his brother's shadow for the first time and took greater control of their criminal empire. He wanted a new headquarters, a better base from which to operate, and settled on a completely derelict premises which would enable him to build a fine drinking establishment in keeping with the Krays' status. Many pubs in the East End used to have gyms or small boxing rings attached (an indication of the popularity of the sport in those parts) and Reggie wanted one as well. A couple of months after Ronnie walked free, the club had its opening night with Henry Cooper, the famous English boxer who once put Muhammad Ali on the canvas, cutting the tape. It was the twins' first legitimate business and proved highly successful among celebrities, businessmen, crooks and punters alike – an authentic taste of the East End. Up until that point, the elder brother Charlie had never seemed interested in the exploits of the twins but now they had a 'proper' business, he wanted to get closer to them again. He convinced the boys to open a second bar and a gambling establishment called the Wellington Way Club, which also proved successful from the word go. Violet could not have been happier – her boys were working together and the twins were living back at home. Ronnie spent a lot of time, at weekends particularly, just watching television quietly on his own, next to the fire, but life was good. He was moodier and more erratic than before his spell in prison but the boys spoilt their mother with the proceeds of their legal and illegal dealings. However, in private, faced with the growing unpredictability of his brother's actions and his general state of mind, Reggie grew increasingly doubtful of his brother's ability to help the business. The boys had a business associate called Daniel Shay who lived in an affluent area of north London. Shay and Reggie were extracting protection money from a number of small businesses and shopkeepers but one store owner in Hampstead went to the police. The two men were caught red-handed and Reggie was sentenced to eighteen months behind bars for his part in the crime. Shay would get three years. With Reggie now 'away', Ronnie spent less time on legitimate business interests and put more energy into planning hits and orchestrating conflicts to improve their standing in the underworld. As a direct result of these moves, Charlie took a big step back and spent more time with his wife, Dolly – there was trouble brewing and he wanted to be a long way from it.

Towards the end of 1960, Ronnie met a man by the name of Peter Rachman, who was a well-known central London landlord. His style was to buy run-down tenanted buildings and immediately force up the rent. As working-class and immigrant families had to move out, so he moved in prostitutes, drug dealers and other undesirables with more disposable income. He used a gang of thugs to intimidate those who didn't want to play ball and soon the vast majority of the original tenants were searching for new places to live. It was a highly lucrative strategy and soon Rachman owned a sizeable portfolio. Ronnie caused some trouble for the property man, who later agreed to pay for protection for his rent collectors and enforcers. The first cheque bounced and Ronnie went on the warpath. The feud would run and run, Ronnie always looking to 'get even'. Eventually, the clever Rachman offered him the chance to get involved with some new people as a peace offering, in the area of gambling.

Gambling was still illegal in Britain at this time. The Krays had stakes in several illicit gambling haunts and were attracted to a deal to become 50 per cent owners in Esmeralda's Barn in Wilton Place. This remains one of London's premier areas and a place where the rich and famous hang out. The twins earned an estimated £100,000 a year from their stake and increasingly Reggie wanted to spent time on this part of the business to the detriment of the rest. In this atmosphere and in these surroundings, he was more open about his homosexuality and took young boys back to an apartment which he had inherited as part of a gambling debt. He needed the company but heavy drinking and drug-taking were beginning to cloud his judgement. It was a period of change for the boys, for when Reggie was finally let loose from Wandsworth he fell in love with a pretty sixteen-year-old Irish girl, Frances Shea, propelled by thoughts of a more stable life, kids and home-cooked food. Ronnie had little time for women, except his mother, and saw the girl as a threat to their relationship and the business empire. The twins argued and rowed like never before. Then came an incident which would help to reconcile the brothers. They were arrested near Bethnal Green for 'loitering with intent to steal parked cars'. The local police were frustrated that they could not seem to touch the Krays for a string of other things and wanted to pull them in for something. Ronnie hired the famous female barrister Nemone Lethbridge, to defend them and got eight witnesses to provide a string of alibis. The high profile and very public court case was heard on 8 May 1961 at the magistrates court in Marylebone and all charges were dropped. A massive celebration party was held at Esmeralda's Barn and many of the twins' 'new friends' turned up. Ronnie proposed a popular toast to 'British justice'. National newspapers covered the story and the whole incident propelled the Krays to even greater heights. It was as if they could do no wrong and their new-found 'West End' image was bringing business offers on a seemingly daily basis. They had certainly never had it so good.

Representatives from the American Mafia, along with French, Corsican and South American gangs, had meetings with the Krays – they spread the rumour that they had the police in their pocket, something that the previous highly public court cases helped to promote. Their activities grew and broadened – one highly profitable scam was to open a business with premises and a front person. The company would start trading, open lines of credit with suppliers and so on, then, at the right time, the business would place large orders with a number of companies, quickly sell the goods and close the business. The people involved would vanish, leaving banks, creditors and the police chasing fresh air. During all this, Ronnie continued his downward mental spiral: a boxer who insulted him to his face was slashed and needed seventy stitches; two men were hired to shoot someone who had had the audacity to pick a fight with an associate of the Krays. The hitmen ended up shooting the man's brother by mistake and his injury was so severe that he lost his leg. In July 1964 a leading British newspaper ran the headline 'The Picture We Dare Not Print' above a story which alleged a gay affair between a member of the House of Lords and one of London's top gangsters. The German magazine *Stern* named Lord Boothby and Ronnie Kray as the men involved. Boothby denied the allegations and received an apology and an out-of-court settlement. Later that year, the Krays were arrested and charged with extorting money for protection. They had demanded half of the West End club Hideaway from its owner Hew McCowan and had threatened his life. The jury could not reach a verdict and by the time of the retrial, the Krays' lawyers had dug up sufficient material on McCowan's past for the judge to call a halt to proceedings. The great irony was that McCowan was forced to sell out to the Krays at a much reduced price and they held a massive party in Hideaway immediately after the court hearing.

On 20 April 1965, at St James's Church in Bethnal Green, Reggie married Frances. It was a star-studded occasion and the whole family turned out in their Sunday best. It was not the married life that Frances had wanted – Ronnie was always around, socializing with gangsters, and she was never allowed to be without a 'minder', even on a shopping trip. After just eight weeks, she calmly packed up her belongings and moved back in with her parents. It was the end of their short marriage. It was a marriage that Reggie had desperately wanted to work but he had fallen in love with the wrong woman. His lifestyle and associates frightened the young girl who seemed to want just a quiet, peaceful life and none of the trappings of her husband's success. Even the unavoidable fame that was thrust upon her was something she never felt happy about. It had been a meeting of two different worlds which were never going to be compatible. Frances was never able to come to terms with the break-up of her marriage and the new world she had entered into. In her own mind, it was as if she had become a leper in her own neighbourhood. She tried to commit suicide several times before succeeding. Reggie organized the funeral and, fortunately for many, Ronnie couldn't make it because he was on the run, this time as the result of an extortion case involving a member of the police. Reggie took the death of his wife badly and it was now his turn to drink heavily, which made him even more dangerous. He went on a violent spree, shooting one man who he thought had insulted his wife, shooting another in the leg over a relatively minor issue and slashing the face of a third man in a fight.

At around the same time, in the first half of 1965, the Royal Bank of Canada was raided and the following month a similar bank in Ontario was also raided. Hundreds of thousands of negotiable bonds were stolen and the American Mafia were looking to launder a proportion of these in the UK. The Krays, making a fee of an estimated 25 per cent, took a large part of the shipment and handled its circulation. They used a shady international businessman called Alan Cooper who in return asked the twins for help with a pair of south London hoods, the Richardsons, who were giving him trouble. The Richardson gang was dangerous and had some well-known violent men on their team – most notably George Cornell and Frankie Fraser, often called 'Mad' Frankie Fraser. On 8 March 1966 a major gangland fight broke out at a nightclub in south London. The Richardsons handled the protection for the place but another group of villains, including Dickie Hart, cousin of the Krays, had a bust-up with several bouncers. Guns were drawn, shots fired, people scattered and bodies lay all over the place. Fraser and one of the Richardsons had been injured, Harry Rawlings, a member of their gang, was shot in the shoulder and Dickie Hart lay dead on the ground. The police were on hand swiftly and many of those involved were locked up but the twins took the death of their cousin very personally. It was not entirely clear that Cornell had been involved in the shooting, but Ronnie was in no mood to stop and ask questions. He heard that Cornell had been to see one of the injured men before going for a drink in a well-known East End pub called the Blind Beggar. Cornell was sitting quietly on a bar stool, pint of beer in hand, when Ronnie entered, put a gun to his head and pulled the trigger. Blood and human tissue literally flew all over the bar, windows, glasses and seating. The murder weapon was dropped in the River Lea and was found some months later; it still sits as an exhibit in Scotland Yard's museum. This killing was as much about power on the streets of London as it was about revenge. The Krays knew they had to be seen as top of the tree and any weakness would be exploited. The twins fled to Morocco for several weeks until things had cooled down and, as was typical of so much gangland warfare over the years, no witnesses came forward and the killing went unpunished by the law.

Jack 'the Hat' McVitie was in many ways typical of London's East End gangsters – a tough, short-tempered street brawler who seemed to like nothing more than a big drink, an argument and a good fight. The only time in living memory that he wasn't fighting was when his hand had been badly broken by a crowbar. He was a freelancer who had worked for many of the leading gangs, including the Krays, and when Ronnie approached him to deal with a close associate, Leslie Payne, McVitie agreed. He was allegedly given £100 and a handgun and promised a lot more. McVitie never got round to the killing and refused to pay back the money – Ronnie was not best pleased and when the word got back to him that McVitie had brandished a sawn-off shotgun at a couple of friends of the twins, it was time for action. On 28 October 1967 the twins were drinking in one of their usual haunts, the Carpenters' Arms just off the Vallance Road, and had planned to go to a party in Stoke Newington just a couple of miles away. News came through that McVitie was in the area and they concocted a plan to get him invited to the bash. The twins got to the venue in plenty of time and removed all the other party-goers, then sat and waited patiently. As McVitie entered the house, Reggie put a semi-automatic pistol to his head and pulled the trigger. The gun jammed and McVitie thought for a moment that it was one big joke. Reggie shoved McVitie forward towards the glass window, and thrust his head through before pulling him back again. With a mixture of blood and sweat, and pleading his innocence, McVitie received a devastating attack from Reggie, who, armed with a butcher's knife, stabbed him many times in the face, chest and stomach before finally impaling him through the throat.

The woman who lived with Jack 'the Hat' reported him missing and the police started a witch-hunt. There were lots of people who had seen him at various times that evening but very little information was forthcoming. The twins thought it better to lay low and spent a few weeks getting drunk in the countryside some miles north of London. The local police suspected the Krays were behind the murder but had no proof. The twins had been on the Scotland Yard radar for some years and they thought it was time they were put behind bars for good but greater resources would be needed. A special unit was set up, headed by Leonard 'Nipper' Read and the team set about building a case. The squad was sworn to secrecy about their plans and whereabouts and each member underwent regular handgun practice. They started by investigating all the nightclubs, bars, gambling dens, supposedly legitimate offices and so on that the Krays had been involved with. A list of potential witnesses was drawn up and each in turn was pulled in and interviewed. After much disappointment, the first big break came from Leslie Payne, who was willing to talk because he felt he was probably next on Reggie's hit list. Secretly stowed away in a small hotel in Marylebone, Payne gave his testimony, detailing all that he knew over almost ten years of associating with the Krays. On 9 May the net fell on the Kray organization when over sixty officers arrested the Krays and twenty-two of their crew, taking the whole lot to Savile Row police station. The twins would see just how thorough the investigation had been as witness after witness was named – the barmaid from the Blind Beggar, Billy Exley, a former bodyguard, Payne himself and plenty of others.

Once all the preliminary material had been presented, it was clear there was enough evidence for the case to be transferred to the highest criminal court in the land, the Old Bailey. After a little more than eight months on remand, the

Krays went on trial in early 1969. In March the twins were found guilty of killing McVitie and Cornell, although they were found not guilty of a number of lesser charges. The trial gripped the nation and the Krays each received a life sentence, with instructions from the judge that they should spend no less than thirty years in jail. Their criminal empire was effectively finished for good due to the severity of the sentences – many believe this reflected the establishment's desire to see men like this put away for life rather than sentenced for the actual crimes of which they were found guilty. Either way, an amazingly violent reign of terror in London's colourful past had ended. Ronnie Kray died in Broadmoor Prison in 1995 and Reggie was allowed out for the day to attend the quiet funeral. Reggie was released from prison after thirty- one years in 2000 and died of cancer soon after. Their lives were immortalized in the 1990 film *The Krays*, in which Gary and Martin Kemp, formerly of Spandau Ballet, played the twins. The film successfully communicates some of the gritty reality of the East End of London in the 1950s and 1960s and the lives of the Krays, but to really understand that world and those times and the lives of the twins one would probably have to have been there.

Lucky Luciano

At the turn of the twentieth century, America needed a vast number of migrant workers to help propel its economy forward. Work was often hard and the hours long, but, compared with rates of pay in other parts of the world, it offered an opportunity too good to miss for many individuals and families. The Mafia, also known as La Cosa Nostra, meaning literally 'our thing', was well established in Italy and helped many groups of people to make the crossing. One such family was the strongly Roman Catholic Lucianos from a beautiful small town in Sicily called Lercara Friddi, not far from Corleone and the capital, Palermo. Included in this intrepid band was a ten-year-old boy Salvatore, who would become better known as Charles 'Lucky' Luciano. Even at this young age 'Lucky' would know that the Mafia code was to keep your mouth closed, something ingrained in generations of Sicilian people. In current times, we tend naturally to think of the Mafia as being just a criminal organization but over a hundred years ago it was thought of very differently. Set up as a group to help protect families from bandits, unscrupulous police and invaders from overseas, members of this most secret of organizations were hailed more as heroes than condemned as villains. As the Mafia established itself in New York, Chicago, Boston and then other cities in America, it evolved, taking advantage of the tremendous illegal opportunities that existed. It is not known quite how or why this change occurred and certainly the Mafia in Sicily and on mainland Italy had been connected with certain criminal behaviour, but this was on a totally new scale. Perhaps the direction was changed by a few of the early settlers who established a path for others to follow. Certainly Italians who made the crossing to America had a swift decision to make: to work legitimately, which was hard, or to join the often flamboyant and relatively wealthy crime gangs.

What makes people become evil criminals or murderers? It is a question that has been asked again and again over the years and perhaps there is no definitive answer. The turning point is different for every person – it can be one event that takes them down the wrong path or they are influenced by their surroundings or by people close to them as they grow up. Lucky Luciano certainly started down a criminal path just about as early as it is possible to do so – at the age of ten he began his first racket, charging Jewish kids for protection, and if they didn't pay they got a good beating. He also started shoplifting and was charged for the first time later that same year. He hung around with older boys and wanted to impress them, never shying away from a fight or an opportunity to put some money into his pocket. One small, Polish Jewish kid, by the name of Meyer Lansky, refused to pay and Lucky was amazed at how tenaciously he fought for his size. Lanksy, born Maier Suchowljansky in Grodno, was an exceptionally bright kid who would became a major influence on organized crime in USA. Instead of becoming enemies, the two boys joined forces in the protection scam and became life-long friends. During their early teens, they worked for a number of gangs, mostly selling narcotics; schooling simply didn't provide the money, excitement or power that they both craved. At eighteen, Luciano was arrested and convicted on charges of possession and dealing in heroin and morphine, and spent six months in a reform home. By the following year, and although younger than several of the other members, he became leader of the notorious Five Points Gang, and was named by the police in connection with a string of gangland murders. It was known that this band of hoodlums were involved in all aspects of the drug trade, plus bootlegging, extortion and prostitution. Luciano would rent places, put prostitutes upstairs and drug dealers downstairs or on street corners – this would allow his thugs to protect both revenue streams at the same time. Many customers who dabbled in drugs also made the odd trip upstairs to spend some time with the prostitutes.

Giuseppe Masseria was the main man on the streets at that time. Also know as 'Joe the Boss', he was the official head of the Mafia in New York and had a hand in everything. Masseria was an old-school crook, liked doing business with Italians, had an extensive network of city officials on his payroll and was inclined to proceed cautiously, especially when looking at new partners, deals or areas of business. He felt that diversification and expansion were dangerous and that the Italians should stick to what they knew and what they were good at. Luciano, on the other hand, saw opportunities slide by and was keen to get things moved forward. Lucky was walking down Sixth Avenue one morning on the way to a meeting, when three hoods forced him into the back of a limo, put tape over his mouth so no one could hear him and then beat and cut him in a vicious attack. Luciano thought he was going to die and passed out, waking several hours later on a deserted beach across the far side of New York Bay. Shaken and with blood still coming from parts of his head, face and torso, he started to walk back to his home but was picked up by the police. Luciano knew he would be questioned about the affair and tried to bribe his way out at first. The authorities were hearing nothing of it and took him to the closest hospital for a scan and treatment to the open wounds. However, the two investigating officers wanted to know what had happened and who had done this to him. In true Mafia style, Luciano refused to say anything, denying recognizing any of the men who had attacked him. The medical team were most concerned about a deep cut to his right cheek, which had given his right eye a pronounced droop, something which would stay with him for the rest of his life. It made him look evil and even when in later life he took to dapper dressing, he could not shake off the gangster look. He discharged himself and went straight to Lansky's house, where he found out that Masseria was behind the hit. Luciano was not sufficiently powerful on his own or with his immediate gang to take on the Boss. He realized it was time to join forces with a rival and set his sights on the next biggest gang run by Salvatore Maranzano. The two men, although initially sceptical of each other's true aims, got along well and a raging two-year battle for control of the underworld between Luciano and Maranzano on the one hand and the Boss on the other erupted on the streets of New York. This bloody and brutal confrontation, often referred to as the Castellammarese War, was about settling old scores and deciding who was smart enough to be a bigger player. It is estimated that over thirty gangsters lost their lives in the 'war'.

Luciano knew there could be only one winner in this particular conflict and for him to become number two in the organization he needed to make a decisive move. In 1931, 'Lucky' had set a trap for Joe the Boss, but it had not worked; this time he swore that he would get even. In a Coney Island restaurant, Luciano, along with several close colleagues including Meyer Lansky and Bugsy Siegel, marched in and shot Masseria in a hail of bullets that killed him immediately. This made Maranzano the clear winner and he set about orchestrating rival factions into five units, all reporting back to him. Lucky's plan had worked and he was made number two in the most powerful criminal organization in New York, and possibly America, at that time. Maranzano, not content merely to obey the age-old gangster adage of keeping your friends close and your enemies even closer, had different plans for Luciano. He saw him as a real threat and planned to have him assassinated. Not for the first time, 'Lucky' lived up to his nickname and found out about the plans, sending Lansky along with four other gunmen in a pre-emptive strike. The men walked into Maranzano's premises carrying government agent badges and went straight into the main man's office. Maranzano was found several hours later stabbed to death.

Luciano was now the boss and things would never be quite the same again. He was more gregarious generally, especially with members of the criminal set. His closest friends would include some of the most notorious Mafioso gangsters of that time – Joe Adonis, Vito Genovese, Frank Costello and Bugsy Siegel. 'Lucky' was no second-rate, simple two-bit crook and had always marvelled at the success of the Roman Empire at its peak. He wanted to structure his organization along similar decentralized lines, with territories and different activities grouped together, a new vision for the future expansion of organized crime. No more racial or religious issues as with the old regime – this was business and anyone who could be trusted to bring in the money was good enough for 'Lucky'. The activities soon expanded into new areas, which proved profitable from the very start – they included establishing more luxurious gambling dens, expanding the loan-sharking operation, manipulating labour groups and blackmail. One of the most lucrative sources of cash was running gambling operations in Havana, Lansky's brain child and for which he had personally undertaken the negotiations with Batista, the Cuban dictator. Luciano trusted Lansky implicitly and recognized that he was often the brains of the outfit, being a sounding board for every new venture or business deal.

Luciano and Lansky, with the help of Bugsy Siegel, Frank Costello and Albert Anastasia, also set up something that was completely revolutionary in the world of American gangsters – it was a special group of hired killers, most of them Jewish, at least in the beginning, who would carry out contract assassinations. At first it was called the National Crime Syndicate but quickly became known as Murder Inc. It was decided that these killers would be used strictly for business reasons and would not be employed against politicians, reporters, government officials or members of the general public. Murder Inc. was run, for the most part, to regulate the various Mafia gangs, its partners and affiliates right across America. It was reportedly responsible for hundreds of hits in the 1930s alone and among its victims were Abe Wagner, Dutch Schultz and eventually even Bugsy Siegel himself. Murder Inc. effectively closed its doors in 1940 when many of the gang were arrested. One of the leaders, Abe Reles, who had been personally involved in an estimated 200 murders was one of the men charged. Facing the electric chair, he provided a great deal of evidence for the authorities, but before he could provide the full story of the group's exploits, he died mysteriously in police custody after falling seventy-five feet from a hotel window.

Every assignment handed down by one of the Mafia bosses was called a 'contract', which is where the term 'contract killing' came about. Because the group only operated under very specific instructions and usually cleared up their mess after them, they were extremely difficult to trace. Murder Inc. employed not just the best killers but also men who tracked the whereabouts of victims, wheelmen who stole cars and provided any other tools needed plus a specialist team who would move in to dispose of bodies and evidence.

Special Prosecutor Thomas Dewey assembled a strong team of New York's finest detectives and law enforcement officers, tasked with breaking the big rackets and Mafia gangs across the city. Having tried all angles, without much success for the usual reason of not enough substantiated proof, he reluctantly tried his luck with the prostitution business. This was a massive part of 'Lucky's' operation. He not only enjoyed the profits from the business, but would also regularly sample the girls too – reportedly every night for several years. However, these habits did not come without a cost as he suffered several times with gonorrhoea and once with syphilis. Dewey and his team raided no less than forty-eight brothels known to be under Luciano's control and right away the girls and the madams began to spill the beans. Many of the girls had been worked long hours, six days a week, and were poorly looked after. If a prostitute had not pleased one of the top guys, she would be beaten and thrown out onto the streets. The amount of evidence gained by the task force in a short space of time was huge and the case seemed rock solid. Dewey had promised a safe passage to some of the prostitutes in exchange for their testimony – many of them wanted to start a new life in Europe. Most of the officials and newspaper journalists believed 'Lucky' was clutching at straws as his attorneys uncovered documents that seemed to suggest that a large number of tickets to Europe were purchased by Dewey's department during the year of the trial. Evidence obtained from the use of financial incentives or coercion could be seen in a different light by a jury. Many of Luciano's gang and close associates knew about the Dewey investigation and a well-known hard man, Dutch Schultz, came up before Luciano as he desperately wanted to remove Dewey. The rest of the group knew that this was not a good idea as it would draw a huge amount of unwanted heat right on to them. Schultz was so incensed that he stormed out of the meeting, promising to assassinate him anyway. The Mafia bosses were left with no alternative and a hit on Schultz which would be handled directly by Murder Inc. was swiftly planned.

Luciano had been visiting America's Midwest, for a mixture of business and pleasure, when the police caught up with him. They served a warrant, and arrested him immediately, taking him in to police custody. Although denying all charges, 'Lucky' was worried – perhaps his luck really was running out this time. The jury heard a compelling case and the vast majority of the witnesses were convincing as evidence from dozens of brothels corroborated the witness statements. The seemingly endless string of witnesses included more than twenty-eight prostitutes – one of whom was permitted to take a shot of whisky while on the stand to help her keep the morphine shakes at bay. Being linked to prostitution was a crime not as bad as some of the other activities that Luciano was reputed to be involved in and many in his camp thought that even if he were to be found guilty his sentence would be light. A tremendous, persuasive summing up was delivered by Dewey himself, in which he described Luciano as a monster who needed to be put behind bars for a considerable time. The jury reached their verdict swiftly – guilty on all charges. The judge sentenced the thirty-eight-year-old gangster to thirty to fifty years behind bars. The severity of the sentence set a new benchmark in the American judicial system and Luciano could hardly believe his ears.

War can bring great profit to some and great loss for others. It was difficult from a cold, dark cell in upstate New York's legendary Dannemora Prison in the winter of 1942 to see how Luciano might benefit from the Second World War, but he found a way. 'Lucky', or inmate 92168 as he was know to the guards, was still able to direct his operation through meetings with friends and family – after all, money drove everything and he certainly had plenty of that. At the same time, Pearl Harbor had changed everything and American forces had moved into Europe, planning to invade North Africa, other parts of the Mediterranean, Italy and later France. For strategic reasons, the Allies wanted to tie up as many German troops as they could in North Africa and Italy, so when the time came for the bold strike over the English Channel, they would be facing a weakened army. It was also thought that if Mussolini's Italy could be made to fall, a major pillar of the Third Reich would be gone and morale affected. The British forces had already made inroads in North Africa, driving Rommel's army back to parts of mainland Europe and now it was time to move against Italy. Everyone expected Sicily to be the first piece of the jigsaw because of its location. The Allied Forces couldn't work around it as shipping across large areas of the Mediterranean could be hit from this island. Sicily is a beautiful place but would have looked very different to any invading army – mountainous and with only a few places to land a major force. They needed help and who else had better contacts with the Mafia right across Sicily than Lucky Luciano.

There is much conflicting information about exactly what was discussed between the US Army and Luciano. There were several sightings of Luciano in Sicily in 1942 and reports that he had formed part of the initial invasion forces. All of these seem fairly fanciful. Mostly the opinion seems to be that Luciano co-operated fully with the heads of the Allied Armed Forces and had many meetings with them before Sicily was invaded and during the campaign on mainland Italy. It is also widely believed that he was in touch with many of his contacts in Sicily and on mainland Italy, acting as a go-between for counter-intelligence. One thing is certain – Luciano was transferred to a much less rigorous penal institution by the name of Great Meadow Prison later that year. It was also clear that the Mafia in Italy wanted the end of the German occupation as much as they wanted to be rid of Mussolini, who had tried to curb their power as he believed there was no room in Italy for any power other than himself. Luciano was certainly in a position to offer substantial information and aid to the Allied Forces in their progress through Italy. It was rumoured that Luciano was also asked to help crack a pro-Nazi ring of saboteurs that had infiltrated the docks in New York – America was nervous, especially about its lengthy coastline, as the German U-boat threat was a very real one for several years. Again the sources are conflicting but it is highly likely that Lucky did indeed work for the authorities and managed to weed out some undesirable elements who had managed to get themselves jobs as part of the war effort. The American government and its armed forces could not be seen publicly to be doing deals with the Mafia or Luciano, for that matter, but they needed help and war was war. From 1942 onwards Lucky was doing 'easy time' – allegedly able to enjoy wine, beer, special food and, occasionally, the company of women. This was until 1946 when the governor of New York granted him a full pardon. In a strange twist of fortune, the governor at that time was none other than Thomas Dewey who would probably have liked few things better than to keep Luciano locked up. However, his hands were tied. Lucky walked free and did not have to serve any more of his sentence, but Dewey made sure that he would not be allowed to live in America again. Lucky was certainly still living up to his name.

At just before 9.00 a.m. on 10 February 1946, Charles 'Lucky' Luciano set sail for Italy on the SS *Laura Keen*. Meyer Lansky, Frank Costello, Santos Trafficante Jr, Joe Adonis, Vito Genovese and many other members of his organization were at the dockside to wish him bon voyage. He moved to Rome initially where he rented a suite in the palatial Quirinale Hotel. There were many conditions placed on Luciano by the Italian government along with many assurances given to the American authorities. One such golden rule was that Luciano wasn't supposed to travel more than a few miles from Naples without armed guard – something he would do from the very start. He had money, he had many friends in high places and was something of a celebrity in many parts of Italy – within months many of the other shackles had simply been shrugged off and Lucky began to get involved in business again.

He continued to believe that having 'friends' within the political system was essential, he even harboured political ambitions and had many discussions with Don Calo, an important man across the whole south of Italy, about setting up the Sicilian Separatist Party. Don Calo was a leading figure in the Sicilian hierarchy as well and even though a new political party was proving difficult to get off the ground, the two men went into partnership building a new factory producing confetti. It was heavily guarded twenty-four hours a day, lorries would leave in the middle of the night and the whole venture was shrouded in mystery. Several years later the factory's secret came out – far from being a confetti factory, it was, in fact, a highly advanced drug-processing laboratory.

It was suspected that opium from Turkey and the Far East was coming into ports across southern Italy and then being processed into drugs to be sold on the streets. It was also thought that he had created a partnership with the French Connection, a drug-running organization based in Marseilles. Much if this is hearsay as nothing was ever proved; Italy seems to like colourful characters almost as much as court cases involving eminent politicians. Luciano wanted to maintain his public persona as he believed it would help to keep the authorities off his back. He gave many interviews, including one to *Life* magazine, and promoted the impression of someone leading a simple, respectable life. The gangster had come home to his roots.

Early in 1947, Luciano somehow obtained a passport and boarded a flight to Cuba for the infamous Havana Conference which was attended by many of the leading American Mafia bosses and the leaders of other criminal organizations. He was still a force to be reckoned with although many thought his influence was beginning to drain away. He confided in very few people, but the main reason for his trip was to forge an alliance between the Sicilian and Corsican Mafia to dramatically expand the production and distribution of hard drugs to both America and Europe. The initial focus was on heroin, which hadn't been widely available before the war and was still commanding a good price on the streets. The Corsicans' power base in Marseilles proved to be an ideal entry point into France and from there the drugs could be moved to Germany and beyond. The demand was much greater than Luciano could supply so he set up a network of agents in Cuba who would help broker deals with South American cartels. These new partnerships also sourced opium from other parts of the world, which helped keep production levels high when shipments were caught. Heroin began flooding onto the streets of major American and European cities and at prices that were much more affordable. They were building a business empire at a rate and size beyond even Luciano's ambitions.

Lucky had been a drug-taker and heavy drinker for many years, living his life to the full in most ways possible. His heart grew weak and he had suffered several heart attacks in the early 1960s. On 26 January 1962 he had a meeting with a scriptwriter at Naples airport, following a deal with a Hollywood film company to produce a movie of his life. While waiting in the lounge, he suffered a massive heart attack and died before he could be taken to a hospital. Even in death, Luciano was controversial. He had wanted to be buried in New York, where he had spent his formative years. The authorities did not want the body to enter America but the federal court in New York ruled that his burial in United States soil could not be blocked because a corpse was technically not a citizen of any country and therefore not subject to immigration laws or deportation controls. His final resting place is St John's Cemetery, Queens, New York. It looks like Lucky has had the last laugh after all.

The French Connection

Many films depict a glorified image of gangsters, crime and criminal behaviour which rarely provides any sort of real backdrop to the events being portrayed. Probably some are better for it, but most need some central reality to enable the viewer to believe in the characters, the intricacies of the storyline and the plot development. *The French Connection*, released in 1971, and its sequel, released in 1975, were like few films either before or since. They tell the gritty story of a tough New York cop trying to intercept a huge heroin shipment coming into America from France. An interesting contrast is established between the principle characters, 'Popeye' Doyle, played magnificently by Gene Hackman, a short-tempered, hard-drinking, hard-working guy, and his nemesis Alain Charnier, a suave and sophisticated Frenchman – in reality a menacing drug lord. Doyle finds out about a big shipment of heroin and begins to tail the suspects in the hope to finding the identity of the French Connection. After an initial bust, the main culprits get away, which leads him to the port of Marseilles on the southern Mediterranean coast of France. Popeye and the local police work together to uncover one of the biggest narcotics smuggling rings on either side of the Atlantic and after lots of violence and bloodshed, the drug bosses are put behind bars. The films are obviously works of fiction, but, as so often, they are grounded in reality.

It has never been proven categorically that the French

Connection exists; quite possibly, it is merely the work of an over-imaginative journalist. Whether it is a single person, perhaps the boss of a crime network, or a whole gang of villains evolving over time in a similar way to the bosses in the great Mafia families of New York, has not been established beyond doubt. However, there is no doubt that Marseilles became, from the beginning of the twentieth century, the crime capital of France and a gateway for illegal goods from the Middle East, Africa and other parts of the world into mainland Europe. The activities of the French Connection are for the most part focused on drug dealing and, in particular, the sourcing and movement of heroin. Much of the trade saw large shipments enter Europe and America, sometimes via Canada. It has been a very secretive organization which has seen many upturns and downturns in its fortunes. In the period between the First and Second World Wars, much of the serious, organized crime in the south of France was controlled by one of two men: Emile Buisson or Antoine La Rocca. Buisson came from a tough background – his father was a drunk and was addicted to highly potent absinthe, which for a number of years was banned in many countries, including the United Kingdom, for its harmful effects. His mother gave birth to nine children but due to the conditions in which the family lived only four survived. Overcome by the demands of caring for her children, the beatings administered by her husband and the lack of adequate nutrition, she was eventually taken into an asylum. Things got worse for young Emile when his father was also sent to an asylum on charges of having sexually abused his children.

Buisson took to thieving in a small gang while still at school and was sentenced to his first prison term at the age of only sixteen. This coincided with his being drafted to perform national service so he spent much of his term in a penal outpost in North Africa. The conditions were uncompromising but Buisson enjoyed combat and was awarded the Croix de Guerre for bravery. Once back in France, he reverted to criminality with gusto, his exploits culminating in the violent robbery of a major bank branch in Troyes in late 1937. He shot one man in the leg and was seen by passers-by firing his gun randomly as he escaped by car. Police picked him up early the following year but his trial was delayed because of a backlog and the start of the Second World War overshadowed everything. He managed to escape from prison and held up two further banks in 1941, killing a number of bank staff in the process. While many in France sat out the war, joined the resistance or actively collaborated with the Nazis, Buisson continued with his life of crime. The maintenance of law and order in an occupied country is not easily accomplished, something of benefit, no doubt, to criminals like Buisson. After the war a number of botched attempts to bring him to justice failed, but the police finally caught up with him in 1955. This time justice was swift and he was convicted of multiple murders, robbery, theft and a long list of other misdemeanours. Early the following year, he was executed by means of the guillotine.

La Rocca was born and bred in Naples. He took under his wing a gangster by the name of Francois Spirito who was to become a major player in his own right. La Rocca hired a Corsican hitman by the name of Jerome Colombani to help him rid the town of unwanted African competition. Several North African gangs had moved in and set up illegal import operations. La Rocca and Colombani drove around late at night and spied on their targets – when the time was right they opened fire. Their weapon of choice was the German-manufactured Mauser semi-automatic. At the end of one particularly industrious night, four men lay dead, dozens had been injured and an unknown number had gone back into hiding or returned to North Africa.

La Rocca's stakes in prostitution, people-smuggling, extortion and drug-running grew at speed, but things were getting hot for him on the popular French coastline as police amassed significant evidence against him. After killing a local pimp, La Rocca moved back to Naples from where he flew to Alexandria where he displayed his skill in developing criminal businesses with remarkable speed. When the authorities caught up with him, he managed to escape to Buenos Aires in Argentina, a city well known as a last resort for fugitives. At this time he had less interest in and influence over the French network, even though trips to cities in neighbouring Italy and Spain allowed him to meet many of the leading players; day-to-day affairs were being run by Spirito. La Rocca was eventually assassinated by Henri Ruiz at a nightclub called El Monica, which, the police later established, La Rocca co-owned. Spirito knew that he couldn't run the growing operation alone and enlisted the help of the notorious Paul Carbone. Although the men disagreed on many issues, they developed into a formidable force. Spirito saw the potential in opium and expanded his operation importing the illegal substance from Egypt and the Middle East, while Carbone trafficked prostitutes to all corners of France and beyond. Together they produced fake passports, immigration forms and other documents, ran guns, organized protection rackets, supplied illegal gambling machines, produced and transported heroin and cocaine, and bribed police and government officials – a diverse criminal empire, all of it orchestrated from Marseilles. However, the two gangsters made increasingly regular trips to Paris to keep a close eye on the selling and cash collection end of the business – something close to the hearts of both men.

The relatively smooth expansion and development of the drug business via links to powerful Mafia families in New York was interruption by the outbreak of the Second World War. When France fell the gangsters had new masters to contend with – the Nazis. Many of the Marseilles-based gangsters worked for the resistance but plenty of them appeared content to sit out the war knowing that running their criminal empire would have been all but impossible. There was, of course, plenty of illegal activity: buying and selling guns, forging documents, supplying scarce resources, but many aspects of the pre-War organization were simply not possible. Even criminals felt the full impact of the war. Carbone joined the resistance and died heroically during the attempted derailment of a German train with high explosives. Spirito was arrested in much less heroic circumstances just after the war and spent the remainder of his life behind bars. Following the war, a new era in France's colourful underworld began. The heroin labs that had been developed near Marseilles before the war had had to be destroyed during the occupation and the post-War trade saw a change to the importation of street-ready heroin and, later, cocaine. Turkey was still a major player because of the number of farmers that grew the opium plants and paid the government to turn a blind eye. The police had little idea of the scale of the problem but seizures were up and many felt this was just the tip of the iceberg. On 17 March 1947, twenty-eight pounds of heroin was found on the French liner *St Tropez* and, less than two years later, fifty pounds of opium were found on board the French ship *Batista*.

The assassination of President Kennedy in December 1963 has given rise to more conspiracy theories than perhaps any other crime in modern history. A new twist came to light in the late 1980s, which sought to connect the assassination to France's Mediterranean coast. In a documentary called *The Men Who Killed Kennedy*, an investigative journalist, Steve Rivele, presented information from an interview with a French criminal called Christian David, who was serving time for drug smuggling and a variety of other offences in a US prison. David claimed that the contract on Kennedy had originated in Marseilles via Antoine Guerini. This man was a well-known gangster at that time, reputed to be the Mafia boss of the town and the head of the French Connection.

As well as being a member of the French Connection heroin network, David had also been a leader of the so-called Latin Connection, a Corsican drug-trafficking network, and he had also served as an agent for a number of intelligence services around the world. David claimed to have been aware of a conspiracy to murder Kennedy; in fact, he said that he had been offered the contract in May or June 1963 in Marseilles. According to David, three killers had been hired on a contract put out by Antoine Guerini, the leader of the Corsican Mafia in Marseilles. David declined the job on hearing that the assassination was to be carried out in the USA as he felt that it would be much too dangerous. David was reluctant to give the names of two of the killers as they were still alive and were members of the Corsican Mafia which bound him to an oath of secrecy, on pain of his own death. He did, however, name the third, deceased man as Lucien. Rivele established that this was Lucien Sarti, a Corsican drug-trafficker and contract killer active in the 1960s and 1970s who had been killed in Mexico City in 1972. David confirmed that Sarti was indeed one of the killers.

Apparently the killers had been flown from Marseilles to Mexico City where they had spent about a month before being driven over the US border, making use of Italian passports, to Brownsville, Texas. They were picked up there by a member of the Chicago Mafia and driven to Dallas where they were put up in a safe house. They spent several days taking photographs of Dealey Plaza and arranging a 'crossfire' to involve three guns. David asserted that two of the killers were in buildings behind the presidential limousine, one of them almost on a level with it, which Rivele took to mean that there was a gunman on ground level, probably in the Dal-Tex Building, which would explain the initial reaction of Nellie Connally, the wife of the governor of Texas who was riding in the presidential limousine – turning around to look – captured on Zapruder's film. According to David, Sarti had worn a uniform of some kind as a disguise during the assassination. He said that there were four shots altogether: the first, fired from behind, hit the president in the back; the second, also fired from behind, hit John Connally; the third shot was fired by Sarti from the front and struck the president in the head; the fourth shot, fired from the rear, missed the limousine completely. Two of the shots were apparently fired more or less simultaneously.

In the ensuing panic, Sarti was apparently able to escape to the safe house where he stayed with the others for over a week until things had quietened down. The hitmen were then flown by private plane from Dallas to Montreal, from where they returned to Marseilles.

Asked if there were anyone who could substantiate his story, David told Rivele to look for a man named Michel. Taking this to be Michel Nicoli, a former drug-trafficker turned government informant who had 'disappeared' as a protected witness, Rivele searched for him, travelling thousands of miles to three continents and speaking to hundreds of people. Finally, in June 1986, almost by accident, Rivele met the one person in the US government, a top-level official in the Drug Enforcement Administration, who knew where Nicoli was. This official agreed to put Rivele in contact with Nicoli, saying that he was the best witness that he'd ever worked with, that if Nicoli said something was true, invariably it was found to be so. Nicoli corroborated David's story.

Attitudes towards drugs were hardening and, in 1972, the Turkish government finally agreed to a complete ban on the growing of opium. There were, however, some up-and-coming gangsters who weren't put off by these difficult market conditions. The French underworld, during the1970s and 1980s, was controlled by the Zemours family, who took up this challenge. The father, Raymond, was originally a wine merchant from Setif in Algeria, and had four sons Roland, William, Gilbert and Edward. The oldest son, Roland, had already come to Paris with friends of the family and was beginning to get himself into trouble. The wine business served as a front for a whole range of illegal activities ranging from fencing stolen goods and protection rackets to prostitution, property and drugs. They bought, usually with a combination of force and some cash, a series of nightclubs, casinos and gambling dens and then sat back as the profits rolled in. At its peak, the gang had 200 members in Paris alone, although around forty were known to have been killed in attacks by rival groups in the space of only a couple of years. Many of the running street battles were with Sicilian mobs who wanted a greater slice of the Parisian drug business. Four Italian gang leaders were assassinated in quick succession and hostilities escalated to such a degree that even the Zemours had to resort to outside bodyguards. The police used their contacts and influence with rival gangs to lay a trap for all the Zemours. They managed to orchestrate the coming together of all four male members of the family in one place and on 28 February 1975, in a café close to the Latin Quarter, the trap was set. Things didn't go exactly to plan for the authorities as a fierce gun battle ensued in which William was killed, Gilbert wounded from a shot in the back, and another gang member, Joseph Elbaz, was also killed, his body left behind in the narrow, cobbled streets.

After this incident relative calm prevailed on the streets of the major cities of France – certainly in terms of an absence of gangland killings, drive-by shootings and bombings. That is until early in 1982 when Marcel Francisci, one of the five men suspected of running the French Connection, was shot dead as he returned from holiday. He was a Sicilian and reputed to have many friends in the European and American underworld and in the South American drug cartels. The Zemours were thought to have been behind the killing and less than three months later Edward Zemour was killed by a hitman inside his Miami home. In July of that same year, Gilbert was executed in a similar manner as he walked his dogs. The only remaining brother Roland went into hiding and the Zemours's empire crumbled quite quickly.

In the 1990s French godfathers seemed to have come and gone with remarkable regularity – usually leaving for their final resting place not long after taking the top job. French authorities believe that, irrespective of the people involved, drug imports are at record levels as well as people smuggling and the traffic in young women brought in from many parts of the world to work in the seedy, 'red light' areas of cities across Europe. Francis Vanverberghe, often referred to as 'the Belgian', was reputed to be the man on whom the film-makers based one of the central characters in the first *French Connection* film. He was one of the last surviving, powerful crew from the 1970s and 1980s until he was shot dead in a betting parlour in 2004. The killer escaped on a motorbike and no one has ever been arrested in connection with the murder. Jacky Imbert, known as 'Mad Jacky' by many of his Mafia colleagues, was convicted of extortion charges in a Marseilles court in 2006 and represented perhaps the last of the big bosses to fall. Imbert had led a charmed life since first appearing in front of French authorities in 1963 for killing the well-known gang leader Andreani Baptiste. He was also connected with the murder of Antoine Guerini and managed to survive an assassination plot when three hitmen caught up with him in the small port of Cassis. The killers left him for dead with twenty-two bullets in his body. After six months of quiet rehabilitation, he was able to exact revenge in the traditional manner.

The story of the real-life French Connection is one of narcotics distribution and selling. The people and gangs that made up the organization varied over time while the business grew exponentially in response to the demand for drugs on the streets. Although Marseilles was the base for many of the activities for years and still remains the nerve centre, new routes for smuggling have opened, often in smaller, less developed ports in France, Italy and many of the developing countries on the Mediterranean such as Albania, Croatia and Slovenia.

Bonnie and Clyde

Many ordinary citizens during the Great Depression of the 1930s saw notorious gangsters and bank robbers as somehow victims of injustice, driven to desperate acts by increasingly desperate times. It was as if these people were just expressing what many others felt. The widely held belief was that these desperate acts were not the fault of the perpetrators, but a direct outcome of the state of the economy, exacerbated by a woefully inept government. Many of the southern states of the USA fell on particularly hard times and young people struggled to see how they could ever make ends meet, let alone build a good future for themselves. It was as if the American dream had collapsed along with Wall Street in 1929 when the nation's wealth plummeted by almost 40 per cent overnight. In many rural areas, people couldn't afford their repayments on farms, property, equipment and stores, and foreclosures hit record levels. Another sign that went up on shop fronts in towns and cities across many states stated simply: 'Out of Business'. This was the backdrop to a dramatic love story like no other before or even, perhaps, since.

Bonnie Elizabeth Parker was born on 1 October 1910 in the small, rural Texas town of Rowena. A good student, who had a flair for writing and drama, she moved to Dallas with her mother when her father died. As she grew up she attended the First Baptist Church every Sunday morning with her mother and grandmother and to everyone who knew the family it appeared close and loving. Standing just 4 foot 11 inches, Parker was slim, very pretty, had ringlets in her hair and was also close to her two siblings. She would turn heads with her looks and her smile. There was a deep streak of impetuosity within her and at the age of just sixteen she met and married a young man by the name of Roy Thornton. We know little about this relationship but it seemed doomed from the start. Within a year he was spending time in prison, thereby ensuring that their union would struggle to develop. In 1929, Parker informed Thornton that the marriage was over. Although she struggled to find the courage to make this decision, she knew in her heart that it was the right one. She had no shortage of admirers after this but she had no serious relationships. Working as a waitress to make ends meet was not the life that she had dreamed of at all.

Clyde Chestnut Barrow at 5 foot 7 inches was taller than Bonnie and eighteen months older. He was the fifth of seven children and had a handsome, roguish charm. He was born on 24 March 1909, also in a Texan backwater, Telico in Ellis County, into a poor, working-class family. His first nickname was 'Champion', supposedly because of his competitive nature, and he was popular with his peers. His parents moved to the outskirts of Dallas, where his father ran a gas station on Eagle Ford Road. Barrow would later say that he never forgot the humiliation of having to live under a flyover with other transient families when they first arrived in Dallas. He felt they all deserved better, especially his hard-working father. Barrow was arrested for the first time when just twenty years old for a series of poorly thought out and badly executed robberies. Barrow dropped out of school early and spent the days sleeping and the nights hanging out in pool halls, the nearby freight yards and on street corners. His life of crime hadn't got off to a good start but he was undeterred. He stole cars and other goods (he was once arrested for stealing turkeys), learnt how to crack safes, burgled stores and lifted produce from neighbourhood shops. He did hold down a couple of legitimate jobs from the age of eighteen to twenty but he was bored by the mundane nature of what he had to do. He yearned for a more exciting existence.

There are several versions of how Bonnie and Clyde met, but the most credible is as follows. One of Clyde's sisters worked in a local neighbourhood diner in Oak Cliff, Dallas, and he decided one evening to pay her a visit as she had broken her arm. Business was slow and while the two were chatting, Barrow heard a loud noise coming from inside the kitchen. His sister advised him to go and say hello to her friend who was called Bonnie. This chance meeting, in January 1930, resulted in love at first sight for both of them and would change their lives for ever. They talked into the early hours and continued to see each other over the next couple of months. However, this flowering love was to be cut short – the police arrested Barrow for a string of offences that had taken place in Waco the year before and he was soon behind bars for a two-year stay. This must have been difficult for Bonnie to come to terms with as she had already been through a similar trauma not that long before. There are a number of reports of trouble during Clyde's first stint in prison, the most notable being that he actually killed a fellow inmate by the name of 'Big Ed'. It was alleged that this man had tried to sexually assault Barrow and was later found beaten to death with a blunt instrument. The true identity of the murderer probably went to the grave with the men concerned but another inmate would take the rap as he was already a 'lifer'. Many believe that this was a turning point in Clyde's life; he had never shown ultra-violent tendencies before and this was not the act of just another car thief. Bonnie, against her mother's express wishes, took time off from work and went to visit her lover. Clyde had become good friends with a fellow prisoner by the name of Frank Turner and both wanted to find a way to escape. They came up with a plan but they needed a gun and Clyde persuaded Bonnie to smuggle one into the prison. Her next visit was just a couple of weeks later and she had brought the 'present' as instructed, leaving it in the agreed place. He told Bonnie to go to Dallas and wait for him – promising that he would take her with him even though police cars cruised the streets outside the Barrow gas station and her neighbourhood.

Clyde and Turner made their escape after beating one guard and threatening to shoot several others. They both sensed Dallas would be too hot for them, so they absconded to Illinois and robbed a series of small stores, service stations and market traders to get some much needed cash. The gains were small and the young men continually needed more money as they moved from town to town, stealing and robbing as they went. On 19 March they were recaptured by police in Ohio after their car was recognized by a passer-by and the two men were taken back to Dallas to face trial. Clyde was sentenced to fourteen years hard labour at the fearsome Eastham Prison Farm in Huntsville which had a reputation for being tough and uncompromising. In John Neal Phillips's book *Running with Bonnie and Clyde*, he relays how 'guards would sit around and draw straws for who would have the pleasure of beating the next unfortunate prisoner'. He also goes on to describe the penal institution as 'a place so vile as to make any veteran of its confines dread the consequences should he ever break the law of Eastham'. Some of the most notorious prisons in America were found in the southern states, a region that prided itself on being very religious by nature – America's Bible Belt clearly thought that the idea of forgiveness wasn't a realistic one as harsh punishment was meted out to anyone who broke the law.

Clyde picked cotton and laid stone from morning to night under the broiling Texas heat and in gruelling conditions with the only highlights being the loving letters that he received from Parker. Prisoners at Eastham were only allowed to receive letters from blood relations, so on entry Clyde had filled out the official papers stating that Bonnie was his wife. She wrote often, expressing her love for him and describing how she longed for him and couldn't wait for his return. Clyde's mother campaigned tirelessly on his behalf for a more lenient sentence and he was paroled after having spent less than two years inside. The whole process was aided when Clyde got a fellow inmate to let an axe slip on his foot, something that his mother was quick to tell the authorities. He walked free in February 1932, on crutches, smiling and with two toes fewer than when he had arrived. Bonnie and Clyde immediately began spending a lot of time together and their love affair blossomed in a way that was apparent to everyone. Even during this happy time, Clyde felt as though he had been treated unjustly and set about forming a new gang, to which end he recruited former Eastham inmates Ray Hamilton and Ralph Fults. They were not keen on having a girl along with them, but, for Clyde, this was non-negotiable – Bonnie was part of the gang. She was coming along and Bonnie and Clyde would never be separated again.

The Barrow gang set off on an infamous spree, beginning by robbing a hardware store in Kaufman, Texas, on 18 April 1932. Fults was shot and captured during the ensuing battle with the police, as was Bonnie, but as she was unknown to the police, they believed her story that she was just an innocent bystander and she was released soon afterwards. Just twelve days later the gang held up a store in Hillsboro, killing the ower John Bucher in the process. It is not easy to step back in time to imagine how ill-equipped and under-resourced the law enforcement agencies of that time were compared with those of today. There were no surveillance cameras and existing investigative techniques were fairly unsophisticated. To prosecute criminals the police needed good, reliable witnesses who were willing to testify and who could positively identify perpetrators even if the crime had been a quick, smash-and-grab raid carried out under cover of darkness. Often, number plates were spotted, and Clyde, having once been caught out in this way, always made sure that his plates were changed before morning.

Many nomadic criminals like Bonnie and Clyde must have thought that they could keep on running and stay one step ahead of the law. The gang stole cars and just about anything else they wanted but being on the road was no bed of roses. Barrow had a tremendous talent behind the wheel of a car, something that got them out of more than a couple of scrapes, but finding safe places to eat and sleep was not easy. One member of the gang was always on watch and peaceful rest was virtually impossible. There was considerable discord at times within the Barrow gang which led to constant changes in its make-up.

The gang criss-crossed state boundaries from Texas to Illinois to New Mexico to evade capture and arrest. They believed that this would keep the individual state police forces guessing as to their whereabouts and what was coming next. On one such trip to Stringtown, Oklahoma, they attended an outdoor dance but were spotted by a local man who called the police. Sheriff Eugene Moore confronted them and was shot dead while Sheriff C. G. Maxwell was wounded by shots which scattered the entire crowd. In another high-speed getaway, the Barrow gang narrowly escaped capture, departing down a dark, country lane just before reinforcements could get to the scene. In October of that year, Clyde killed a grocery store owner in Howard Hall during a hold-up and two months later he shot Doyle Johnson, the owner of a car they were trying to steal. He showed no remorse; it was as if he was simply taking what was due to him. Clyde continued to believe that stealing different cars and changing number plates would make them difficult to spot, but their growing fame made simple things like filling up with petrol increasingly risky.

The turn of the year saw no let-up in the activities of the violent gang. By this time they were national celebrities and the police were under increasing pressure to put them away. In January, Malcolm Davis was killed in Dallas trying to arrest them and two more police officers were murdered three months later close to their Missouri hideout just outside Joplin. During this time, the outlaw band had several new members that came and went, most notably Clyde's elder brother Buck and his wife Blanche. Clyde knew that the gang faced growing numbers of local police as well as special teams which were being drafted in to hunt them across state borders. They lay low in a new hideout for a couple of months but their money ran out, forcing them to take once more to the roads, this time on an amazingly violent summer spree. Bonnie was severely burned and partially crippled in a car crash in June and Clyde shot the highly respected Marshall Henry Humphrey in an attempted hold-up that went wrong. In July the gang was being repeatedly spotted by members of the public and was being followed almost continually, managing to keep just one step ahead of the pursuing pack. Their luck finally ran out on 19 July when a shootout took place at a cabin in Platte City, Missouri, where Buck was wounded and Blanche received facial injuries while trying to escape. Five days later, at the Perry Hospital, Dexfield Park, Iowa, Buck died from his injuries. Blanche was arrested and later given a lengthy sentence. In the meantime, the two lovers made another daring escape, driving their car down side roads under the noses of the police and in a hail of bullets.

Bonnie and Clyde were greatly saddened by the death of Buck and the imprisonment of Blanche and planned a visit to their respective families in Dallas. Bonnie, in particular, was very homesick and missed her mother, Emma Parker, who she used to write to quite regularly. They were spotted going through a small town and the Dallas police were waiting in yet another ambush planned for them. Amazingly no one was killed and the infamous pair escaped, driving at high speed across fields and getting only minor wounds. They needed a change of car and held up an unsuspecting district attorney on the highway and liberated his much loved vehicle, which was later abandoned in Miami, Oklahoma.

On 21 December, showing that no job was too small – they held up and robbed a single person walking down the road in Shreveport, Louisiana. As Christmas came, Clyde turned his thoughts to breaking out Raymond Hamilton, Joe Palmer and possibly others from Eastham Farm Prison.

Jimmy Mullens had been sharing a cell with Hamilton and had been promised one thousand dollars for anyone who could spring him out.

The routine at Eastham was well known to the outlaws as it hadn't changed for many years: a group of guards would oversee the work squad from close range and a further guard on horseback equipped with high-powered rifles would be situated some way away, ready to react quickly. A gun had been hidden close to where the prisoners were working and Palmer was the first to reach the spot. Reports vary about what happened next but one guard was fatally shot in the stomach and another was shot while trying to ride back to the prison to raise the alarm. Bonnie and Clyde had parked their car just out of sight but could hear the commotion and from their vantage point under some trees they fired several rounds from a rifle over the heads of everyone. Two guards turned and ran for cover and only one stood his ground over the remaining inmates, preventing a mass breakout. Palmer and Hamilton made it to the trees and into the car and they were soon heading rapidly towards the dusty town of Hugo, Oklahoma, where Bonnie and Clyde had planned to switch cars.

Neither Palmer nor Hamilton would stay with Bonnie and Clyde for very long. They were too 'hot' and the men had different views on what to do next with their freedom. However, within months both had been recaptured and returned to prison and Palmer was later convicted of the murder of the prison guard, for which he was sentenced to death. The same fate awaited Hamilton for his part in a string of offences. Jimmy Mullens was the state's main witness, having received immunity for his lesser charges. For the romantic twosome, it was perhaps the beginning of the end. They continued to travel and tried to lie low during daylight hours but things weren't getting any easier as their faces appeared in newspapers and police handouts and on billboards. On 1 April, the couple had an encounter with two police officers from the town of Grapevine, Texas, namely

E. B. Wheeler and H. D. Murphy, who were both fatally shot by Clyde. Only five days later in a similar incident two unsuspecting policemen stopped to investigate a vehicle that had stalled by the side of the road. They had no idea of the identity of the two people inside and realized too late. Constable C. Campbell was killed and Police Chief P. Boyd was wounded and kidnapped and thrown into the back of the truck, though he was later released. The FBI had already been involved in tracking the gang, but their efforts were doubled after this latest spate of high-profile incidents – the circulation of 'Wanted' notices and hand-bills was increased, every clue was swiftly followed up and police teams right across the southern states were working together for the first time.

Anything to do with Bobbie and Clyde became instant front-page news across America but particularly in the southern region where large numbers of people would visit places that had won instant fame as a result of shootings, sightings or robberies. However, someone new made the news at around this time. It was a retired Texas Ranger by the name of Frank Hamer. He had been commissioned to find and kill Bonnie and Clyde, and quickly cut a deal with Henry Methvin to use him as bait. Hamer had promised Methvin a full pardon if he delivered the outlaws, and an ambush plan was hatched. Methvin was to send word to Bonnie and Clyde to meet him at his parents' home in Bienville Parish, Louisiana. The couple knew the place well as they had used it as a safe house many times on their journeys, getting to know many members of the family. They also trusted Methvin, who had taken part in a number of robberies with them. It seemed a perfect plan. Hamer had figured that as Bonnie and Clyde had been on the road for so long they would both welcome the opportunity to enjoy a period of rest and relaxation among people they knew. Clyde duly received Hamer's message and changed his plans to keep the rendezvous, suspecting nothing, only looking forward to meeting up with an old friend and trusted ally.

Hamer kept very quiet about his plans – even within the

ranks of the police authorities. Very few people indeed knew what was planned for fear of a leak to the papers who would bribe anyone for stories or news of the couple. After waiting two full days and nights, the time had come for Hamer to put his plan to the test. All of the men involved were feeling the pressure and the mood was tense. The hit squad included Ted Hinton, P. M. Oakley, B. M. Gault, Bob Alcorn, Henderson Jordan and their leader, Frank Hamer. At around 9.10 a.m. on 23 May 1934 Hamer's nervous group of officers heard the roar of a car approaching rapidly across the bumpy track from Highway 154, between Gibsland and Sailes. The men were spread out, hiding in the bushes and trees along the dusty track close to the house. They could make out the licence plate (15-368), which was from Arkansas, but Hamer needed to know for sure that this was Bonnie and Clyde and not another false alarm. Two of the officers present, Ted Hinton and Bob Alcorn, could identify the gangsters so they looked out from their hiding place. They positively identified the couple to Hamer who had already decided that no warning would be given. There was a momentary pause, then, as the car was no more than fifty yards away, the order was given to the officers to open fire with the aim of killing both occupants of the car. In a short space of time, each officer pumped the entire contents of his gun into the approaching Ford 34. In a matter of seconds, about 130 rounds, many of them from very close range, hit the car. The officers were close enough to see two figures slump in their seats as the car shook and bounced from the impact of the direct hits. When the shooting was over, Bonnie and Clyde lay dead, having been shot more than fifty times each. It had been a short, violent and destructive love affair from the first with neither of them willing to separate from the other.

There is still some controversy as to whether Bonnie Parker deserved to die so young. There were many at the time who felt that her love and feelings for Clyde had overtaken everything else. It is not known what legal authority there was to kill her or even if she had ever killed anyone herself. She had certainly taken part in prison breaks, kidnappings and robberies but none of these warranted the death penalty in any of the states where they had occurred. Former Barrow gang members W. D. Jones and Ralph Fults testified that they had never even seen her fire a gun. One thing was for sure, Hamer was not going to hold up proceedings for one second to ask questions or to find out. Several of the police posse kept stolen guns that they found in the back of the car as souvenirs. This was approved by Lee Simmons, the acting district police boss, who was happy to reward such courage. Each officer became a national celebrity in a matter of minutes and the reputation of police authorities across the southern belt of America was restored.

The final resting places of both criminals can be found in Dallas, Texas. Clyde Barrow was buried in Western Heights Cemetery and Bonnie Parker in Crown Hill Memorial Park. The poem below was handed by Bonnie Parker to her mother the last time they were together. Reports from the meeting suggest it was very poignant as the still very youthful, pretty, diminutive daughter talked about being on the run and how she expected not to see her mother again. The poem is undoubtedly an amazing piece of writing, self-aware and insightful, written by a woman who was still very young at the time of her death. Below is the poem exactly as written by Bonnie.

The Story of Bonnie and Clyde

You've read the story of Jesse James
Of how he lived and died
If you're still in need for something to read
Here's the story of Bonnie and Clyde.

Now Bonnie and Clyde are the Barrow gang,
I'm sure you all have read
how they rob and steal
And those who squeal are usually found dying or dead.

There's lots of untruths to those write-ups
They're not so ruthless as that
Their nature is raw, they hate all law
Stool pigeons, spotters, and rats.

They call them cold-blooded killers
They say they are heartless and mean
But I say this with pride, I once knew Clyde
When he was honest and upright and clean.

But the laws fooled around and taking him down
and locking him up in a cell
'Till he said to me, "I'll never be free
So I'll meet a few of them in hell."

The road was so dimly lighted
There were no highway signs to guide
But they made up their minds if all roads were blind
They wouldn't give up 'till they died.

The road gets dimmer and dimmer
Sometimes you can hardly see
But it's fight man to man, and do all you can
For they know they can never be free.

From heartbreak some people have suffered
From weariness some people have died
But all in all, our troubles are small
'Till we get like Bonnie and Clyde.

If a policeman is killed in Dallas
And they have no clue or guide
If they can't find a friend, just wipe the slate clean
And hang it on Bonnie and Clyde.

There's two crimes committed in America
Not accredited to the Barrow Mob
They had no hand in the kidnap demand
Nor the Kansas City Depot job.

A newsboy once said to his buddy,
"I-wish old Clyde would get jumped
In these hard times we'd get a few dimes
If five or six cops would get bumped."

The police haven't got the report yet
But Clyde called me up today
He said, "Don't start any fights, we aren't
working nights, we're joining the NRA."

From Irving to West Dallas viaduct
Is known as the Great Divide
Where the women are kin and men are men
And they won't stool on Bonnie and Clyde.

If they try to act like citizens
And rent a nice little flat
About the third night they're invited to fight
By a sub-gun's rat-tat-tat.

They don't think they're tough or desperate
They know the law always wins
They've been shot at before, but they do not ignore
That death is the wages of sin.

Someday they'll go down together
And they'll bury them side by side
To few it'll be grief, to the law a relief
But it's death for Bonnie and Clyde.

Yakuza

Criminal organizations vary tremendously from country to country, in terms of how they do business, how they are structured and what illicit activities they are involved in. A society's culture is a major influence on how crime in carried out and how criminal gangs develop and act. Social revolutions, huge political upheavals, religious movements and the migration of large masses of men and women can all affect how criminal groups evolve. Japan's people, its history and many of its beliefs are quite strikingly different from elsewhere in the world and its gangsters, too, are unique in the global underworld. Japan comprises a series of long, slender islands; most of the population, though, live on the largest island, Honshu. The Sea of Japan separates Japan from Russia and North and South Korea to the west, while to the east lies the open Pacific. To the south and west lies the restless giant, China. Oppression in Japan has come in many forms and the true origins of the Yakuza lie in their role as protectors of the poor rather than as predators on the rich.

Yakuza can be traced back as far as the year 1612, when *kabuki-mono*, literally meaning 'the crazy ones', armed themselves with specially sharpened swords to protect villagers and townspeople. The *kabuki-mono* were also sometimes referred to as *hatamoto-yakko*, meaning 'servants of the shogun'. Many films have been made of this era but Akira Kurosawa's magnificent epic, *Seven Samurai*, made in 1954, remains the best. It tells the story of a group of villagers who decide to hire a professional warrior to protect them from the annual raid of bandits who steal food and other possessions.

The *kabuki-mono* were eccentric samurai who wore strange clothing (a rarity in Japan at that time) and whose behaviour was often unpredictable. Their often strange haircuts and large swords – occasionally two of them worn on either side of the waistband – made them instantly recognizable and much feared. Their loyalty to one another was remarkable – well beyond the loyalty that they felt towards their own family members or close friends. At the height of their power they amassed enormous fortunes, but in the Tokugawa era, a time of widespread peace, their numbers dropped as the need for their services declined. Many became *ronin* – leaderless bands of outlaws, roaming the countryside, stealing and robbing. Many modern-day Yakuza members deny that they are the descended from the *ronin* and claim that their true antecedents are the *kabuki-mono*, protectors of the defenceless. Power, however, has corrupted many groups, no matter how noble their original objectives may have been.

The number of present-day Yakuza members is difficult to assess accurately – estimates vary wildly, but it is thought that there are around 5,000 gangs operating in Japan, comprising almost 200,000 people. Gangs of Yakuza operating overseas, particularly in America, should also be added to this total. The Yakuza have a guiding principle of the *oyabun-kobun* relationship – *oyabun* means literally 'role of the father' and *kobun* is the 'role of the child' or 'son'. Each gang is like a family with a father at the head, making all the important decisions, and the children obediently following orders. The chain of responsibility beneath each boss is more complicated with regional heads, a senior adviser, or advisers, and a headquarters chief. This structure is usually established above *wakashu* (junior leaders) and, below them, *shatei* (seen as younger brothers). Anyone wanting to join a Yakuza needs to be proposed by a guarantor and part of the initiation is to drink sake with the boss; in the Mafia equivalent a member will draw blood from his trigger finger. If a Yakuza member displeases either the main man or his guarantor, his punishment is the amputation of the last joint of his little finger. Another serious offence may result in the severing of the second joint of the same finger; further offences result in similar mutilation of the remaining fingers.

From the turn of the twentieth century, Yakuza gangs have fallen into one of three categories – *tekiza* (street peddlers), *takuto* (gamblers) or *gurentai* (hoodlums). The last of these factions, since the 1930s, have modelled themselves on the American gangsters of the time such as Al Capone, using similar means of extortion and bribery to build a power base and assets. It was, in fact, the period just after the Second World War that saw the fastest growth in numbers and activities caused by a desire for more individual freedom. The Japanese government were allowed to perform very few tasks and the Yakuza stepped into the breach, replacing their samurai swords with modern-day weapons, even though these had been outlawed by the surrender terms of 1945. With the growth of the Yakuza gangs came great violence in the form of big turf wars between rival gangs. With the Japanese government's hands tied, the way was open for many of the criminal gangs to prosper by taking control of assets, property and commercial business operations. The man who was widely credited with bringing many of these bitter factions together was the group's first twentieth-century godfather, Yoshio Kodama. He was able to deal with influential right-wing political forces, while at the same time placating the various criminal gangs. He had developed contacts before the war when the government had need of resources such as copper, nickel and other metals with military uses. He bartered cash, goods and heroin to make these deals work for both sides and his network grew internationally until it included spies and informants in China, Russia and Korea. In many ways, he was seen by the government as a fixer and espionage agent, dealing in areas where they couldn't afford to be seen to be operating. From the underworld's point of view, he wielded great political power, supplying vital information and with access that had previously been extremely difficult to obtain.

By the end of the Second World War, Kodama was worth an estimated $150 million, but he was seen by the Allies as a 'Class A' war criminal. He served only two years in jail, though, before being released under a general amnesty. Once back in business, he was able to call on huge street gangs to carry out his political will and at the same time strengthen his spy network, especially in Russia and China. It is reported that the CIA paid him $150,000 in 1949 to use his connections to smuggle a shipload of tungsten out of China – although the boat never reached its destination, the fee was never returned. He was settling an old score and he wasn't afraid because of his great power in Japan and neighbouring countries, especially when compared with an American agency. Kodama was a fervent anti-Communist and would often order Yakuza groups to break up labour marches or anything that he thought was disruptive. He was also a strong nationalist, one of the leading men in *Kenkoku-kai*, the Association of the Founding of the Nation, a radical pro-Japanese organization the activities of which were often top secret. Many of these things endeared him to high-ranking Japanese political figures as well as his public support for peace, which was ironic given that he was perfectly prepared to use extreme violence to achieve peace.

Kodama showed his true political skill in the 1950s and 1960s, when opportunities where plentiful. He was even paid by the massive G2 enterprise to act as their go-between with the Yakuza network. A few years later, Kodama was one of the pivotal figures in the notorious Lockheed scandal, which revolved around the giant aircraft corporation paying him an amount in excess of $2 million to use his influence with major Japanese companies which were purchasing aircraft at the time. One way in which he did this was to send a gang to disrupt the annual general meeting of Nippon Airways, along with spreading rumours that the company had made a huge loan to the president of the company. Under mounting pressure, the president of the company resigned and a new man was appointed who was much more favourable in his attitude towards Lockheed. In 1976, the head of Lockheed, while subject to a United States Senate investigation, gave revealing testimony that hit the headlines back in Japan. Police were unable to find enough evidence to convict Kodama but found that he had evaded taxes to the tune of $6 million. Public pressure was growing and his empire was beginning to crumble around him. He survived a bizarre assassination attempt when someone tried to fly a plane into his house but time was running out as the authorities were closing in. He was indicted for bribery, violating exchange laws and perjury but before the case could be completed Kodama died of a stroke. This was a great relief for many leading Japanese politicians and businessmen all around the Pacific Rim, as his testimony could have turned the whole region's criminal underworld upside down.

The largest of the Yakuza gangs following the Second World War was *Yamaguchi-gumi*, led by the charismatic and highly influential, Kazuo Taoka. Under his thirty-five-year reign, this crime family outfit grew to an estimated membership of 15,000 and was known to be active in thirty-six of Japan's forty-seven prefectures. The *Yamaguchi-gumi* ran legitimate businesses as fronts while they involved themselves in sport and entertainment as well as illegal gambling, loan-sharking, extortion and prostitution. Taoka's empire started in the giant docks of Kobe, where he did deals to supply cheap labour for many shipbuilding firms. He had been sentenced to an eight-year prison sentence at the age of just twenty-three for killing a rival gang member, and his reputation as a hard street-fighter stood him in good stead for these tough competitive deals. Each Yakuza gang tends to have different characteristics and skills. Some are good gamblers or co-ordinators, others are more politically skilled or better at dealing with overseas drug-runners. The *Yamaguchi-gumi* were known as well-trained fighters and were highly aggressive in whatever business they were in – much like their leader. Taoka expanded his operation into the lucrative Osaka rackets business by removing several of the leading figures in the Korean gang *Meiyu-kai*, with 'strike-first-and-ask-questions-later' tactics, straight out of the Al Capone textbook. In 1978, Taoka had ordered the killing of the head of the Matsuda group and several members of that organization had sworn to avenge his death. One of them, Kiyoshi Narumi, walked calmly into a Kyoto nightclub where Taoko was watching a limbo performance and opened fire. He hit Taoko in the neck and in the circus that ensued the gunman managed to get away. Taoko, bleeding profusely, was rushed to hospital where he survived, but the gunman's body was found in the forest above Kobe. However, the events had taken their toll and Taoka suffered a massive heart attack and died in 1981. His funeral was a spectacle unsurpassed in the entire history of Japanese gangland.

The new Yakuza attempted in most major Japanese cities to control the rickshaw business, labour unions, prostitution, the supply of drugs and black-market goods, gambling (lotto-style tickets and other cards), bribery and extortion. Along with this criminal empire came the need to launder large amounts of money as the popular currency in the arena of international crime was the US dollar rather than the yen. The Yakuza therefore set up or otherwise involved themselves in numerous business ventures which enabled them to trade their own currency for others, especially the 'greenback'. Developing a global infrastructure or being part of an international crime ring never came easy to Japanese villains, largely on account of cultural differences and different ways of doing business. Western gangster culture and deal-making were alien to the instinctively secretive and non-confrontational Yakuza.

Yakuza members favour tattoos as a way of showing allegiance to a particular sect; some of these tattoos are extremely elaborate and cover almost the entire body. Favourite images are gang logos, slogans and insignias, but flowers, dragons, landscapes, guns and sayings are also to be seen. This is another point of difference with gangsters from elsewhere in the world.

One major source of revenue for the Yakuza in modern times, which is unique in the global underworld of gangsters, is payment in return for not disrupting company annual general meetings (AGMs). This may seem very odd indeed, but has been commonplace in Japan for many years. Yakuza threaten to completely disrupt company AGMs by questioning directors about their indiscretions, haranguing company officials for hours about dividend policy, continually side-tracking events where much needed motions are required and getting support for the removal of certain company officials. In the 1990s, the government took steps to try to remove this kind of protection racket but it was not easy as the individuals involved were usually shareholders, if only of one share, or claimed they represented shareholders. In one prominent incident, executives from a major supermarket chain, Ito-Yokado, were arrested in relation to such illegal payments. According to local police a large sum was handed over in a men's toilet. In a second very public case, three officers of a large department store were arrested after allegations that payments of S730,000 had been made.

The relationship between the Japanese and Korean underworlds has been marked by violent antagonism. Japanese gangsters often look down on their Korean counterparts and centuries of warfare have left deep and bitter scars to this day. A Korean street gangster by the name of Chon Gwon Yong wanted to expand his enterprise into Japan and in the 1940s, when many of the Yakuza were being imprisoned or watched closely by American forces, the Koreans were able to do business quite freely. Yong set up an extortion racket in Tokyo's Ginza district and started trading many black-market goods. He brokered deals between the Korean government and several leading Yakuza gangs that allowed outlawed Japanese criminals to set up shop in Korea and developed a highly successful prostitution ring using women imported from other Far Eastern countries. Although no charges were ever brought, he was also involved in the kidnapping of the Korean opposition leader, Kim Dae Jung, from a hotel in Tokyo. Jung was bound, gagged and taken out to sea, expecting at any moment to be slung overboard, but American intelligence agencies had anticipated the plot and intervened. They had no wish to see further political instability and miraculously Jung was returned safely to his home in Seoul.

In the book *Yakuza*, the authors Kaplan and Dubro describe how *Yamaguchi-gum* have expanded into business areas such as narcotics (primarily amphetamines), money-lending, smuggling, rigging sporting matches, seizing real estate, human trafficking, stock market manipulation, prostitution and pornography – hardcore pornography is illegal in Japan. They have also been known to trade in weapons such as rocket launchers and machine guns for narcotics. Much of this barter has taken place in America through their network of agents and overseas members. Japanese gangs are, however, quite different in ideological terms from those found in other parts of the world. The Yakuza gangs do not operate under the same veil of secrecy, it being quite common for Japanese gangsters to have an office with a sign above the front door. Also, simple theft is frowned on in traditional Japanese culture and, as a result, few Japanese gangsters practise this form of criminal activity. In some parts of Japan attitudes towards the Yakuza have hardened in recent years, making it more difficult for them to undertake some of their more traditional forms of making money. In Ebitsuka, a small town around 130 miles from the capital, a gang called the *Ichiri Ikka* had built new headquarters for themselves, which were very garishly coloured. The local people objected and videotaped everyone going in and out of the premises. The leader of the *Ichiri Ikka* was displeased and ordered retaliatory action – windows were smashed, a lawyer was stabbed and another protagonist was cut on his throat with a knife. The police had to move in to stop the escalation of violence and the Yakuza gang eventually agreed to leave the area, fearing negative publicity and growing scrutiny from the law enforcement agencies.

However, the bread-and-butter business for many Yakuza gangs is the sex trade. Revenue flows from the overworked, white-collar Japanese salarymen and also from overseas establishments, to which Asian women are exported and sold into prostitution in America, Europe and other parts of the world. Many of the prostitutes or 'comfort workers' as they are sometimes known, are imported from other Asian countries as well, especially China and the Philippines. In Japan, there is a huge obsession with young women who dress up like schoolgirls in short, pleated skirts and knee-length socks. The fascination with Western pornography has grown insatiably in the form of films, books and magazines – the more the government try to prevent its dissemination, the greater the demand for it. To help drive this business, many Yakuza own their own bars, nightclubs and restaurants, which operate legitimately to some extent while offering 'extras' upstairs or from under the counter. Sex tours have also grown in popularity in Japan, where the Yakuza organize vacation trips to many cities like Bangkok, Taipei and Manila where sex hotels offer prostitutes to satisfy any fantasy or desire.

The Yakuza have been involved in the integration of business and politics from the very beginning, believing that power is money and money, power. In 1987, a new Japanese prime minister, Noboru Takeshita, was elected amid extensive speculation that gangsters had been involved in the process. It emerged five years later than money had been paid to silence a group who had been making things difficult for Takeshita – he swore that he knew nothing about the significant sums involved and was able to continue in politics. One man was found guilty and was removed from public office but many thought he had simply been made a scapegoat. In an amazing episode, which took place in the late 1980s and early 1990s, a Toyko-based company called West Tsusho purchased two American companies, namely the Houston-based Quantum Access and Asset Management International. Nothing strange about that, but the man paid $250,000 for his work as 'finder' was none other than Prescott Bush Jr, the elder brother of President George W. Bush. What makes this an intriguing venture is that West Tsusho is, in fact, owned by Ishii Susumu, the head of the Yakuza group known as *Inagawa-kai*. Many believe political influence was part of this and many other deals done by the Yakuza.

There is mounting evidence of Yakuza involvement in international crime, with members now imprisoned for drug- or sex-related activity, gun-running or human-trafficking, all over the world. Many now wear dark glasses, shave or closely crop their hair and wear black suits. They have become caricatures based on characters from many popular films, such as Tarantino's modern gangster movies. It is perhaps fitting, then, that many Yakuza gangs have built strong bases in America, principally in Hawaii but also in parts of California, Nevada and even on the west coast of Canada. It was William Sessions, then a director of the FBI, who testified in 1991 that the Yakuza (also known as Boryokudan) 'have built one of the largest criminal organizations . . . According to a publicized report of the National Police Agency of Japan in 1988, grossed almost 10 billion US dollars in revenue, one-third from crystal methamphetamine, a relatively new and powerful stimulant known on the street as "ice". The Boryokudan control an estimated 90 per cent of the "ice" flow into Hawaii. The Boryokudan also smuggle guns from the United States into Japan.'

Hawaii is, in many ways, a perfect staging point for the

Yakuza groups. They work with local crime gangs, fuelling tourism from Asia to this most picturesque of places – many visitors also sample the gambling, shows and prostitution which are all on offer courtesy of the Yakuza. Los Angeles has also been a hub for Japanese gangsters, a place where there are vulnerable young women, an enormous drug industry, a wealth of pornographic material and a huge mix of people from many cultures, making the presence of significant numbers of Japanese men nothing unusual. Las Vegas is another favourite location for the Japanese gangsters, providing, as it does, both legal and illegal gambling and just about whatever else anyone might want, twenty-four hours a day. There is recent evidence that a number of establishments in and around Los Vegas are now owned by Japanese corporations, that are linked directly to the Yakuza network. The Yakuza continue to organize many trips for Japanese businessmen and often get substantial 'finder' fees for steering people in the right direction. Having overseas operations brought other benefits and in the 1990s proceeds from drugs and prostitution were used to purchase expensive Louis Vuitton and Hermès products. These were then shipped back to Japan where the market for such goods was very strong. Police managed make inroads into this practice and in 1993 arrested over ninety people including Japanese Yakuza members, Chinese criminals and French customs officials.

The Japanese police force have always been reluctant to co-operate with other law enforcement agencies and provide very little in the way of tangible information on the current state of the Yakuza gangs. Perhaps they are concerned about losing face if the true scale of organized crime were to become known, nevertheless there do seem to be some key indications to suggest that the power base of the Yakuza is being eroded. This may, of course, be a function of the downturn in the Japanese economy or perhaps some gangs are spending a lot of their time moving in on the tremendous potential that exists in China or other rapidly developing

Far Eastern economies. The National Police Agency of Japan did issue a helpful statement in 1997, to the effect that of the 1,600 gangsters jailed in the four months from December 1993, 60 per cent had said that business was poor – one leading *Yamaguchi-gumi* member talked about activity being 50 per cent down. It is possible that the next couple of decades will see international gangs make real strides in these high-growth areas. The Yakuza membership remains large and the secretive nature of many of their activities will stand them in good stead. James Morton, author of *Gangland International*, points out that the number of Yakuza had risen by the end of 1996 by 600 to 79,900. Two-thirds of these belonged to three major organizations: 18,600 to the *Yamaguchi-gumi*; 8,800 to the *Inagawa-kai*; and the remainder to the *Sumiyoshi-rengo*. The Japanese government has brought in new laws which will make some of the Yakuza's illegal activities more difficult for them, but they have a long history of successful manipulation of the political system so their future wellbeing and prosperity should be anticipated.

The Providence Mob

Connecticut and Rhode Island were the only two states in America not to ratify the eighteenth amendment to the American Constitution – an amendment which was probably more unpopular and self-destructive than any other in US history either before or since. It came to be known simply as Prohibition and outlawed the production, distribution and sale of alcohol. It would last for fourteen controversial, colourful and long years. It fuelled organized crime like no other piece of legislation and drove ordinary, law-abiding people into the arms of waiting criminal gangs. The state officials of Rhode Island knew that their region would become a haven for bootleggers and smugglers as it has 400 miles of open coastline, difficult to police at the best of times. Many Americans began to produce gin and other spirits illegally, but people were prepared to pay a premium for 'proper' produce. The Canadian border was close to Connecticut and Rhode Island and even before the Constitution was changed, plans were being hatched for a huge export business, often in the dead of night. Neighbouring states were also affected, Maine and Vermont in particular, but access to the major cities of New York, Boston and beyond was not so easily managed. The dramatic and beautiful East Coast would never be as popular as during Prohibition. Many national borders prove difficult to police today – the border between the USA and Mexico springs to mind – and this is with the aid of modern surveillance equipment and tracking devices. Police officers in the 1920s trying to locate smugglers in the dark at night must have spent much of their time chasing ghosts. In the last few months of 1930, a congressional hearing was called with the specific purpose of discussing the Prohibition amendment. A heated debate followed as America was split over what the next move should be. In one of the most public and widely followed chapters in American political history, the amendment to the Constitution was eventually repealed by 172,545 votes to 48,540 – a majority of nearly 80 per cent.

As expected, criminal gangs had grown in number, size and influence in Providence during Prohibition and they were not about to see their empire crumble just because selling alcohol was now legal. Instead they turned their attentions to extortion, fraud, racketeering, the smuggling of other goods, prostitution, pornography, fixing horse races and other illicit pursuits. The local underworld was highly fragmented but, as in New York, it was heavily influenced by the big Italian crime families. Never quite as organized as Chicago or other major cities, the Providence Mob, under an agreement with the overall Mafia lords, became a separate crime outfit working the whole of New England. There followed a power struggle for who would take control of the business. The Gustin Gang, led by the former boxer, Frank Gustin, had built a huge empire during the 'dry' years and it was thought that Gustin would take the top job. However, his ambitions were cut short by his assassination three days before Christmas in 1931, a day that would prove to be a turning point in the story of the Providence Mob. Gustin had allegedly hijacked some shipments from the Italians, led by Joe Lombardi, and a feud had raged for many months before truce talks were held at the office of the lawyer, Julius Wolfson. Gustin had gone into the lawyer's office while the bodyguards remained on the floor below, as had been agreed between the parties. But the sound of shots rang out and Gustin staggered from Wolfson's office across the hall and died in the chair next to the secretary's, who had fortunately been given the afternoon off. Barney Walsh, Gustin's minder, ran up the stairs and was also shot dead. Although police swarmed into the building, statements were taken and evidence assembled, no one was ever convicted of the killings. It was the end of the Gustin Gang as a major force.

Several men and gangs vied for control of criminal activities in Providence over the subsequent months and years, but it was not until Raymond Salvatore Loreda Patriarca came on the scene that things began to take on a definite pattern. Patriarca was born in Worcester, Massachusetts, on 18 March 1908. He was five foot, eight inches tall with black hair, brown eyes and was of medium build. This son of Italian immigrants whose father ran a liquor store would have no problem finding trouble. As a teenager he managed to build a long list of arrests and convictions, including armed robbery, assault, stealing cars, hijacking and more, spending a total of ten years behind bars before he had even turned thirty. New England's Mafia boss at the time was Phil Buccola, he had been following the exploits of Patriarca for some time as he liked the man's decisive nature and his ability to persuade others to follow him. In 1954, Buccola hung up his boots and decided to retire to Sicily, appointing Patriarca as the new boss. It is not known exactly why this happened although many speculated at the time that he fell out with the New York family that sanctioned his role in the first place. There would now be no rest for anyone involved with his operations right across Maine, Connecticut, Rhode Island and Massachusetts. Everyone was brought together, procedures were strengthened and roles expanded. Patriarca would have liked to take control of upstate New York but this turf was managed by the big Mafia families in New York City directly, something that always irked him. Patriarca soon gained a reputation for fairness but was totally ruthless when crossed. He was famously described by one Boston policeman as 'just the toughest guy you ever saw'. Like many other Mafia bosses, he would gain friends in the government and within the law enforcement agencies, using these relationships to get many rivals put away. One man who was a thorn in his side was the Irishman Carlton O'Brien, a smuggler who had built up a large gambling business. Patriarca saw O'Brien as a threat because he was smart and resourceful and although he did not have a major impact on his activities at the time, Patriarca was keen to act first. Using pre-emptive tactics similar to Al Capone and other Mafia dons, Patriarca's men tracked O'Brien from town to town for days before finding the right place and the right time to shoot him.

Patriarca set up his head office in the small neighbourhood of Providence. His headquarters were a two-storey building with 'spotters' covering the surrounding streets. Many of these spotters actually lived in the area and were paid to keep a look out and help when the legitimate business was busy. The Atwell Avenue office was a front for a vending machine distribution firm and became known as 'Federal Hill' to gangsters right across Providence. Patriarca built up interests across America including two Las Vegas casinos, various bars, clubs, and crime networks in Philadelphia and Florida at the same times as expanding his local activities. He even dabbled in garbage collection, a string of linen service outlets and vending machines. When anyone tried to muscle in on his turf he would have them killed. His empire now spanned loan-sharking, gambling, pornography, hijacking and drugs, all of which proved very lucrative. He would quite happily do business with non-Italian people, something that many of the major New York Mafia families never liked to do, and paid his men well. He liked to run a happy ship and believed better rewards would keep his employees' fingers out of the till. He gained a hard reputation as a loan shark; people who fell into debt were often killed or their assets seized, rather than being offered some leeway to pay off their loans. Very few knew they were borrowing from his outfit at the outset of a deal, but they certainly knew it if they fell behind in their payments.

Patriarca was unlike many of the other Italian family

bosses. He lived in a modest house, not far from his office. He would usually turn up to meetings dressed casually and looking like any other ordinary Italian immigrant. This was a far cry from the thousand-dollar suits of John Gotti or the fleet of large, black cars that followed Capone and others around. He always wanted his legitimate businesses to be successful, perhaps out of pride, or to make sure the front would work effectively. If these businesses were investigated and were seen to be losing money hand over fist, the investigators would want to know where the money was coming from to invest in all his other activities. The distribution operations Coin-O-Matic and the National Cigarette Service were tightly managed and performing well, along with the newer Nu-Brite Cleaners chain. One of his largest money-spinners was organizing floating gambling dens – often referred to as 'floating craps', which at their height were allegedly pumping £250,000 a week into his coffers. He also set up an elaborate scam to fix horse races and managed to involve bookmakers all over the country. His business empire was remarkably diversified. With the proceeds from his illegal operations he bought ski-resorts, ranches and dyeing services, believing these would be more difficult to trace back to him. Everything was held in a convoluted series of companies, many of them offshore, which were virtually impossible to link to Patriarca.

The man who ran the horse racing and several other loan-sharking and gambling operations for Patriarca was Jerry Angiulo, who was highly thought of within the family. His debt collection methods were harsh, though broadly in line with those of the boss. According to well-known New England hard man Phil Waggenheim, these worked on a kind of sliding scale. If payment was three weeks late, a debtors arm or leg would be broken. If payment was six to eight weeks late, the debtor would meet with an 'accident': his brakes would be tampered with, he would be run off the road or his home or business would be blown up. Sometimes a defaulter's wife would be beaten up or a child would be abducted on the way home from school and his or her leg broken. If someone owed more than $15,000 or was arrogant about having fallen behind, he would be killed.

The relationship between Patriarca and the New York Mafia families, the Genovese and Colombo families in particular, was good. They shared information, met quite regularly to discuss new ideas and there were few problems with the way territorial lines were drawn. The Connecticut River was considered the border between the gangs but the discussions in the early 1960s centred around something quite different. The major gangs had always been able to function without too much interference from central government. However, President John F. Kennedy had come to power promising, among other things, that he would be tough on crime. He appointed his brother, Robert F. Kennedy, as Attorney General and provided him with the powers and resources that he needed to mount a more effective fight against organized crime. The Kennedy clan had deep personal and political roots in Providence and in that part of the US generally. The family was keen to show that they meant business and showing that they could make a difference in Providence would win them much political kudos. A major investigation into Patriarca's affairs was initiated which made extensive use of wire-tapping to gather information. As usual, few people were prepared to go on the record against the mob and many knew that the gangsters had paid 'friends' in high places. The Kennedy brothers hated the Mafia, particularly Patriarca, the mob boss in their home town. During the McClellan Committee hearings, Patriarca taunted the brothers with the jibe that they didn't 'have the brains of [their] retarded sister'. And Bobby Kennedy is reported to have told a friend that he and Jack were 'going after that pig on the hill', referring to Patriarca and his 'Federal Hill' headquarters.

By the mid-1960s the law enforcement agencies had had some luck. Patriarca had pushed around several gang members and associates – given the sheer scale of the operation it would have been difficult not to have done so. The FBI took advantage of these disgruntled mobsters by turning several of them into government witnesses, providing them with protection under the witness protection scheme. Patriarca had employed Joseph Barboza, a contract killer of Portuguese extraction who had once boasted of having murdered twenty-six men and who, in 1966, had been arrested for carrying a concealed weapons. The bail was set at $100,000, a large amount of money at that time, and Patriarca was expected to come up with this money. After much deliberation, Patriarca decided not to post bail so two close friends of Barboza set about trying the raise money. When Patriarca heard of these plans, he immediately sent out a gang to kill the two men. The FBI played some of the wire-tap recordings of Patriarca relating this incident back to Barboza and, over a period of several months, they got him to talk. Barboza had been sentenced to five years behind bars for his weapons charges and he thought that his days, in any case, were numbered. He testified against Patriarca who was charged with conspiracy to kill the prominent local bookmaker, Will Marfeo, who had been shot to death in the phone booth of a Providence restaurant while startled diners looked on. Patriarca was found guilty and sentenced to six years behind bars.

Patriarca's power and reach meant that he was able to continue to control much of his empire from within the walls of his Atlantic prison cell. Several other gangs tried to muscle in on Boston, Providence and other towns, but each time they were repelled. Patriarca's gang continued to fight for every inch of turf and every business operation, even without their respected leader. Patriarca emerged from jail in 1975 but things were never quite the same as before. Informants came forward more freely and wire-tapping particularly helped the FBI to develop a better understanding of how Patriarca organized his businesses. At times like this, people from within a gang generally feel that the time is right to move up in their organization, as has been seen time and again in New York, Chicago and just about every other city in the USA.

Cennaro Angiulo had also spent time in and out of prison, but he aspired to the top job. He had gained entry into the Mafia by organizing much of the gambling in parts of the region and had paid substantial sums of money to Patriarca. In 1978, Patriarca was in court again, this time for being a key player in a plot to assassinate the Cuban leader, Fidel Castro. In 1983, he was charged with conspiring to murder Raymond Curcio back in 1965 and the following year he was arrested for ordering another killing. On 11 July 1984, ambulance services were called to an emergency on Douglas Avenue in the northern suburb of Providence. It was the house of Raymond Patriarca's long-time girlfriend and, to the amazement of the medical team, the man lying on the ground having suffered a huge cardiac arrest was Patriarca himself. He was pronounced dead at the hospital, aged seventy-six.

Succession in any of the major crime gangs, especially the Mafia, is always a difficult time. The changing of the guard, the passage from one era to the next, is a time when all kinds of things emerge from the woodwork. It is also a time when players make their move, when grudges and old scores are settled. Patriarca's death was no exception to this rule for the Providence Mob. Patriarca had left instructions before he died that his son should be given the top job, but key New Yorkers would have to back this in the face of others who were bound to lay claim to the position. Angiulo was in prison awaiting trial when he heard the news that the New York families had ratified the appointment of Raymond J. Patriarca, known to everyone as 'Junior', as the next boss. He was not happy. It was true that Angiulo was not well liked by several of the families, especially the Genovese clan, but he was a safe pair of hands. The man had a strong record of delivering the money and profitable businesses – something very close to their hearts, but the fact that he was in the sights of the police counted against him. As it turned out, within two years, Angiulo, two of his brothers and a close member of his gang were convicted of racketeering charges and he was sentenced to a hefty forty-five years in jail.

The young Patriarca was doing many of the right things – he went to see Tony Salerno, the head of the Genovese family in New York, to discuss the future and rewarded the influential Ilario Zannino for his support. However, others questioned the leadership skills and vision of the new kid on the block. Many believed that William Grasso, who had become Raymond's 'under-boss', had better connections and a more loyal following. On a warm summer evening on the banks of the Connecticut River in 1989, Grasso's body was found – he had been shot in the head from behind, in the old, Sicilian fashion. A year later, Patriarca was indicted, along with around twenty other New England gang members, on a range of charges. An extensive investigation had been going on since before the death of his father, and the law enforcement agencies saw their chance to tip the balance of power in their favour, especially as the new boss hadn't been as secretive as his father in many of his dealings. The list of charges was impressive, covering illegal gambling, extortion, running rackets, murder, attempted murder and drug dealing. The FBI had managed to place a hidden camera in an office where they thought initiation ceremonies into the Mafia had been taking place. After weeks of getting nothing useful on film, they struck gold and for the first time a 'family' initiation was captured for all to see. It was material that would be played at many subsequent hearings all over America as it proved unequivocally that the secret organization existed, something that the Mafia families had rejected since the very beginning. It also showed that entry into the Mafia was a significant step and not something taken lightly by those involved.

In February 1991, Patriarca was reportedly replaced as head of the Providence Mob and speculation was that the public embarrassment caused by the initiation ceremony tape was the last straw. He was replaced by Nicholas Bianco, who had been consulted by many on major decisions for several years, having built up experience from working for Raymond. Bianco was cut from very much the same cloth as his mentor – his personality was low key, he was usually casually dressed, and he came across as a private man. He was, in fact, someone against whom law enforcement officers struggled to compile evidence for a successful prosecution. A good example of this was two murder charges which were brought against Bianco in the mid-1980s, both of which ended up being dismissed. The trial of Junior Patriarca and many other members of the New England underworld was a long, drawn-out affair in the Hartford federal court house. Eventually, after all the usual stalling tactics and attempts to get to the jury, Patriarca was found guilty of violating racketeering laws and was sentenced in June 1992 to eight years and one month behind bars. In the end he served fewer than six years and, on his release, tried to start a new life as a property developer. If found to have any further links with organized crime he would have been in violation of his parole conditions and he would have found himself back inside.

The authorities eventually managed to gather enough evidence against Bianco to bring a string of charges, the most serious relating to racketeering. He too was found guilty and he was sentenced to eleven years in jail. He never regained his freedom as he died on 14 November 1994, aged sixty-two, in a secure medical facility in Springfield, Missouri.

The criminal era and the power of the Mafia across the whole region were far from over, however. After a number of gangsters were locked up in a fairly short space of time following one of the most successful FBI investigations of its type ever, one man came to the fore as the next boss. Frank Salemme was that man and for the first time in forty years the power base of organized crime moved from Providence to Boston. Salemme had spent fifteen years in jail for his part in the attempted assassination of John

Fitzgerald, an attorney acting for Joseph Barboza. In the early years of the 1990s, Salemme settled some old debts and put a marker down that he was the man in charge – six men were known to have been killed and these were just the ones that the police knew about. Several of the established gangs felt that Salemme needed to learn some humility, and in March 1994 three of his closest associates were killed and another wounded. Further shootings and retaliation continued across the streets of Boston and far beyond. On 20 October that same year, Joseph Souza was shot dead while making a telephone call and just a few days later Michael Prochilo only narrowly escaped injury when he ducked just in time as a masked gunmen opened fire as he sat in his car. Although both men were far from being at the centre of the gang, Salemme went into hiding, fearing any public appearance could be his last. The authorities caught up with him, though, in West Palm Beach, Florida, the following year and he was indicted on several counts. While he was 'away', he had left the business to be run by his younger brother, John J. 'Jackie' Salemme, but before long, Jackie too found himself facing the inside of a federal court house. It was not long before he was behind bars and another colourful chapter for a criminal dynasty of Providence was over. In a famous statement US Attorney General Donald K. Stern told a packed press conference that, 'Organized crime isn't as organized as it was fifteen years ago – and we're here to say we've got it on the run.' Only time will tell if Stern's assertion is correct, but any gangs and gangsters which follow in the footsteps of Patriarca and Salemme will be hard pushed to achieve the same degree of notoriety as Patriarca and Salemme.

Canadian Gangsters

When looking at the gang-related criminal activity in Canada, it is important to know that the country has three distinct areas and that for many years these regions were quite strongly autonomous and independent. Much of this has to do with the tremendous distances involved and the time required to move from one area to another, but there are significant cultural differences involved. Canada's social landscape has been influenced initially by the French, then by the English and, more recently, by Canada's powerful southern neighbour, the USA. Canada's immigration laws differ from those of the USA, which has enabled a large number of Asians to make their home there. As is so often the case, a trickle of immigrants from a particular area leads to a much stronger flow as others follow, knowing that they have some contacts and a stronger opportunity to build better lives for themselves. As well has thousands of hard-working Asian migrants, a number of criminals have been part of this migration to Canada and recent years have seen a growing sophistication in criminal activity. Canada's first piece of anti-drug legislation came in 1908, almost by accident, at a time when most other countries were still combating longer-standing forms of criminal activity, Mackenzie King, Minister of Labour for Canada, was concerned about rising labour problems in Vancouver among the Asian population; an investigation revealed that opium was readily available to the workers. King believed that banning the substance would help to curb some of the problems of social integration that were being experienced, so a new act was passed which made it illegal to possess or to use the drug. King's report also outlined his view that the use of the drug could spread to local young men and women, dulling their senses and leading to degrading behaviour. With the wisdom of hindsight, it is certainly possible to link opium and its derivatives with degrading acts, although for many it does anything but dull the senses.

The 1950s and 1960s were a period of tremendous criminal expansion throughout Canada but it was Montreal that became the undisputed hot-bed of illegal activity, forming trading links with some of America's mob organizations and gangs located on the Pacific Rim. A godfather was also emerging, a former professional wrestler and someone who would survive at the top of his chosen profession for thirty years. Vincenzo Cotroni was born in Calabria, Italy, in 1911 and made the long boat journey to Canada with his family in 1924. He claimed to be illiterate and just a simple carpenter, but in his early twenties he developed a colourful life of crime. In the years leading up to the Second World War, he was charged by the authorities with theft, assault, selling alcohol without a licence and theft, but he served only short sentences on each occasion. He was also charged with the rape of a girl in his local neighbourhood, a charge which was dropped when he married his alleged victim the following year. He also narrowly escaped prosecution for voter intimidation in the course of a local election.

During his early days in wrestling he used to meet Armand Courville, someone who was to have a dramatic influence on his life. As well as helping the youngster get into sport, Courville also opened the door to serious organized crime. They would join forces and open a nightclub business in the buzzing red-light district and from this base they would drive a network of drug smuggling, extortion, prostitution and counterfeiting. Cotroni's rise in the gangland world was nearly stopped in its tracks when he got mixed up in a feud which had started after a deal between the American mobsters Joe Bonanno and Stefano Magaddino went wrong. The disagreement involved a number of Canadian gangsters, many of whom were big fish in a small pond. This made them feel comfortable in their own world but many learnt that when you upset the Mafia, you need to find a very quiet hiding place. These were men that Cotroni wanted to do business with and he managed to avoid the ensuing confrontation, retaining much of his Mafia-related activity in the Montreal area. Cotroni set up a tight-knit family enterprise with only twenty main members making all the decisions. Although small by American, and even by Canadian, criminal standards, Cotroni's gang had good connections and set up partnership deals with other gangs, forging a series of legal front businesses, which included nightclubs, real estate and meat packing. Like all prosperous gangsters, Cotroni and his second in command, Paulo Violi, were also involved in politics – persuading several notable candidates not to stand for local and national elections and having 'friends' run instead.

Cotroni was sailing close to the wind, especially with regard to his burgeoning drug-running business, much of which came over the border by truck and in containers via shipping contacts. In 1973, the American authorities caught up with his brother, Frank, and charged him with offences related to drug-trafficking – he was extradited to America and the following year he received a sentence of fifteen years behind bars. During this period, Violi was summoned to meet the Carlo Gambino family in New York. He had requested Vic Cotroni join him, but the the Mafia family had refused, believing the Cotroni name to be too hot. People were trying the split the organization apart so that they could move in on Canada's growing rackets and Violi couldn't see why things should change. Pressure was beginning to mount and Violi's own brother, Francesco, was murdered by a Toronto-based family who wanted to take control of Montreal. He was backed into a small area at one of their importation company premises and shot several times in the face by two unknown contract killers. Paolo Violi, in prison for contempt of court, became a marked man and he too was murdered, this time while having a drink and chatting with friends in a quiet downtown bar. The empire was beginning to collapse and Vic Cotroni, suffering from cancer, handed over the reins of power. The family would never again achieve quite the same degree of power and influence as they had once had.

In more recent times, the Montreal mob has been made up of many members of the New York-based Bonanno family, headed by Nicolo Rizzutto, a Sicilian with a reputation for being a hard man in the classic gangster mould. Rizzutto made his way to the top of the tree through his drug connections, heroin in particular, and was able to move the focus of the outfit away from less lucrative loan-sharking, prostitution, extortion and gambling. He had seen from parts of America what potential there was if an efficient network of street sellers and a transportation infrastructure was put in place. As the economy and general prosperity grew in Canada, so would the demand for cocaine, crack and other hard drugs. Rizzutto was finally arrested in 1988 and was charged with cocaine possession and trafficking. He received a sentence of five years.

The story of organized gang crime in Toronto is quite different. Rocco Perri is probably the nearest thing the city has ever had to a gangland boss. He was born in 1890 and came to Canada at the age of thirteen and it was not long before he was making a living from supplying alcohol as many young, pretentious hoodlums did. In 1923, the police, while on a regular patrol of the dock area, stumbled on a gang unloading a substantial quantity of whisky. The police called for back-up and finally went in en masse – a furious gun battle ensued and one of the smugglers was killed. The men all worked for Perri but the weight of evidence did not favour the authorities and the charges relating to his involvement were eventually dropped. The police were onto Perri and wanted to get him behind bars – they regularly raided his warehouses, premises and offices, disrupting his business operations however they could. Adding to the frenzy was a growing feud between a Ukrainian gang which was alleged to be behind a notorious alcohol poisoning incident which killed thirty-five people in Niagara Province. Finally, Perri was sent down, but it was not for drug-running or any of the other major crimes that he had orchestrated – it was for perjury. He started his six-month sentence in 1928. After his release, he tried to drive his business empire forward but things were getting more competitive and difficult. In 1930, his first wife Bessie, who was still involved to a great extent in the business, went down one evening to put the car into the garage – a lone gunman was waiting and she was shot dead. She had been the brains of the organization, keeping good records and statements of deals. From that point, Rocco Perri's ability to manage and control his various illegitimate activities diminished markedly.

Toronto has a less well-known son by the name of Antonia Nicaso. One night he was asleep in his bed when he heard two men outside his house. When he went to investigate the men had fled, but when the police arrived, an inspection of his car showed traces of dynamite and wires for a bomb. Nicaso writes articles and books on the Sicilian Mafia and his life has been threatened many times, although never in this way. The mob had long used Toronto as a spot to smuggle drugs into Canada and as the business grew, they wanted more independence from New York. Articles appearing in a number of Canada's regional newspapers had been very accurate in their description of how criminal businesses were being conducted and many in the underworld felt control would not pass to them with this level of intrusion. Greater organization and co-operation was needed and the Sicilian gangs pulled together and formed a union called 'the Consortium'. This was truly ground-breaking, acting like a governing body, and unlike a lot of other gangland agreements, it included rival groups such as the

Russians, the Hell's Angels and the Colombian cartels. Nicosa had identified how each area and patch had been split up and how a set street price for the main drugs was recommended. Finding out how this agreement worked had proved more than a little tricky as many of those involved operate according to the old Sicilian saying that 'your mouth is for eating'.

British Columbia and its capital, Vancouver, was always seen as the third of the three major provinces of Canada. In the 1960s, the Gentile Family ran most of the high value extortion rackets, bootlegging, drugs and gambling but were infiltrated by several members of the Co-ordinated Law Enforcement Unit (CLEU), one of the greatest police achievements in the whole of the country. Today's Vancouver underworld consists of eight major gangs who have, in total, over 400 active members – the rivalry is intense and violent, from the mostly Chinese Lotus gang to the Red Eagles (emanating from a Hong Kong group of the same name), and from the Filipino mob to the Hispanic Los Diablos. However, the most powerful of all the gangs is undoubtedly the biker group, the local band of Hell's Angels. In the early 1980s, the Hell's Angels got involved in a dispute between the Russian Filonov brothers and the Asian Lotus gang. A hitman by the name of Ngoc Tung Dang, often referred to as Tommy Dang, was hired by the Russians to cause trouble for the opposing gang and then things went from bad to worse. Lotus, who had links to the Hell's Angels, involved them in the feud and, over the following months, a spate of kidnappings, ransom demands and assassinations ensued. The most notable of these was the assassination of John Raymond Ginetti who was shot in the back of the head and his body left for his wife to find the following morning. There were also a number of shootings in the same neighbourhood, with one drive-by shooting leaving over forty bullets marking the front and inside of the Hell's Angels clubhouse. The two Filonov brothers had underestimated the speed with which their opponents would retaliate and they were soon tracked down. The first, Sergey, was killed by two Angels outside a motorbike shop, and Taras was found dead having been tortured and shot to death with a shotgun. A semblance of calm was restored and an uneasy peace ensued.

The biggest and most fundamental trend in recent times in Canadian gangland has been the rise of the young Indo-Canadian gangs who have been becoming increasingly sophisticated in their criminal behaviour and who have adopted a national approach to crime. Much of their revenue derives from drug smuggling and dealing, in everything from heroin, cocaine, crack, marijuana to a range of other less well known, but in many cases equally harmful drugs. The gangs have legal backing, which has frustrated a number of attempts to remove leading members from the streets. Their fronts have been integrated into their crime operations to provide almost perfect cover. One notable success, however, was the high-profile arrest of Kuldip Singh Chaggar, a lawyer from Vancouver who had represented a number of Indo-Canadian gangs in court cases across the country. In a well-planned sting operation, Chaggar was arrested and convicted of tampering with a witness in a drug-related case involving men thought to be leading Indo-Canadian bosses. He was found guilty and received a one-year sentence.

Sukvinder Singh Dosanjh became something of a gangland star of the Indo-Canadian gangs from the late 1990s as he eluded the authorities and appeared in the papers connected to a string of murders and other criminal acts. However, in late 2005 Dosanjh was killed in a well-arranged collision which ushered in a new era of street violence. Another member of his gang was found shot dead, slumped in his car near the centre of downtown Vancouver, and no fewer than ten other murders took place between rival gangs in fewer than six months. Much of this activity was related to a turf war, an attempt to control key streets and blocks which are difficult to police and where hard drugs are bought and sold on a daily basis. Another alarming consequence of this outbreak of violence has been that nearly all gang members now carry weapons and are well schooled in how to use them. This period of heightened police activity and feuding between rival gangs has led to several gang leaders deciding to retire and leave their enterprises to others. They have made so much money from drugs that their return to their places of origin has caused quite a stir. Villages in India such as Aitiana, Burjlittan, Noorpur, Punjab and Sudhur have seen the return of relatively young, rich men able to buy thousands of acres of land, huge houses and expensive cars. One such migrant was identified as Randhir Singh, also known as Dhira, who returned to Aitiana after just four years in Canada during which he had amassed significant wealth. He was arrested having been caught red-handed with a truck-load of drugs and spent time behind bars, but still managed to retain a large part of his fortune.

Increasingly, the spread of violence perpetrated by south Asians involving guns, drugs and honour killings stretched right across Canada becoming a national problem for police authorities. With the growing prominence and resources of the major gangs, this Canadian problem has surfaced elsewhere in North America and in Great Britain, Malaysia, Australia and Thailand. Clearly, it is not just a single-country problem as with many of the big gangs, though the situation seems to be more acute or advanced in many of Canada's urban areas than it is elsewhere in the world. According to the Canadian police, the east Indian gangs are actually small players who only get a lot of attention because they are so flagrantly violent. They get involved in shootouts regularly, often over nothing more than a dirty look or love rivalry. To date, the police have had less success with convicting Indo-Canadian gang members due to their close-knit and, for the most part, well-organized nature. These gangs have specialized in the distribution and selling of marijuana although the authorities believe that the transition to cocaine and heroin is a small one. Many column inches have been dedicated to possible reasons why the Indo-Canadians have become so violent and, in particular, why so many have joined the ranks at such a young age. Parents have been seemingly unable to halt the flow and the desire to obtain wealth and its associated status seems to be gathering pace. This is indeed a far cry from the reserved and very religious nature of most of the people just one or two generations ago. According to a report in the *Vancouver Sun* on 1 October 2005 Canadian police claim that young Indo-Canadian gangsters are becoming increasingly sophisticated and adopting names and logos like the infamous outlaw motorcycle clubs. A year ago police felt that Indo-Canadian gangs, despite dozens of murders, were less organized than traditional crime groups. But today there is a level of sophistication exhibited by these rival groups as they tussle over turf in British Columbia's lucrative drug trade.

Consider the following incidents of Indo-Canadian gang-related killings during just six months in 2005, taken from an official report released by the head of British Columbia's Integrated Gang Task Force.

> 30 September 2005: Hardev Singh Sidhu, 27, was found shot to death in a car at the corner of 136th Street and Grosvenor Road in Surrey. He is believed to have been involved in the drug trade.
>
> 28 August 2005: Hartinder (Harry) Gill and his girlfriend Lexi Madsen were gunned down at a busy intersection in Abbotsford. Gill was facing an attempted murder charge at the time of his death and was well known to police. His house was hit by gunfire in July.
>
> 13 May 2005: Surrey resident Dean Mohamed Elshamy, 30, was found slumped in a late-model grey Audi in the parking lot of a Mac's store at the corner of 72nd Avenue and Scott Road in Surrey. While Elshamy is Egyptian, the intended target of the hit is believed to have been his buddy, Sandip Singh Duhre, who was uninjured in both the May shooting and a second incident in July 2005.

7 May 2005: Inderjit Singh Rai, 23, shot to death about 2:30 a.m. in the 9800-block 140th Street in Surrey.

2 April 2005: Sukh Jawanda, killed on a rural road in Abbotsford. His friend was injured in the shooting.

Traditional Sikh values include 'image, status, reputation and respect', and many local people believe that a way of gaining respect on the streets is through carrying a gun and knowing when to use it. There is certainly a tremendous gender difference within the Indo-Canadian gangs as women have virtually automatic respect and are excluded from being involved. It is possible to speculate as to why this criminal and ultra-violent trend among South Asians has been so dramatic – being marginalized from mainstream society and the feeling that they are not offered equal opportunities in the workplace has certainly lead to frustration. Peer status from ordinary, manual jobs is now considered low and, as we have seen, status is one of the bedrocks of their culture. Having different religious beliefs, especially when people look and dress differently, can cause integration problems plus the usual family structure that was in place in their homeland is not so evident abroad. The problems are far from being just Canada's alone and we have seen minority groups take the step into violent criminal gangs all too frequently.

The original source of many of the drug shipments arriving in Canada is, as for many other countries, the warm, mountainous countryside of Colombia. The major cartels have been connected with a string of shootings in the early 1990s and now a series of former associates have been working with the Federal Bureau of Investigation. This is usually in exchange for a shorter sentence. One very popular turncoat from this period was Larry Mazzi, a former hitman for the Mafia, who was hoping for leniency in the same way that Salvatore Gravano received a sentence of just five years in prison. Mazzi managed to provide useful evidence to help convict and trace a number of leading drug traffickers but was not as helpful as Gravano and was astounded when he heard Brooklyn federal judge Charles Sifton say that he was going to jail for ten years.

The judicial system is trying to send a loud message to the Indo-Canadian gangs – one high-profile hearing involved the gangster Jethinder Singh Narwal, who was found guilty on all but two counts out of the fifteen offences with which he was charged. He was sentenced to a seventeen-year prison term and cannot expect favourable parole terms. The court heard how he used kidnapping, assault and threatening behaviour to drive his drug-related business. The case was slightly complicated by the fact that several of the kidnap victims were known felons and there had been a long-running feud between several gangs. This did not sway British Columbia's Supreme Justice Sunni Stronberg-Stein, who handed out the maximum term for these offences. A report on the case stated that even with a witness (Khark Grewal) providing some conflicting evidence, Stronberg-Stein was convinced and in his final summing up said, 'Mr Grewal's testimony about the identification and role of the accused in his kidnapping, unlawful confinement, extortion and assault, and the possession of a dangerous weapon – a handgun – is confirmed and supported by independent evidence. I am satisfied the Crown has proved beyond doubt the accused's guilt.'

The Yardies

The term 'Yardies' entered popular usage in the eighties, meaning Jamaican gangsters or those of Jamaican descent. Originally the term referred to people coming from the 'back yard', or back home in Jamaica. Usually Yardies work in large groups and are prepared to use violence against anyone who says anything against them. In the past, their downfall was making rash decisions, an inability to handle the police and other authority figures, so getting unwanted attention at an early stage plus their general disorganization when compared with larger gangland groups. Yardies, though numerous in the UK, have tended to share a distrust of anyone outside their own gang, and are often drawn into gunfights or knife battles, rather than exploring other solutions. Many are also characterized by wearing excessive jewellery, baseball caps and talking with load, screeching accents – not exactly blending into the background. The term should not be confused with the same name, which is sometimes given to people living in the government yards, in the Trenchtown neighbourhood of Kingston, Jamaica. This island was very badly hit by hurricanes and many people live in extreme poverty in makeshift accommodation in these yards making use of communal, government-funded cooking facilities.

In the years immediately after the Second World War the economy of Great Britain began to prosper and grow – by the 1950s the demand for labour had outstripped supply and to maintain this industrial and commercial development, the government actively encouraged immigrants to its shores. Many Afro-Caribbeans saw this as a chance for a better life and greater opportunities for their families. Most were unskilled and lived in cheap council housing built in inner-city areas. There were enough jobs for just about everyone and although many lived in fairly basic conditions, the situation benefitted everyone. However, by the late 1960s and into the 1970s, the United Kingdom saw high inflation, a dramatic slowdown in economic growth, trade union strikes and a rise in unemployment. Many of the new citizens had encouraged others to join them and a proportion of immigrant children were getting to employment age, jobs were not as easy to find, the provision of good, affordable housing was struggling to keep pace, and racial unrest was just around the corner. The problem was acute in many areas close to the centre of London but was also present in Liverpool, Manchester, Birmingham and Glasgow. It would be a problem that police would struggle to contain for decades and which would add to the appeal of a criminal lifestyle.

Along with many hard-working and diligent West Indians came convicted criminals and fugitives, looking to start a new life often on the wrong side of the law. Many of these transients would live close together, enjoying the company of people with similar ethnic and cultural backgrounds, forming enclaves which were difficult to police. These enclaves of Jamaican clubs and bars soon became hotbeds for gangs and criminal activities. Although the shores of America are much closer to the West Indies, the US immigration policy for Afro-Caribbeans was much tougher than that of the UK, helping to push emigrants towards the UK. Many entered the UK as 'tourists' but then disappeared from sight, assuming different identities and carrying false documents. Often they had been propelled by widespread poverty back home. As it was difficult to police the huge number of people entering and not leaving the country, the Yardie gangs soon had plenty of potential foot soldiers to call on. The classic profile of a Yardie member is single, male and between the ages of eighteen and thirty-five. Crime is generally their sole occupation and many have strong links with the music business, as singers, producers, agents, bouncers, promoters or simply as fans. One of the main problems facing the police is actually tracking these criminals down – many have a string of aliases and forged papers to go with them. Often drug dealers have offered users a free hit of crack for birth certificates, passports or other documents, helping criminals to create a new identity and disappear into the urban abyss. The police have tried to infiltrate gangs, but to date they have had limited success. The most high-profile police informer was probably Delry Denton who in 1995 agreed to go undercover in exchange for not being deported back to Jamaica. While working with the authorities, he sexually assaulted and stabbed to death Marcia Lewes, a crime for which he received life imprisonment.

In the early 1980s, many gangs were poorly organized and resorted mostly to small-scale robbery and prostitution along with fencing stolen goods including cars, household goods and jewellery. Very few had any sort of national network to call on, let alone international contacts. This would change as the gangs focused on one single product – drugs. The large South American producers, especially those from Colombia and Mexico, built up contacts via Jamaica and shipments of cocaine and heroine began to increase at an alarming rate. The range of drugs commonly available by the mid-1980s was staggering; marijuana had given way to crack cocaine as users graduated to harder drugs. Ecstasy and other pills became openly available at clubs, bars and other places across the length and breadth of the country. Firearm ownership among the general public has historically always been very low in the UK, but the Yardies had a substantial income stream to protect and were not about to give it up to rival gangs or to law enforcement agencies. The most significant of the London gangs towards the end of the 1980s was run by Errol Codling, also known as 'Rankin Dread'. He was targeted by Scotland Yard for special attention as he was becoming a major influence on the drug scene. By 1988, enough evidence had been compiled and Codling was arrested and deported back to Jamaica. This single event signalled the start of a huge turf war. In September of that year one of his main rivals, Rohan Barrington Barnet, was shot twice in the chest and later died. A couple of months later, Steven Mendez was shot dead in the back of his car by a neighbourhood gang. The Yardies were becoming more organized and more violent, and the stakes were getting higher.

For many years the various regional and national police departments seemed to be in denial that a serious, country-wide Jamaica gang problem existed, but by the early 1990s, the evidence was irrefutable. The precise number and size of gangs operating in the UK has proved difficult to establish with precision as there are so many small, street gangs operating beneath the radar. However, similar patterns of drug distribution were beginning to evolve all over the country, from Liverpool to Nottingham, and from Cardiff to Newcastle. Manchester was being referred to by police as 'Britain's Chicago' as street shootings hit an all-time high, largely as a result of high-tech weaponry becoming easier to come by, with guns being imported from Russia and the countries of the former Soviet Union. Many of the larger Yardie gangs target a city and take over the drug trade and local gangs find it difficult to fight back as they lack the resources to arm themselves to the same degree. Their general method is to establish a network of heavily armed regional safe houses, from which cities furthest from London would be supplied and the use of extreme violence is commonplace. The Yardies don't have a monopoly on the drug trade in the UK, but they have a significant lead on anyone else and the lion's share of the overall supply. Many other groups and nationalities have tried to take over in other areas – the Chinese Triads often use fraud, extortion and loansharking to raise cash; Eastern European gangs are heavily into prostitution, pornography, human smuggling and contract killing; and Turkish gangs focus on import scams and arms dealing.

The following account describes the conviction of Yardies involved in a murder in London in 2000; it is representative of the many such incidents which are becoming a staple of the news in the UK.

Four members of a Yardie gang known as the Lock City Crew – Winston 'Escobar' Harris, 38, Stephen 'Beamer' Murrary, 26, both from Kensal Green, Jermaine 'My Lord' Hamilton, 22, from Kilburn, and Leonard Cole, 27, from Finsbury Park – have been jailed for life for their part in a turf war murder at the Bridge Park sports centre in north-west London, while a fifth man, David Lewis, 49, from Wembley, was cleared of all charges. The victim was twenty-nine-year-old Dion Holmes who died from a bullet wound in his heart on 1 May 1999. The gang had initiated a 'war' to defend their turf against a rival Brixton gang. The sports centre, near Wembley stadium, had served as the headquarters of the Lock City Crew who had stored arms, drugs and ammunition there. The four convicted men are all Jamaicans who have outstayed their legal right to remain in Britain. The judge made no recommendation as to the deportation of the men at the end of their sentence, noting that the Home Secretary would make whatever decision was appropriate at the time. According to Richard Horwell, prosecuting, the gang, armed with handguns and a sawn-off, pump-action shotgun, had 'descended on the sports centre complex on a mission of revenge and retribution'. They had apparently felt, following a parking incident earlier in the day outside the centre, that the group that they targeted had shown 'a certain lack of respect to them and their territory'. One of the men locked the doors to prevent people from leaving and shots were fired both from the sawn-off shotgun and a handgun. The incident which caused all the trouble had involved a woman parking outside the entrance of the complex, not in a parking bay. When she was asked to park properly an argument had ensued. She had later returned with her husband and abuse and insults had flown, sparking the fatal crisis.

One significant announcement came in April 2006 when the Serious Organized Crime Agency (SOCA) was set up to tackle organized crime. The Agency was formed by the amalgamation of the National Crime Squad (NCS), National Criminal Intelligence Service (NCIS), that part of HM Revenue and Customs (HMRC) dealing with drug trafficking and associated criminal finance, and a part of UK Immigration dealing with organized immigration crime. SOCA's website states that it is 'an intelligence-led agency with law enforcement powers and harm-reduction responsibilities', something that will be put to the test over the years to come. Certainly it will need to move swiftly to prove that it can pull together different law enforcement functions and skills more effectively than has been achieved previously.

Yardie gangsters have spread their drug dealing and gun crime across the UK to such an extent that they now pose the biggest policing challenge apart from international terrorism, according to Detective Chief Superintendent John Coles, the officer in charge of Operation Trident, the 225-strong unit set up by the Metropolitan police to combat gun crime, particularly in black communities in the UK. He said that Jamaican criminals are increasingly targeting villages in Somerset, and that the police have taken action against Yardies in both Sussex and East Anglia. Yardies are even present as far north as Aberdeen. The Yardie problem has spread beyond inner-city, black communities and now poses a threat to people in the home counties and beyond.

Yardies are entrepreneurs who will go wherever there is a market for their drugs, taking their violence with them. The crack cocaine market is now understood to be more dynamic than had previously been thought, both in terms of scale and activity. And increasingly Britons of West Indian origin are working with other groups.

Information on 500 criminals involved in trafficking and dealing in crack cocaine compiled by Operation Trident reveals that while Jamaicans are the major players, accounting for 40 per cent of the crimes investigated, the rest are committed by British-born criminals, most of whom are black. The crack trade and gun crime go together closely, particularly as the Yardie's stock in trade is ruthless and often indiscriminate violence.

Each year, Operation Trident investigates about seventy murders, about a third of all murders in London, and has succeeded in bringing prosecutions in 70 per cent of those murders, up from 20 per cent previously. The unit has also recovered 170 guns in a three-month period. However, it is this very success that is probably helping to push Yardies to venture further afield to sell crack. Any town or city where drugs are sold is vulnerable to Yardie violence; forty-three forces in England and Wales have devoted resources to combating Yardie crime. In far-off Aberdeen, heroin users were lured to crack by dealers who offered a free rock of crack with each wrap of heroin.

The drug culture has brutal, disturbing and far-reaching consequences, not only for users, but for just about everyone in society. It is estimated that around 250,000 cars are stolen in Britain each year. Many of these are transported in containers to India, South America and Australia, but an increasingly significant percentage are turning up in the West Indies as payment for drug shipments to the UK.

Late one Sunday night, or rather very early one Monday morning, in 2000, a queue of young people waiting to get into a private party playing soul and reggae in Chicago's nightclub in south London were suddenly sprayed with bullets from one or more automatic weapons. Eight of them were wounded, including a twenty-seven-year-old man with serious chest injuries; two other men were also injured, one of them in the ankle by a ricocheting bullet. Five young women were hurt, including a fifteen-year-old girl hit in the arm and chest. A passing motorist was also taken to hospital to be treated for shock. The incident seemed have been another Yardie-style hit in an increasingly violent turf war which had already been raging for more than two years. In 1999, twenty-nine people were killed in Yardie-related 'hits'. Up to August in 2000 there had been six murders and twenty-one attempted murders. Particular Yardie hotspots have been Brixton, elsewhere in south London, Harlesden in the north and Dalston in the east.

One of the challenges with combatting Yardie crime is the loose and disorganized nature of the gangs. Also distinctive is the way in which extreme violence can be provoked by seemingly utterly trivial disputes, such as a gang member's girlfriend being barred from a nightclub.

Another tale of Yardie depravity concerns thirty-year-old Rohan 'Chunky' Chung who, despite having been deported from the UK for gun offences, returned in 2006 to shoot dead two sisters and their stepfather in a revenge attack aimed at another member of their family who, he claimed, had double-crossed him in a drug deal. The victims were twenty-seven-year-old Connie Morrison, thirty-four-year-old Lorna Morrison and Noel Patterson, who was sixty-two. The eight-month-old son of one of the women was left lying in the blood-soaked room for sixteen hours. Chung had apparently repeatedly used false names to slip in and out of the country while running a Yardie gang supplying cocaine to London dealers. Chung and his accomplice, Michael Letts, both received three life sentences.

Bugsy Siegel

Benjamin Hymen Siegelbaum was born in 1906 in the poverty-stricken slums of Brooklyn, New York. He was one of that generation of gangsters which rose to infamy during the Depression and the years that followed. His parents were poor Austrian Jews who had come to America in search of a better life for their five children. Brooklyn was a teeming cauldron of people from all over the world struggling to make ends meet, the perfect breeding ground for gangsters and criminals of all kinds. It was on the streets of Brooklyn that Benny got his nickname, Bugsy, from a slang term for crazy behaviour. It was a nickname which he hated and he would pick a fight with anyone who used it in front of him. Some kids deliberately make trouble, but trouble seemed to follow Bugsy everywhere he went during his childhood. He was not one to shy away from a fight and he was welcomed into his first street gang on Manhattan's Lafayette Street with open arms. He got involved in various crimes including protection rackets, theft and buying stolen goods.

It was within this gang environment that Bugsy met Meyer Lansky – it was a meeting that would change his life. There are a number of accounts of how the two men met and became friends, but one common strand is that Lanksy helped the impetuous and fearless Siegel away from a street fight just before the police arrived. Lansky had already started working with Charles Luciano and had great plans in the world of crime. A new gang was formed which included Lepke

Buchalter who later ran Murder Inc., Abner Zwillman who would one day run a large section of the New Jersey racketeering empire and Arthur Flegenheimer (who would become better known as Dutch Schultz). Soon Bugsy developed a reputation on the streets for great bravery; he was also known as a man who would shoot first and ask questions later. He grew to a height of nearly six foot and had a mop of thick black hair and piercing blue eyes. Many Hollywood studios were looking for exactly this type of character to cast in gangster roles, but this wasn't the world that excited Bugsy – he needed real danger, not the made-up thrills of a screenplay. Once he had a little money, he began to dress smartly and he liked to catch the eye of the pretty girls. Athletically built and with a quick wit, Bugsy seemed equally at home chatting with the rich and famous as with the humble street peddler. While Lansky was happy to stay in the background, Bugsy enjoyed the limelight and 'respect' that he received from virtually everyone the two gangsters had dealings with.

Charles 'Lucky' Luciano had been fingered for a large drugs deal that had gone wrong and had been sentenced to a year behind bars. After serving six months, he was allowed out on parole and wanted revenge. The man who had shopped him was a nineteen-year-old Irish boy who was the son of a well-known New York policeman. Lansky convinced Luciano to keep a low profile and not approach the lad who had informed on him. He told him that Bugsy would handle this one. In was well into 1916 when Bugsy and Lansky found their opportunity to kidnap the unsuspecting young man. Even after a massive police search and full help from the media, the body of the boy was never found. It was the first time Bugsy had been involved in murder – and it wouldn't be the last. One woman who lived in the block next to the Irish lad had apparently seen the incident but was 'persuaded', by means of a brutal beating, not to talk. Several years later, in a strange quirk of fate, Bugsy met the woman in a New York bar and the woman decided to taunt him. Bugsy didn't react while others watched but left the bar and waited in his car for her to walk home. In an alleyway close to her home, Bugsy cornered the woman and ferociously raped her. She was later spotted by some neighbours and the police were called, she named Bugsy and the following day he was arrested. Bugsy had spoken to Lansky about the incident and he knew what to do. After Bugsy got out on bail while awaiting trial, he paid a visit to the woman. The police received a note from her soon afterwards, stating that she wanted to drop the charges and that no amount of persuasion would change her mind.

By the early 1920s, the Jewish gang led by Bugsy Siegel and Meyer Lansky was a force to be reckoned with. Their relationship with Luciano was an unusual two-way street as gangs from different ethnic backgrounds in New York at that time rarely got on, let alone collaborated or did business together. It was known on the streets that these particular Jews were OK and the Italians and Sicilians effectively allowed them to work wherever they wanted. Bugsy had the freedom to roam across the whole of Manhattan, staking out new targets, developing deals and committing robberies. Times were beginning to get tough as the American economy entered its most stagnant period and a huge number of pawnbrokers and moneylenders sprang up. These people typically had little in the way of guns or other weapons with which to defend themselves and needed protection. They were easy prey for Bugsy who would typically walk in bold as brass, beat people up with his bare hands, rob the place and walk back out again. The gang were beginning to have some serious money lying around the office and Lansky wanted to put it into the local bank for safe keeping. Bugsy went to take a look at the premises and wasn't impressed with the level of security. The money was never deposited and just two weeks later a gang of masked robbers led by Bugsy broke in, surprised the ageing security guard, and stole an estimated $8,000 from the safe. Lansky was to have a growing problem with what to do with the pile of cash that Bugsy was generating.

The gang had developed a very profitable illegal gambling operation out of several locations around the affluent Upper East Side on Manhattan Island and a big game could be found most nights of the week. One evening a venue that had many of the regulars in attendance was raided by a gang of Italians led by Joe Masseria, who could call on the services of a 200-strong gang. He was systematically pushing smaller gangs out into the suburbs and away from the wealthier areas. The bodyguards and organizers were powerless and Bugsy wanted to go straight round to Masseria's place with guns blazing. Lansky managed to restrain his partner's impetuous urges and sent low-profile colleagues over to case the offices. However, he knew they needed to fight this war or be pushed out into the minor league. Late one evening, when most of their members were still present, the Masseria gang got a well-planned wake-up call: a massive barrage of gunfire came from a dozen well-chosen vantage points and completely overwhelmed them – those that were still standing fled for their life as they thought they had been attacked by a mighty force. Eventually the police turned up in enough force to halt the shooting and Lanksy, Meyer and others in their gang were arrested. The only charge that would stick was disorderly conduct and the maximum fine was imposed – the princely sum of two dollars. The reputation of Bugsy, in particular, as a hard, fighting man was becoming legend on the streets of New York.

As Prohibition hit the country, Bugsy and Lansky's battle with Masseria and his men raged. Masseria had managed to partially rebuild his team and was one of the first to start a lucrative alcohol importation business through Canada and the Caribbean. Bugsy believed that the Italian had got off lightly and was still gunning for him – he arranged to hijack a large booze shipment and shot three of Masseria's gang in the process. He knew getting to Masseria would not be easy so he used his friendship with 'Lucky' Luciano to do just that. Luciano had arranged to have dinner with Masseria, under the pretext of discussing new business. When Luciano left the room to go to the bathroom, Bugsy burst in and gunned Masseria down. This killing opened the way for Lansky's brains and Siegel's brawn to expand their fledgling bootlegging business. New trucks, fast boats and even pipelines were purchased as the market for the 'real stuff' mushroomed in and around New York. Bugsy had helped set up a series of small gambling dens and these grew in size as people wanted to chance their arm and have a drink at the same time.

Siegel had been friends with Al Capone since they were boys. They were not members of the same gang, but they spoke often and had collaborated on occasion over a number of years. Capone got himself into trouble when a beating turning into a killing which could be traced back to him. He called Bugsy and asked for help. Capone went into hiding and spent several weeks in Bugsy's aunt's house until things cooled down. Capone moved to Chicago soon afterwards and joined Johnny Torrio's gang but kept in touch with Bugsy and Lansky. The underworld in Chicago at that time was run by Jim Colosimo, also known as 'Big Jim', who was nervous about getting into bootlegging, something that Capone saw as a huge opportunity. Discussions were under way and the team of friends hired hitman Frankie Yale to travel up from New York to sort out Colosimo. The following week, news came through that he had been found with a bullet in his head. There was an immediate shift of power as Torrio and Capone stepped up and arranged for shipments of alcohol to be shared between the Bugsy/Lansky gang and their Chicago mob. A very productive and profitable partnership had grown beyond their greatest expectations.

Friendships in the underworld can be blessings in disguise, or quite the reverse. Dutch Schultz, another natural-born killer, was a member of the Bugsy/Lanksy gang for some time, but had gone his own way during Prohibition. Lansky always felt that Schultz was too much of a loose cannon and that he was bound to bring trouble in his wake.

At one stage Schultz was forced to go underground to avoid tax evasion charges and had the Special Prosecutor Tom Dewey all over his operation. Schultz left his business to be run by Bo Weinberg, a man from the same part of the world as Bugsy. The two men knew each other well but when Schultz came out of hiding and found his empire had been reduced to a fraction of its former size, he wanted to make some fundamental changes. Schultz met with Bugsy and the two men discussed various options before finally agreeing that Weinberg would have to be removed and that Bugsy would handle this. Bugsy stole a car and picked up Weinberg under the pretext that they were to have dinner together. But Bugsy brought the car to a halt by the East River, got out, calmly walked around the car, lit a cigarette and knifed his friend in the throat. He then knifed Weinberg in the stomach to ensure that all the gases still within the body would escape and not allow it to float – one of the tricks of the trade. Weinberg's body was never located and probably found its last resting place at the bottom of the murky river.

The summer of 1932 was a turning point for both Benjamin Siegel and Meyer Lansky. They had grown more powerful, their business empire was now providing tremendous cash returns, but the number of their enemies had grown too. One evening, the Fabrazzo brothers, a pair of contract killers hired by a rival gang, planted an explosive in Bugsy's head office. Bugsy was chatting to Lanksy when he spotted the bomb and managed to throw it out of the window just before it exploded, injuring himself in the process. Despite having pieces of bomb embedded in his face and body and multiple cuts from which blood was streaming, Bugsy was not about to sit around. He found out who was responsible and hunted the two men down. The body of Andy Frabazzo was found in a sack in a neighbouring suburb and his brother, Louis, was gunned down on a street corner under the cover of darkness. One brother remained, Tony, who wasn't involved in the original attempted murder, but who nevertheless feared for his life. Siegel went round to his house one evening and Tony's father came to the door – Bugsy said he was a police detective and needed to speak to his son. When Tony came to the door, he was shot three times and died instantly. Bugsy knew that he would be the prime suspect, so he had devised a cast-iron alibi, which held firm, but he had made even more enemies and Lansky knew that it was time for a change of scene for him. He sent Bugsy to Los Angeles to develop an organized crime network there.

Bugsy arrived in California in 1936 with his wife and two daughters and rented a mansion befitting his status and power. He had several contacts in Los Angeles and soon started mixing with Hollywood society, something that he was clearly adept at and that he enjoyed. To the locals having a real gangster rather than just actors was a novelty and he gained access to the rich and famous. Siegel had always had an eye for the girls but when he moved to the West Coast, he was like a kid in a candy store. His womanizing reached new heights as he found himself surrounded by beautiful, sun-kissed women who seemed endlessly available to him. Bugsy was unlike many other gangsters at that time in that he was charming, suave and charismatic and clearly had a way with women. In Los Angeles he became even more vain, spending most afternoons in the gym and allegedly using beauty creams every night to stop his face from sagging. Soon, however, it was back to business – Harry Greenberg, sometimes known as Harry Schacter, had been one of the members of the New York Mafia families but had moved to Canada when things had got a bit hot for him. He was still on the payroll, but many of his colleagues were concerned as to whether he would keep his secrets to himself. Greenberg moved to California and Bugsy got a call to see if he would 'take care' of him. He was asked not to get involved personally, but simply to co-ordinate and oversee a team to handle the job. Bugsy, however, wanted to show that he was still a man to be reckoned with when it came to this sort of work. He also confided in a friend that he enjoyed killing and had missed it. On 22 November 1939, Greenberg was returning to his home with the newspapers when a gunman stepped out from the palm trees, riddling the unsuspecting man with bullets. Greenberg's whereabouts had been established by a local hood called Whitey Krakow and several months after the assassination he was heard in public discussing Siegel's part in what had happened. The underworld was a small place and news quickly reached Bugsy, who was incensed. In July the following year the body of Krakow was found, having been shot several times from close range.

The story of Las Vegas is inextricably linked to the life of Bugsy Siegel. The reality is that this man wasn't the first to see the opportunity, or even the one with the vision to turn the parched, desert town into the gambling capital of the world. During the Great Depression, the state of Nevada decided to legalize gambling to help the economy. At the same time Bugsy eventually managed to find a partner by the name of Billy Wilkerson to develop some property. Together they planned to build the best, most luxurious integrated hotel, casino and entertainment centre in the town to attract punters from right across America. Wilkerson ran out of money during the building phase and Siegel saw his chance to become the sole owner – something that he had secretly always wanted to be. The money for the project came from New York and the bosses were naturally very nervous of this massive enterprise, which was starting to absorb cash like the parched desert soil absorbed water. Bugsy, however, ploughed on with his dream, called the Flamingo, which opened with a blaze of publicity and star-studded promotion. There are many stories about how the Flamingo got its name, but the favourite theory seems to be that this was Bugsy's pet name for his long-term mistress, Virginia Hill. The Flamingo was on a scale rarely seen anywhere in the world at that time; the budget, however, was in bad shape, having spiralled out of control to 400 per cent more than had initially been agreed by its financial backers. Bugsy was a gangster, not a professional businessman or builder, and tales of supply companies robbing him blind were widespread. Some of these found their way back to the already nervous New York investors and they were not happy.

Lansky found out that Bugsy had opened a Swiss bank account and some of the money earmarked for the building of the hotel was being redirected. Luciano, Costello, Adonis, Genovese and other members of the Mafia Syndicate met in Cuba to discuss what they were going to do. It went to a vote and unanimously they agreed to remove Bugsy and the contract was given to Charlie Fischetti, a regular, highly experienced assassin. Lansky fought for his friend's life and was able to secure agreement that the hit would not be made until after the opening. Perhaps if the Flamingo was a massive success and the money was returned, he would be able to save him after all. The opening of the casino saw the Hollywood stars turn out in force – George Raft, Jimmy Durante, Clark Gable, Lana Turner, Joan Crawford and many others filled the tables and had their photographs taken. However, the publicity wasn't sufficient to get enough people to travel to the desert at that time and as the sun fell behind the surrounding mountains, the punters soon left, making the grand opening an expensive flop. Bugsy was also well behind with the actual hotel, which would not open for another three months. Business did start to pick up as people saw the impressive facilities and heard stories of the high rollers who frequented the casino. Although cash was coming in, it was a trickle compared with what had been spent over budget. On 20 June 1947 at around 10.20 p.m. Siegel was relaxing in his Hollywood home with a couple of friends, having just returned from a haircut, manicure and supper. The forty-two-year-old was suddenly caught in an explosion of gunfire, which came from outside the front window. One of the first shots hit Siegel in an eye, dislodging it and sending it flying right across the room where it was later found. Although several subsequent bullets missed their target, ineffectually hitting the walls of Bugsy's mansion, Siegel was dead and his bloodied body lay on the floor. He had died the way he had lived – violently. The two survivors of the attack lying on the floor of the room heard a car pull out of the driveway, but they saw nothing.

No one was ever arrested for Siegel's murder and only five people came to his funeral – all of them relatives. Lansky sent one of his top casino guys from Florida to take charge of the Flamingo and all of the top management were unceremoniously and immediately axed. The hotel and casino complex did go on to be highly successful, often filling its 3,500 rooms and offering top entertainment, but it was sold by the mob to a large corporation which knew how to run such a venture. The Flamingo became firmly established in the history of Las Vegas and remained one of its principal attractions for many years, thereby turning, at least to some extent, Bugsy's dream into reality.

The Triads

'Two men can keep a secret as long as one of them is dead' is a motto much used by members of criminal gangs when speaking about the Chinese Triads. It says much about their clandestine and violent nature. The Triads have become one of the most powerful crime syndicates in the world and their drug network, in particular, has reached just about every major city in the Western world. It is fairly unusual for a criminal organization to have long, complex oaths, vows or affirmations. Usually, being prepared to commit serious crimes is sufficient to be accepted as the member of a gang. Swearing oaths is more conventionally for churchgoers or children on summer camps. Given the rarity of oaths in gangland, it is even more surprising that one gang would have thirty-six of them. Traditional Triad members were expected to abide by the following list of oaths:

The Triad Oaths

1. After having entered the Hung gates, I must treat the parents and relatives of my sworn brothers as my own kin. I shall suffer death by five thunderbolts if I do not keep this oath.
2. I shall assist my sworn brothers to bury their parents and brothers by offering financial or physical assistance. I shall be killed by five thunderbolts if I pretend to have no knowledge of their troubles.

3. When Hung brothers visit my house, I shall provide them with board and lodging. I shall be killed by myriad knives if I treat them as strangers.
4. I will always acknowledge my Hung brothers when they identify themselves. If I ignore them I will be killed by myriad swords.
5. I shall not disclose the secrets of the Hung family, not even to my parents, brothers, or wife. I shall never disclose the secrets for money. I will be killed by myriad swords if I do so.
6. I shall never betray my sworn brothers. If, through a misunderstanding, I have caused the arrest of one of my brothers I must release him immediately. If I break this oath I will be killed by five thunderbolts.
7. I will offer financial assistance to sworn brothers who are in trouble in order that they may pay their passage fee etc. If I break this oath I will be killed by five thunderbolts.
8. I must never cause harm or bring trouble to my sworn brothers or Incense Master. If I do so I will be killed by myriad swords.
9. I must never commit any indecent assaults on the wives, sisters or daughters of my sworn brothers. I shall be killed by five thunderbolts if I break this oath.
10. I shall never embezzle cash or property from my sworn brothers. If I break this oath I will be killed by myriad swords.
11. I will take good care of the wives or children of sworn brothers entrusted to my keeping. If I do not I will be killed by five thunderbolts.
12. I have supplied false particulars about myself for the purpose of joining the Hung family I shall be killed by five thunderbolts.
13. If I should change my mind and deny my membership of the Hung family I will be killed by myriad swords.
14. If I rob a sworn brother or assist an outsider to do so I will be killed by five thunderbolts.

15. If I should take advantage of a sworn brother or force unfair business deals upon him I will be killed by myriad swords.
16. If I knowingly convert my sworn brother's cash or property to my own use I shall be killed by five thunderbolts.
17. If I have wrongly taken a sworn brother's cash or property during a robbery I must return them to him. If I do not I will be killed by five thunderbolts.
18. If I am arrested after committing an offence I must accept my punishment and not try to place blame on my sworn brothers. If I do so I will be killed by five thunderbolts.
19. If any of my sworn brothers are killed, or arrested, or have departed to some other place, I will assist their wives and children who may be in need. If I pretend to have no knowledge of their difficulties I will be killed by five thunderbolts.
20. When any of my sworn brothers have been assaulted or blamed by others, I must come forward and help him if he is in the right or advise him to desist if he is wrong. If he has been repeatedly insulted by others I shall inform our other brothers and arrange to help him physically or financially. If I do not keep this oath I will be killed by five thunderbolts.
21. If it comes to my knowledge that the government is seeking any of my sworn brothers who has come from other provinces or from overseas, I shall immediately inform him in order that he may make his escape. If I break this oath I will be killed by five thunderbolts.
22. I must not conspire with outsiders to cheat my sworn brothers at gambling. If I do so I will be killed by myriad swords.
23. I shall not cause discord among my sworn brothers by spreading false reports about any of them. If I do so I will be killed by myriad swords.
24. I shall not appoint myself as Incense Master without authority. After entering the Hung gates for three years

the loyal and faithful ones may be promoted by the Incense Master with the support of his sworn brothers. I shall be killed by five thunderbolts if I make any unauthorized promotions myself.

25. If my natural brothers are involved in a dispute or law suit with my sworn brothers I must not help either party against the other but must attempt to have the matter settled amicably. If I break this oath I will be killed by five thunderbolts.
26. After entering the Hung gates I must forget any previous grudges I may have borne against my sworn brothers. If I do not do so I will be killed by five thunderbolts.
27. I must not trespass upon the territory occupied by my sworn brothers. I shall be killed by five thunderbolts if I pretend to have no knowledge of my brothers' rights in such matters.
28. I must not covet or seek to share any property or cash obtained by my sworn brothers. If I have such ideas I will be killed.
29. I must not disclose any address where my sworn brothers keep their wealth nor must I conspire to make wrong use of such knowledge. If I do so I will be killed by myriad swords.
30. I must not give support to outsiders if so doing is against the interests of any of my sworn brothers. If I do not keep this oath I will be killed by myriad swords.
31. I must not take advantage of the Hung brotherhood in order to oppress or take violent or unreasonable advantage of others. I must be content and honest. If I break this oath I will be killed by five thunderbolts.
32. I shall be killed by five thunderbolts if I behave indecently towards small children of my sworn brothers' families.
33. If any of my sworn brothers has committed a big offence I must not inform upon them to the government for the purposes of obtaining a reward. I shall be killed by five thunderbolts if I break this oath.

34. I must not take to myself the wives and concubines of my sworn brothers nor commit adultery with them. If I do so I will be killed by myriad swords.
35. I must never reveal Hung secrets or signs when speaking to outsiders. If I do so I will be killed by myriad swords.
36. After entering the Hung gates I shall be loyal and faithful and shall endeavour to overthrow Ch'ing and restore Ming by co-ordinating my efforts with those of my sworn brethren even though my brethren and I may not be in the same professions. Our common aim is to avenge our Five Ancestors.

There are many myths and legends regarding the origins of the Triads; certainly the oaths lead one to think that they had some unusual ways of working. The most plausible and widely held belief is that they began as freedom fighters in a resistance movement against the Manchu emperors. These men came from the north of the country and were seen by anyone in the south or central plains as outsiders, establishing a dynasty by force in the seventeenth century. Folklore has it that the Manchu used a band of fighting monks to crush a rebellion, but they then turned on the monks who they saw as a possible threat to their authority. Five monks escaped and set up their own monasteries, supposedly safe havens from crime and the tyrannical rulers of the land. They had followers who swore allegiance and acted in secret. Like Japan's Yakuza or Robin Hood's band in England, those who fight oppression are often seen centuries later as people who could do no wrong in the eyes of the poor.

From the beginning, the Triads were a most secretive organization. Although individual gangs were often small, they were able to punch above their weight as they enjoyed the support of the overwhelming majority of the public and could muster an army of followers for their cause. The White Lotus Rebellion in the eighteenth century ran for many years, as did the Kwanhsi uprising in the middle of the nineteenth century. These men fought to restore the ideals of the Ming dynasty and were often to be seen wearing red garments, the colour associated with that period. The family name of the Ming emperors was Hung, a term which as can be seen from the oaths was synonymous with the Triads during their early years. The Manchus were finally overthrown in 1911, but there were no members of the official Ming dynasty left to rule so a warlord by the name of Yuan Shik Kai became head of the country. There was a severe north-south divide, not just in the politics but in the way the regions were being run and in the late 1920s, the Triads took control of the south of the country while the north became part of a Communist state, later to be run by Mao Tse Tung.

It is no wonder that crime and the size of the Triad gangs grew rapidly from the turn of the twentieth century – China was still very poor, mostly because it had been robbed of its gold, minerals and heritage for centuries, but the economy was beginning to grow. As Japan invaded most of the major cities in China at the start of the Second World War, they arranged deals with the Triads who had managed to gain control of a great deal of the infrastructure. Gangsters were used to help the police and the army to suppress any unrest associated with anti-Japanese activities or sentiment. The gangsters were paid well for their help, through a Japanese front business called the Lee Yuen Company. Once again, following the end of the war, the Triad's target became Communism and their membership began to grow again. In southern China this campaign was run by Kot Siu Wong, who had his headquarters at 14 Po Wah Road, Canton; this is where the name of the 14K Triad is thought to have originated. Hong Kong became the place where all the major Triad groups needed a foothold and it was estimated that in 1950 there were well over 300,000 Triad members living in that one, small province alone. The following years saw greater violence between the Triads and the Communist state and many Triad members were hunted and imprisoned or executed. As a result many Triads moved their operation overseas to places like Taiwan, Thailand, San Francisco, Perth and Vancouver. Taiwan became a particularly strong base for the Triads where they have creamed off a multi-billion dollar fortune from government infrastructure projects alone. Their stranglehold on the major construction deals revolves around their ability to prevent many others from doing work and having an international network of companies who will offer favourable terms to call on.

Estimates of the size and scope of the Triad's activities vary widely. This is difficult to assess due to the widely dispersed nature of many of the gangs which now operate far from China. However, a recent article offered the following breakdown of the four major Triad groups.

> United Bamboo: 10,000 members, mostly second- and third-generation immigrants. Activities include construction, security services, debt collection, loan sharking, gambling dens, hostess clubs, restaurants and other small businesses.
>
> Four Seas: up to 2,000 members, again mostly second- and third-generation mainland immigrants involved in similar activities but including massage parlours and brothels as a major source of revenue.
>
> Tian Dao Man: several hundred members, mostly active in Taiwan in debt collection, massage parlours, prostitution and running small businesses.
>
> Sung Lian: several hundred members active in prostitution, debt collection and massage parlours.

The importance of Hong Kong in the development of the Triad operation cannot be overestimated. It is the link between their past and their present wealth. It is estimated that around fifty-seven different Triad gangs remain active in the Hong Kong underworld and many of the larger groups are firmly based there. Typical activities include illegal gambling, prostitution, car theft, drug trafficking, money laundering and counterfeiting intellectual property in the form of computer games, other computer software, music CDs, and movies in all formats such as video, DVD and other optical discs. Triad groups tend to operate very differently from the traditional Mafia model of a boss of bosses with a loose affiliation of regional bosses below him. Triad gangs are often made up of smaller groups of individuals who specialize in one particular activity or form just part of a chain of activities. Members rarely come together except when they are being threatened by another gang or when a big opportunity comes along. This structure usually has a leader heading fifteen to twenty active members with each small gang reporting to a higher power quite regularly. Triads often use numeric codes to identify different positions within larger and more diverse gangs. Number 426, for example, refers to a fighter, 489 to a mountain master, 49 to the lowest level and 25 to an undercover spy. All the small gangs benefit from the protection of the larger organization behind them and often useful contacts are sent down the chain by the boss. Most Triad members are extremely unlikely ever to meet their main boss.

When new opportunities present themselves or when rival gangs are in competition, there is often a show of force. Gang leaders round up as many members as they can for a show of strength and solidarity. They try to avoid fighting for a number of reasons, one of which is cost – weapons and ammunition are expensive, in addition to which many groups have to bolster their actual membership by hiring mercenaries. In 1990, one gang wanting to show its strength to local rivals monopolized the queues for a new apartment block with over 700 people. The action backfired as the police found out about the plan and moved in to arrest many of the conspirators. Many were found not to be members of the gang, but just hired drug addicts or hawkers from other districts. All the participants were given white gloves by the leader of the gang to signify their allegiance and the gang became known as 'The White Glove Gang' thereafter. Recently, Triad gangs have become more businesslike, interacting and integrating with other groups from China, Taiwan, Macau and Hong Kong. The scale of the problem faced by the police is formidable – there are 27,000 police officers in Hong Kong compared with an estimated 100,000 active Triad members. The authorities have been slow to introduce new laws to help the police, and consequently the judicial system has been struggling to convict many known felons. The first legislation to create a vital Police Protection Unit came during 1995 and to this day many essential laws needed by the law enforcement units are not in place. Some senior policemen do work with Triad groups in an effort to find out when rivals are planning big drug shipments or opening new houses for prostitution but this has led to public fears about bribery and corruption.

The sheer scale of the Triad's illegal activities has at times dwarfed the authorities' ability to keep track of it. Triad involvement in Taiwan, especially by the United Bamboo gang, has reached every part of the country, into leading corporations and affecting hundreds of occupations. The Triads walk a fine line and often bid for large government contracts through entirely legitimate companies. The key to the whole process, however, is their ability to use all their financial power, their control over the labour unions and their 'friends in high places' to get awarded deals at the right price. During the 1990s, Regis Chen was the chairman of the state-owned BES Engineering Corp, responsible for handling many major government contracting projects. In 1994, they were looking to bid for the Hsipin freeway with a budget of an estimated $4 billion – the main rival was the Chun Kuo group who have strong affiliations with United Bamboo. Chun wanted an unchallenged run for this work and started an eighteen-month campaign of intimidation, involving personal threats, the bribery of BES workers and sabotage. In 1995, the boss of BES resigned, believing he was in a battle he just couldn't win, leaving Chun Kuo to win the contract. The freeway would have serious problems, with tunnels collapsing and parts of the surface having to be replaced within a year of being laid. This led to a massive investigation and United Bamboo had to keep a very low profile in relation to this kind of work – but only for a while. According to some estimates, the extent of crocked deals over a six-year period had resulted in the Triads, along with certain officials and politicians, earning an estimated $26 billion. Some of this money had gone into maintaining proper businesses in Taiwan and using them as fronts for further illegal activity, but most had gone into already well-filled Triad coffers. The power of the Triads, especially United Bamboo, now rivals the government itself.

United Bamboo is not one of the oldest Triad groups, but it is certainly now one of the most powerful. It was started around fifty years ago by a handful of sons of senior officers in the Chi'ang-kai army which had moved from China to Taiwan rather than face an all-out war with Mao's advancing forces. The young rebels started on the streets outside Taiwan's capital, Taipei, setting up gambling dens, loansharking deals and protection rackets. They quickly found it necessary to have a legitimate business front, which is how they ended up getting involved in construction, and in the latter days have taken to wearing black suits, white shirts, a black tie and dark sunglasses. It is a close-knit group, many having grown up together and marrying into each other's families, which has led to a structure more democratic that the Japanese Yakuza or America's Mafia. United Bamboo tends to work more like a team, allocating tasks and responsibilities according to the most efficient way of getting a job or deal done. When differences of opinion arise, they vote on how to proceed and accept the decision of the majority – not exactly the way Al Capone would have handled things.

Democracy can be a tough and, at times, uncompromising two-headed master. In Taiwan, which is certainly not alone in this, many leading figures are elected with the financial help and influence of others. Once they are in a position of power and influence, it is payback time. Unfortunately for officials in many parts of the Pacific Rim, they all too often find themselves at the mercy of unscrupulous people with ulterior motives who are able to meddle with government policy, legislation and contracts. It is a vicious cycle that can take decades to bring to an end and many countries struggle with this problem, to some extent, for generations.

In fact, it is not even democracy, but a form of criminality which can affect whole nations, often for decades. The Taiwanese Justice Minister for much of the 1990s, Liao, stated that many voters were actually paid by individuals to put a tick next to their names. He added that, 'Most voters have no notion that getting NT$500 or NT$1,000 is wrong. We tried to arrest many voters. Now we realize we must catch the offending political candidates. We must seize their assets.' Corruption has been especially rife at regional level, where certain officials have ruled with a rod of iron. Particularly notorious was Cheng Tai-Chi and Huang Ching-Ping who are waiting on death row for the result of their appeal.

Protection rackets in China, Taiwan, Hong Kong and many other places in the Far East now operate not just for individuals, shopkeepers, restaurants and club owners but major companies as well. *Business Weekly* magazine identified sixteen publicly listed companies that have had to turn to protection in the course of business disputes. Protection usually means contacting one of the major Triad gangs and getting them to 'persuade' an opposing firm or labour union to change course. United Bamboo has the largest network by far in this line of work, but other gangs operate very successfully in the smaller towns and cities. Another way in which senior government officials or high-ranking commercial figures get involved with the Triads is as silent partners in ventures such as clubs, restaurants, massage parlours and houses of prostitution. In exchange for a licence to continue trading or a favourable contract, monthly cash payments are made by the owners of these establishments to people who are effectively above the law. For America, Europe and many other parts of the world, China's accord with organized crime is a cause of great concern as many of these activities have a significant impact on the streets of towns and cities all over the world. China's economy is projected to continue to expand at great speed over the next couple of decades which will bring many problems with it for the power of the Triads is inextricably linked to the level of prosperity. It is likely that the decision-making and strategy of major international companies will be influenced not just by their boards of directors and what is good for their shareholders, but also by the Triads. Sinister forces will be at work, affecting both legitimate business deals and the spread of criminal activities in the Far East. For companies and individuals alike, it will be difficult to come to terms with this development as representatives from listed businesses are usually perceived to be acting fairly and properly. Even when criminals are caught there will be the whole issue of extradition and where crimes have originated, something that several governments have been at odds about recently. Certainly laws relating to criminal behaviour differ to a large extent from country to country and this is a growing problem for law enforcement agencies. Criminals, especially those seen as white-collar criminals, can often plead to be returned to their native country for a 'fair' trial – in such circumstances true justice is unlikely to be served.

For many years the major Triad gangs did not seem to raise their head above the parapet in many countries, seeming content to wait in the background and move in slowly under the radar of both other criminal groups and also the local law enforcement agencies. Perhaps this says something about the culture of the gangsters themselves and how they are perhaps less ego-driven than many of their European and American counterparts who come in with a big show of force. Their desire for wealth and power is, however, more than equal to that of other criminal outfits.

Writing in the UK's *Police Review* in 1991, Detective Superintendent James Bocock commented on the development of the Triads: 'Quite distinct from these street gangs, there exists a number of very close-knit groups whose criminal empires are networked throughout the United Kingdom and beyond. They are shrewd, ruthless individuals who have no compunction in resorting to extreme violence in order to punish, intimidate or impose their will on vulnerable Chinese businessmen.'

There has been a Triad presence in Holland from the 1920s, when poorly paid sailors from Hong Kong and the Chinese mainland were used on merchant ships. Many ended up in Amsterdam as job prospects were good and it was friendly towards Asians. However, with domestic matters to sort out, many Triads retained just a small working force and it was not until the 1970s, when the infamous 14K gang arrived in force, that things began to hot up. They set up a travel agency business and a modern casino as a front and a way of laundering money. In the background were other activities, which included prostitution, pornography, extortion rackets and drug dealing. There was a long-held suspicion that the travel agency business was helping the gangs to smuggle large amounts of cocaine, heroin and crack into mainland Europe, but there have been few prosecutions to back this up. One rival Triad gang, the Ah Kong, was trying to muscle in on 14K's strength in Amsterdam and this came to a head in the mid-1970s when the leader of this band, Si Hoi, was shot dead outside a restaurant in the city centre. His replacement Chan Yuen Huk was also a marked man who was killed soon after arriving in Europe. Although hit by several bullets, his bodyguard managed to survive the attack.

Other countries were beginning to see similar trends. Germany, France, Australia, New Zealand and Spain were all targeted and the South African police reported a series of killings in Johannesburg and Cape Town, which were attributed to the Triads. The same situation was occurring right across the wealthier parts of South Africa, where gang rivalry was becoming an international affair as testified to by newspaper headlines. Local criminals were being pushed by the Triads as they attempted to get a foothold. In a short period in Cape Town in the early 1990s, one man was found dead in a river with the bolt from a crossbow in his back, another was killed while eating in a restaurant, and a third burnt so badly he was almost unidentifiable. All were attributed to gang violence involving Triads. Many of the Triad gangs were incorporating new illegal activities in their traditional business model, things such as trading in rhino horns, dried shark fins, gold and precious stones. One owner of a fishing warehouse on the docks was beaten up because he wouldn't pay protection money – his body was later found floating in the bay with nine bullet holes in it. It was a stark warning to law officials and businessmen alike that the Triads needed to be dealt with quickly and that fire would be needed to fight with fire.

Any global expansion of the Triads would not be complete without a significant presence in the largest arena for organized crime by far – North America. Immigrants have long been arriving in droves on the West Coast and San Francisco in particular became a major destination for criminals and hardworking Chinese alike. Its China Town remains the largest grouping of Chinese people outside China in the world. During the 1990s the Triads became heavily involved in smuggling the purest form of heroin available on the streets, called China White, and they often brought in specially trained illegal immigrants to help with the distribution and selling of it. Many of these people were also made to work in the brothels and sweatshops to repay the cost of their transport from China or elsewhere. During this period it was estimated that up to 100,000 illegal immigrants came in from China each year, with one-fifth coming through southern California. Given this amazing number of people, it is no wonder that the power now being wielded by the Triads has grown considerably, making them a major league player in the world of criminal gangs.

Sammy 'The Bull' Gravano

Salvatore Gravano was born on 12 March 1945 in Brooklyn, New York. He was to become known throughout the entire underworld as 'Sammy the Bull' or often, simply, 'The Bull'. His parents had come over from Italy separately, his father having jumped ship in Canada and entered America as an illegal alien. The name Salvatore was dropped in favour of Sammy when the boy was quite young and this became popular with the whole family as it was the name of a favourite uncle. Sammy's father was a painter and decorator and his mother a good seamstress; both of them had to work hard and long hours to provide enough money to feed the family. Gravano was identified at school as being dyslexic and, with no help, he used to struggle to complete his assignments and classwork. It is thought that his hatred of authority probably grew from these early days of being humiliated in front of his peers. Anyone who made fun of him was soon set upon and although not a big or tall child, he would usually come out on top, having no fear of being hurt or of the consequences of his actions. At the age of ten, Sammy was bought a new bike for his birthday and carelessly left it on the street one afternoon. It was stolen and the young boy swore he would find the culprits. After searching the entire neighbourhood for whole days at a time, Sammy eventually tracked down the thieves, two boys who were several years older and considerably bigger than he was. However, this meant nothing to him and he attacked both boys with wild, swinging blows, knocking both to the ground on several occasions. The fight carried on for some time but Sammy would not be beaten and eventually the scuffle was broken up by some men walking from a nearby hostelry. Sammy got his bike back along with a new nickname that stuck immediately – Sammy the Bull.

Salvatore's parents started working together in a dress-making factory and one day while their then teenage son was present, two hoods came in and demanded protection money. Sammy was irate and borrowed a gun from friends in his gang to deal with the matter. However, this wasn't needed as the owner of the business had connections and when the thugs returned they were full of apologies. Sammy, at the age of just thirteen, had learnt that friends in the Mafia could be very powerful. Sammy continued to find school difficult and increasingly he preferred to spend time with his gang, the Rampers, than with his school books. Just before his sixteenth birthday, Sammy fought with a fellow schoolboy and hurt him so badly that Sammy was expelled – his traditional schooling was over and the streets were to become the place where he received his lessons. Some of his free time was spent in the neighbourhood gym. He had no interest in weight-training or running; he liked to be in the ring, man against man, usually taking on men who were several weight categories above him and with considerably greater reach. It was as if he enjoyed situations where the odds were stacked against him or where he had to use his full range of skills to prosper. Sammy is quoted in Peter Mass's book *Underboss* as having said, 'We never burglarized homes. That was against what we wanted to do. It was all commercial places. We'd break in at night, robbing clothing stores, hardware stores, stuff like that. We'd hold up jewellery stores, you know, with ski masks on. They all had insurance.'

In 1964 Gravano was arrested during an attempted burglary and his lawyer tried to have his sentence reduced by stating that the boy would be happy to enlist in the army rather than go to prison. Sammy had absolutely no wish to join the army but was convinced by his lawyer that he would never be called up. Much to the nineteen-year-old's dismay, before the verdict of the court had been finalized, he had received his draft papers and was summarily whisked of to Fort Jackson, South Carolina, for basic training. Although many of his fellow gang mates feared that Sammy would try to buck the system, he had no problem with the physical training and regimentation. On passing out he went first to Indiana, then Fort Mead in Maryland, serving as a bodyguard for one of the top brass. He hadn't forgotten some of the things he had learnt during his time in the Rampers and he ran a very profitable gambling and loan-sharking operation from inside the service. It was a hard environment but perhaps these were exactly the sort of conditions that he liked, he knew where the boundaries were, fought against them and knew how to manipulate the system when he could.

Sammy had no wish to stay on in the army and once back in Brooklyn, he took stock of his future; this would obviously continue to involve petty crime, mostly stealing cars and breaking into business premises, but he was also interested in getting involved in extortion rackets and illegal gambling. He always carried a gun and was involved in a number of shoot-outs; once, while in the back of a getaway car, he was hit by a bullet fired by the man who they had just robbed. The shot hit Gravano in the head just above the right ear; bleeding profusely, he managed to get to the hospital and had to undergo several months of convalescence. At the age of twenty-three, Sammy wanted to move up in the world, away from the Rampers and into one of the powerful Mafia families. He had a contact who introduced him to Joseph Colombo, head of the Colombo gang, but he wasn't offered a job. One night, however, the wheel of fortune was to turn in an unexpected direction. He got into an argument and eventually a fight with two youths, beating them both comfortably. The next day, he was walking close to his home and was picked up by members of the Colombo family, being told simply that he had an appointment with the boss. The two boys were the sons of Joseph and the old man wanted to see who had taken care of his boys. Sammy described the incident as follows, 'I beat up both his sons one time. In a movie house. We had this argument and I got in a fight with Joseph Junior, who was younger than me, and I broke his ass. He went and got his big brother, Anthony, who comes and it's the same result. I'll never forget it. Joe Colombo sent for me, he called me down. He looks at me and says, "You beat up both my sons? You must be pretty tough. Did you know they were my sons?"'

Gravano was welcomed into the Colombo organization and reputedly handled his first hit within a matter of days, the murder of Joe Colucci. Trouble never seemed too far away from Sammy, his first couple of assignments didn't go smoothly but being part of a large criminal empire proved beneficial as witnesses were paid off or, after a little persuasion, they decided not to testify. He was then sent to take care of the completion of some major refurbishments to a Mafia-owned bar. This went reasonably smoothly until Sammy had a go at one of the owners who, like many Italian-American gangsters in parts of New York at that time, liked to play the boss. He was moved away from the club and decided to open his own place with a little help from his friends. The club in Bensonhurst would become his main focus and the centre of his loan-sharking, gambling and operation for fencing stolen goods. The place was successful as a commercial venture in its own right and the steady stream of money being paid back to the Colombo family was helping to overcome negative feelings. It was here that Gravano started dating an innocent-looking seventeen-year-old, Deborah Scibetta, and the two were soon married. Later that year, Gravano also met Michael Hardy, a drug importer and dealer. Together they hatched a plan for Hardy to set up drug deals and for Gravano to impersonate a police detective who would bust the cosy meeting. The money and/or substances would be split equally. It was a simple scam but one which proved effective time and again, robbing unsuspecting small-time street dealers and crooks. This practice created problems with other gang members and in a show of power Gravano's capo spoke to the bosses of the Colombo family. The attitude towards drugs was very parochial among many of the big Mafia bosses and the incident lead to his release. Sammy had quite a reputation in New York and was soon accepted into the Gambino Family, working for Salvatore Aurello.

A leader of one of the largest Gambino outfits called Gravano one evening and told him he would be attending a special meeting, one where he would need to dress formally and would meet some new friends. Sammy was given the nod that he would be sworn into membership of La Cosa Nostra. For many years this secretive organization was strictly for Sicilians only, but the rules had been changed over time to enable it to grow and prosper. Gravano was led to a seat next to Paul Castellano, the head of the Gambino family, and the procedure was soon under way. His index finger was pricked, the rules of the family were outlined and he was kissed on both cheeks. Gravano recalled that, 'He [Castellano] told us that the man we answered to was our captain. He was our direct father. You do everything with him. You check with him, you put everything on record with him. You can't kill unless you get permission. You can't do anything, basically, until you get permission from the family. You don't run to the boss. You go to your captain. That was the protocol. Your captain will go to the administration of the family, which is the boss, the underboss and the consigliere.' This meant that things had to change for Sammy – he could no longer be a loose cannon, running around the streets of New York doing just exactly what he wanted to; he needed to clear things further up the chain of command and consider the impact his actions would have on the family as a whole and on the other Mafia gangs too. Treading on other people's toes was potentially more problematic from now onwards.

Sammy's brother-in-law, Nick Scibetta, had problems with drink, cocaine and picking fights with the wrong sort of people – guys who had connections or who, in some cases, were direct relations of Mafia bosses. Gravano was informed that Castellano had ordered a hit on the young man and was furious but knew there was nothing he could do, he simply couldn't take on the whole of the Gambino family. It was a tough lesson, especially for Sammy's wife. Many felt that she never fully came to terms with her loss. Soon afterwards, Sammy was called to his club in Bensonhurst because they were having trouble with a group of bikers. A massive fight ensued, but the bikers were driven away in the end. In the course of the fight, Gravano had his ankle broken. With his ankle in a large cast and still on crutches, Sammy went looking for the leader of the gang and, when he caught up with them, he beat one man severely and killed the other. Castellano was not amused, he saw this as rogue behaviour and something that needed to be stamped out. However, the Gambino boss needed 'The Bull' to sort out several construction sites, places that needed to be finished or refurbished. Gravano had proved himself in the construction business, something that earned him great credit with his masters. Meanwhile Gravano's club was starting to do great business and the high-profile cocaine dealer Frank Fiala had organized a birthday party that went off very well. He was so impressed with the place, he offered Sammy one million dollars to purchase it, a sum which was well in excess of its value. Sammy agreed the price and contracts were being drawn up. However, before anything had been signed Fiala was running round like he owned the place, hurling abuse and insults at an increasingly irked Gravano. The deal was still being drawn up when Sammy decided to take matters into his own hands and set out, with his side-kick Louie Milito, to find Fiala. After hours of searching, the two men cornered Fiala in an alleyway where his body was later found, having been shot once in the head with two further bullets, one in each eye. The murder prompted the Internal

Revenue Service to initiate a full investigation into Gravano and his club. His luck held as much of the evidence was sketchy and the jury had no option but to acquit him.

The early 1980s saw a shift in the fight against organized crime. New task forces were set up in an attempt to break up New York's Mafia families and FBI Special Agent Bruce Mouw was charged with heading the investigation. As well as tapping phones and planting bugging devices, the task forces tried to get members from inside the gangs to work with them, usually having first amassed considerable evidence against them and threatened them with long prison sentences. In the end, the FBI, working with the New York Police Department, had a breakthrough. Wilfred Johnson, a friend of John Gotti of the Gambino family, decided to become an informant, which was to have major implications over time. The summer of 1983 saw the eagerly awaited indictment of three of Gotti's closest crew and the word went out on the street that Castellano was also recorded on the tapes that were being used as evidence. Suspicion within the Family was rife and Castellano found out that he was going to be arrested and charged with a long list of crimes, including racketeering, drug dealing, extortion, theft, prostitution and murder. Gotti, Frank DeCicco and Gravano met to discuss the matter and for a number of reasons it was decided that Castellano should be hit, and soon. The incidents leading up to the now infamous shootings at Manhattan's Sparks restaurant have been covered in the chapter about John Gotti's criminal career but Gravano remembers the occasion as follows, 'The shooters were there. The four of them wore long white trench coats and black fur Russian hats. You couldn't tell one guy from another. I don't know whose idea that was, I guess John's. But I think it was brilliant. We made an agreement that nobody involved in this from here on out would ever speak to each other about it at any time under any circumstances and wouldn't admit anything to anybody in our family or in any of the other families. The official party line was, we don't know what happened to Paul, but our family is intact.' The hit marked the end of one era and the beginning of another, one in which Gravano would play an increasingly significant role.

The journalists, the police and the people of New York had just recovered from this incident when another came along hot on its heels. A car bomb was planted under Frank DeCicco's Buick and he and an associate from one of the other Mafia organizations, the Lucchese family, walked over to it unaware of their impending fate. Gravano saw the incident unfold: 'Frankie Hearts [Bellino] goes flying backwards. The blast blew his shoes off. And his toes. I go flying across the street. And there's Frankie Hearts with the blood shooting out of his feet. I saw Frankie DeCicco laying on the ground beside the car. With the fire, it could blow up again. I tried to pull him away. I grabbed a leg, but he ain't coming with it. The leg is off. One of his arms is off. I got my hand under him and my hand went right through his body to his stomach. There's no ass. His ass, his balls, everything, is blown completely off. I was wearing a white shirt. I looked at my shirt, amazed. There wasn't a drop of blood on it. The force of the blast, the concussion, blew most of the fluids out of Frankie's body. He had no blood left in him, nothing, not an ounce.' It was an attempted coup by two men to take control on the Gambino operation, but they were to pay a heavy price for their failure. Gravano, on the other hand, was appointed underboss to Gotti, which was a major step up in the organization. Gravano benefited from a significant increase in his power base as well as enjoying greater financial rewards, but he also attracted greater interest on the part of the FBI.

Gravano had become a major player in the New York construction industry, handling much of the work contracted by several of the Mafia families, as well as his own projects. Each Tuesday night, concrete company executives, building contractors and subcontractors, shop stewards in construction unions and Teamsters would visit Gravano's restaurant,

Tali's, in Bensonhurst, to eat and drink and to touch base with Sammy. Gravano was being pulled in two directions – his legitimate business dealings were successful but he was also a major player in the Mafia. Up to this point, he was alleged to have taken part in eight murders and, since having got involved with Gotti, it was estimated that he had been directly involved in a further eleven murders. Several members of his own empire had developed drug addiction problems, something frowned on by the top bosses, and Sammy had to act swiftly to remove them. It is thought that the list of people culled in this way included the well-known figures of Nick Mormando and Mike DeBatt. Gravano later took care of the informant Wilfred Johnson, Eddie Garfolo and then Louis DiBono, about which Gravano had the following to say: 'He was still robbing the family and I asked for permission to take him out. But John had a meeting with DiBono, and DiBono told John that he had a billion dollars of drywall work that was coming out of the World Trade Center. John bit, hook, line and sinker, and refused my request. John said he would handle DiBono personally and become his partner. But DiBono was up to his old tricks double-dealing. He had obviously been bullshitting John. So when John called Louie in for meetings to discuss their new partnership, DiBono didn't show up. John was humiliated. This meant an automatic death penalty. John gave the contract to DiBono's captain, Pat Conte. Conte botched an ideal opportunity to kill DiBono. Then, as Gotti grew increasingly impatient, Conte explained that the problem now was trying to corner DiBono again. Whenever a meeting with him was arranged, DiBono never appeared. It was a joke, what was going on. I couldn't help laughing to myself. I told John why didn't Pat simplify everything. Just call Louie up and tell him to hang himself. Ten months went by. John looks like an asshole. He was too embarrassed even to ask me for help.'

On the evening of 11 December 1990 Gravano and Gotti were holding a secret meeting to discuss how to deal with the

FBI and possible indictments that were being amassed by the authorities. Rumours had been floating around for several weeks that enough evidence had been collected to lock both men away for ever. Suddenly the door was knocked down and the whole place was swarming with police officers and FBI agents. Over the coming days and weeks the men were kept apart and Gravano was shown much of the taped evidence against him. Benjamin Brafman was appointed to represent Gravano and increasingly he felt that Gotti was lining him up to be the fall guy – the one to take the lion's share of the responsibility and therefore the time behind bars. As Gravano said, 'All John had to do was come to me once during that eleven months we were together and say, "Sammy, I'm sorry. My big fucking mouth got you indicted, number one. Number two, let's try to get a severance for you, so you could fight your case. Fuck the public. Let's try to fight this so that one of us, all of us, a couple of us, get out of this fucking mess." If he done that, I would have never co-operated with the government, not in a million years would I have co-operated.' It took months to get the case together, it was huge, not just for the Mafia, but for America. Both men spent this time locked up – as expected, no bail had been offered. In October the following year, Gravano sent word that he wanted to speak to the FBI and less than three weeks later, headline news across America was that he had become a government witness.

On 12 February 1992 the judge and jury heard the opening comments in the trial of John Gotti and Frank Locascio. Tapes were played and evidence presented in an orderly and thorough fashion but it was as if the main show was still to begin. On 2 March Sammy 'The Bull' Gravano took the stand and everyone was hanging on his every word. The FBI had had little success in the past getting top gangsters, Mafia or otherwise, to testify against their fellow criminals, out of fear of reprisals against them or their families. Even gangsters who had received life sentences seemed reluctant to give any help to the authorities. Many of them had spent their entire lives fighting the law enforcement agencies and were extremely distrustful of anything to do with them. Many had also spent the majority of their lives in one or two gangs and considered many of their fellow hardened crooks as more like family even than friends. All this, however, was about to change. A well-known, high-profile figure like Gravano would certainly help others to see the witness protection system as a viable alternative to long years of prison life. Several people tried to get to Sammy during the hearings but without success; his resolve to turn on Gotti had hardened. As Gravano put it, 'Did you see that fuckin' kid [Joey D'Angelo, a member of the Gambino family, who was sitting in the front row of the court during the trial]? I helped him out his whole life. Three years ago, he came to me beggin' for work. Now he comes here and tried to rattle me. Get up, walk out, come back. What's this, a movie? Fuck 'im and fuck them!'

By the time Sammy had given his entire testimony, the verdict was all but known. The evidence was stacked against Gotti and the others and all that was left was to know what sentences were going to be handed out. Gotti received multiple life sentences with no chance of parole, and the others suffered similar fates. On 26 September 1994 Gravano himself was up before the same judge, John Gleeson, who praised him for his efforts in co-operating with the authorities. He was sentenced to five years in prison. However, this was far from the last that would be heard of 'The Bull' as he subsequently testified against Vincent Gigante, the boss of the Genovese family, and Joe Watts from the Gambino clan. His deal with the FBI allegedly didn't require him to speak out against these men but he obviously felt compelled to do so. His time inside passed quite uneventfully, by Sammy's standards at least; there were a few fights and disagreements, but Gravano looked like someone who wanted to get out on parole as quickly as possible. When he was finally released, he moved to a small place in Tempe, Arizona, and started leading a more normal life. His book, *Underboss*, was a bestseller and the royalties were flowing in. He began to feel more confident, at least until his true identity was discovered by the *Arizona Republic* newspaper. This was potentially hazardous as his 'friends' in New York could now track him down if they wanted to. The whole situation took a turn for the worse on 24 February 2000 when Gravano was charged with drug dealing – police saw him as the boss of a state-wide drug ring, distributing and selling ecstasy tablets and other banned substances on an enormous scale. Sammy's wife, his twenty-three-year-old son, his daughter and her husband were also arrested. It was clearly a family affair and one which would lead to twelve different charges of drug dealing, money laundering and possession of guns. Prosecutors were able to take possession of his home, his wife's home, his pool business, bank accounts and even his book royalties.

Things just kept getting worse for Sammy as evidence came to light that he had also bought and sold drugs in New York and new information was put forward which linked him to the murder of Peter Calabro in 1980. The law was beginning to move into uncharted territory; on the one hand, the FBI were incredibly grateful to him for helping put Gotti and others behind bars, but on the other hand, he did not seem to have learnt any lessons. Gravano was clearly bad to the core and would always be a hardened criminal, no matter what impact it had on his life and the lives of his family and friends. Gravano was convicted of drug-related offences and served the first part of his time in a high security prison in Colorado, but many other charges hung over him. It is highly unlikely that he will ever experience freedom again, something he has in common with many of the gangsters he helped put behind bars.

The Columbian Drug Cartels

Since the 1970s, the wild, beautiful and fertile landscape of Colombia has become home to some of the most violent, sophisticated and powerful drug growers and traffickers on the planet. Their enormous multinational empire reaches to the four corners of the globe and provides sufficient cash reserves for them to challenge whole governments. The level of sophistication in drug production and distribution now has few parallels in organized crime, enabling them to hire engineering experts from Russia and America, technology specialists from around the world and buy the most sophisticated weapons. In a recent sting operation, the Colombian government, aided by US forces, were able to track down a high-tech submarine which had been used for some time to smuggle drugs across the border. The history of drug growing is very much linked to marijuana and other softer substances as cocaine didn't become a major export until the early 1980s. Before this time, it was very much a cottage industry, relying on the small-scale movement of goods in suitcases in boats and yachts, and in trucks crossing the borders. The scale of the business is now quite staggering – in 2000, it was estimated that the value of the worldwide trade in illegal drugs was around $400 billion. The various Colombian drug cartels account for a considerable proportion of this business, especially that which relates to the substances which find their way onto the streets of North America. It is estimated that Colombia exports over one hundred tonnes of cocaine every year with a street value in excess of $60 billion. This represents no less than 40 per cent of the country's entire gross national product.

Most people refer to the Colombian drug business as several cartels, although they are not really cartels at all. The term cartel, as in Medellín cartel, refers to a band of individual growers or distributors who operate closely together in a geographic group. Many of these small growers are, however, linked to larger outfits who handle the distribution which requires international contacts and an expensive infrastructure. In the early days, local growers and distributors may have known about their neighbours, but there was very little actual co-operation or sharing of resources. However, since the late 1980s, there has been increasing evidence that many smaller enterprises have tried to club together to fight the authorities and to use the good smuggling routes. The other option, which many have taken, is to sell their produce to larger organizations to handle the processing and onward movement. There are essentially two forms of distribution: a hierarchy and a hub layout. With a 'hierarchical' form of distribution, the producer retains his own band of smugglers and transportation devices. A hub layout requires a number of growers and producers to come together to form a hub, which uses other gangs and local groups to move the produce. Some of the bigger cartels use both methods, especially when distributing substances into areas where law enforcement activities are making inroads into their business. Usually any third parties who provide boats, vehicles, small aircraft and so on will be paid not in cash but in kind, in the form of the particular drug they are moving. The cartels believe that the absence of cash in the supply chain can help to keep people 'honest'.

Since the 1980s, there have been three main cartels in Colombia, namely the Cali, Medellín and Norte del Valle cartels. The highest profile cartel has probably been the Medellín, which was led by the notorious Pablo Escobar and had as members the three Ochoa bothers, Fabio, Jorge and Juan David. At the height of its powers, it was estimated that revenue from all drugs was around $60 million per month. The Medellín cartel has been known to try to produce just about every possible substance which can be sold on the streets for a profit, such as: anabolic steroids (which aid muscle growth and are often sold to gyms); cannabis; LSD (highly hallucinogenic, often referred to as 'acid'); tobacco (particularly cigars, as high-quality Cuban cigars can fetch very good prices in the US where they cannot legally be sold); opium (the raw ingredient from which heroin is made); heroin (prices vary greatly depending on the level of purity); cocaine (one of the most popular drugs along with its derivative crack cocaine, made from the leaves of the coca plant); methamphetamine (a highly addictive stimulant).

The market for cocaine has been in decline in America since around 1985 from a peak of an estimated 10 million regular users. People with a cocaine habit have traditionally been divided into recreational users – often middle or upper-class, who buy cocaine by the gram and snort it – and crack cocaine users who are predominantly poor and where the proportion of highly dependent people is much greater. 'Crack' is significantly cheaper and the vast majority of its users continue to be in the lower socio-economic groups. It is often referred to as the 'loser' drug, for this very reason. The overall downward trend in cocaine use in the USA hides a much more worrying trend in which overall drug use is still increasing. A growing number of younger people try drugs, there are many more different kinds of drugs available and violent crime continues to follow closely in the wake of drug use. Drug use worldwide is increasing and, as in America, the appetite for new substances is always there. Many of the significant drug-producing regions, especially Colombia, have focused for many years on the large single market of America for most of their business to the lasting detriment of the USA. Due the success of the law enforcement agencies, getting large volumes of drugs into the USA has proved increasingly difficult and consequently the large drug-trafficking organizations have been looking to export significantly larger quantities to Europe, Japan, Australasia and Russia. Recently, other developing countries such as China, Thailand and Eastern Europe have become more important targets for the cartels.

It is possible to trace the roots of the Medellín cartel back to the early 1970s but its rise to major prominence occurred when the Ochoa brothers, who came from a well-respected ranching background, joined forces with Pablo Escobar. He was little more than a common thief at that time but he had big ideas. The new team, in turn, enlisted the help of Carlos Lehder, who was a young marijuana smuggler but who had valuable experience of drug production and distribution. These men would dramatically increase the scale of production and establish a highly secretive network of sellers in America and then round the world. Escobar was known for having a 'short fuse' and a violent streak – he is thought to be responsible for the murder of hundreds of government officials, police officers, judges and innocent citizens who just happened to get in the way. It is also alleged that he organized the blowing up of a commercial plane and the assassination of a Colombian presidential candidate. Lehder had bought with the proceeds of drug trafficking a large part of an island just off the coast of the Bahamas, which was to become a rendezvous for the Medellín clan and the ideal base for trafficking drugs into the US and elsewhere.

As the violence and sheer scale of the cash being generated mounted day by day, the early signs of possible self-destruction started to appear – the Medellín cartel started to make mistakes and to act unilaterally. They also underestimated the ambition of the next largest cartel, the Cali who were less flashy, though no less ambitious. The Cali allegedly made a number of attacks on the life of Escobar, targeting his homes, his business addresses and also staking out places that he visited regularly, but they were unsuccessful. They also provided a stream of information about his operation to the American and Colombian authorities. By 1994, Escobar was running for his life as the law was closing in – later that year, after a series of gun battles, he was shot and killed by Colombian police officers. It was the end of the first chapter of drug trafficking in Colombia, but it was far from being the end of the story.

The Cali were far more modern in their thinking and organization – they employed a team of the best lawyers they could find to work out how the DEA, FBI and Colombian government would track them. They also directed the best technical brains in their fields to devise improved bugging and surveillance devices, more advanced than anything that the forces of law and order had available to them. Their organizational structure made use of small groups of people working in cells, with each cell knowing only one aspect of the whole jigsaw. These independent groups, even if tracked down and caught by the authorities, would not be able to jeopardize the overall operation or any of the leadership of the organization as a whole. The only real loss would be the contraband that was being transported on that trip. The bosses bought vast expanses of land and built hideouts right across Colombia, they invested in legitimate businesses which were used to gain the commercially sensitive information and political influence that they required. At the peak of their success, they were thought to control around 80 per cent of the cocaine exported from Colombia to America. The problem they faced was that with the Medellín being completely fragmented, the Cali became the primary target and they were finding it harder and harder to maintain their grip on the operation. In an unexpected turn of events, under the threat of an extradition treaty, the Cali leaders entered into negotiation with the Colombian government – they didn't want to be deported to the USA to spend time in US prisons. With this in mind, they were now willing to hand over a large amount of money and to end their operation in exchange for leniency. By the mid- to late-1990s, virtually all the Cali bosses were serving ten to fifteen years behind bars in Colombian jails, their wealth greatly diminished, but they were not exactly breaking rocks – by all accounts, they were reputedly doing very easy time.

All of the major cartels were feeling the impact of the efforts of the law enforcement agencies and they were only too well aware of the high-profile inroads that had been made into the Medellín and Cali networks. These developments convinced many growers and traffickers to keep their businesses small and thereby more manageable. However, using a chain of informants and undercover officers, the United States DEA and customs officials continued to make sizeable busts and seizures. The most prominent witness to spill the beans was Adler Berriman Seal, known as Barry Seal, a legendary pilot and drug smuggler. He was finally nailed in 1984 in Fort Lauderdale, Florida, where, in the face of a lengthening charge sheet, he agreed to co-operate with the authorities. He had worked for many of the cartels and knew how they operated, so he was able to testify against several top Colombian drug lords, leading to their arrest. Ultimately, however, he was murdered in Baton Rouge, allegedly on the orders of the Ochoa brothers.

Perhaps the greatest threat to the various Colombian drug empires was the extradition treaty which had been signed with the USA. The treaty allowed US forces to extradite anyone it believed was involved in trafficking drugs bound for US streets. Many high-ranking government officials in Colombia supported the treaty, but of these supporters Justice Minster Rodrigo Lara Bonilla was brutally murdered and police chief Jaime Ramirez was shot and killed at the same time as a threat was made to kill all judges if they didn't publicly support the abolition of the treaty. These warnings fell on deaf ears, however, and the situation was exacerbated when, in November 1985, a group of heavily armed gunmen broke into the Palace of Justice, which at that time housed most of the senior judges. It was a classic hostage situation. The army and the police tried to free those held, but virtually all were shot dead in the ensuing chaos and crossfire. In the aftermath of the debacle nothing could be pinned on the cartels, but the USA increased its aid to the Colombian government (in the form of cash, DEA agents, US Customs officials and FBI support) and for a while things seemed to quieten down.

In very recent times a third cartel, known as Norte del Valle, meaning simple North Valley, has grown to greater prominence. They operate principally from the Valle del Cauca region of Colombia, another perfect environment for growing illegal substances of all sorts, with hiding places for refineries, laboratories and hideouts. The leader of the Norte del Valle cartel, Diego Leon Montoya, also known as Don Diego, is listed on the FBI's 'Ten Most Wanted' list, one of the few Colombians to be 'honoured' in this way. Since 1990, it is estimated that he has organized the export of at least 1.2 million pounds of cocaine into America alone and has routinely used murder, kidnapping and brutality to traffic his produce. On 6 May 2004 Montoya and nine of his associates were charged with the illegal trafficking of cocaine, the laundering of the proceeds of drug sales, the bribing of Colombian law enforcement officers and politicians, the kidnapping, torture and murder of informants, and the wire-tapping of American law enforcement agencies. The Norte del Valle cartel have declared war on several other Colombian gangs, leading to the slaughter of hundreds of innocent bystanders. It is further believed that Montoya has also enlisted the help of a paramilitary group called the United Self Defence Force of Columbia (AUC), to help protect distribution routes, offices, laboratories, business partners and associates. This enterprise has now been designated a foreign terrorist organization by the US State Department, who have also posted a reward of $5 million for information leading to the arrest of Don Diego.

Many of the Colombian cartels had relationships with drug-trafficking organizations in Mexico, although it has always been an uneasy marriage as there is so little trust on both sides. The Mexican groups were very powerful and benefited from their close proximity to a two-thousand-mile border with America. However, they grew their own illegal substances, often similar to those being supplied from Colombia, and received shipments from other parts of the world as well. While they may have been partners in distribution they were competitors along the supply chain – a situation that made both groups nervous. The Mexican organizations also had a large network of street sellers right across America, usually made up of illegal immigrants from Mexico. Many had struggled to get good jobs because they did not have valid US visas and as a result they had turned to pushing drugs to earn a living. Earnings from Mexicans living and working illegally in the USA contribute substantially to the Mexican economy – it is thought that after income from petroleum, Mexico's next most significant import is cash sent or brought home by Mexicans living illegally in the USA. A significant percentage of those earnings are generated by drug-related activities.

An interesting offer made by a paramilitary leader suggested that he would broker a deal which would see Colombian drug lords surrender and be extradited to the USA in exchange for leniency. About seventy drug traffickers were reportedly interested in the deal, if it was accepted by Washington. It is unlikely, however, even if such an agreement were to be reached, that it would have much impact on the quantity of cocaine and heroin finding its way onto the streets of the United States.

Despite the elimination of the Medellín cartel in the early 1990s and the downfall of the Cali cartel a short while later, and 'successful' coca eradication campaigns in Peru and Bolivia which have significantly reduced the amount of coca cultivated there, cocaine and heroin are as readily available on the streets of the USA as they were ten years ago.

In the late 1980s when the USA's main target in the drugs war was Pablo Escobar and the Medellín cartel, many US officials claimed that capturing or killing Escobar would severely damage Colombia's drug trade. However, Escobar's imprisonment and subsequent death did nothing at all to diminish the drug trade.

With the subsequent campaign to bring down the leaders of the Cali cartel, similar claims were made, but, again, success in dismantling the Cali cartel did not even slow the flow of drugs into the USA. The result, instead, has been the creation of an estimated 300 mini-cartels which are well aware that the wealth and power flaunted by the Medellín and Cali cartels had made them an easy target for the agents of the Colombian and US governments.

The new drug lords outsource much of their operation: they contract pilots to pick up leaves or paste and deliver the raw material to drug-manufacturing laboratories; they contract other individuals or groups to organize transport to Mexico; they then contract yet more people to distribute the drugs within the USA. This atomization of the drug manufacturing, running and distribution structure makes these new groups much harder to infiltrate and bring down.

In addition, squeezing the drug trade in one area has been shown simply to result in expansion elsewhere, the so-called 'balloon effect'. For example, while aerial fumigation resulted in much-reduced coca crops in Bolivia and Peru during the 1990s, the amount of coca produced in South America as a whole remained constant as production shifted to Colombia where it doubled between 1995 and 2000. In fact, the 'success' in Bolivia and Peru made it easier for the drug cartels as they no longer had to transport coca paste or leaves from Bolivia and Peru to Colombia; their operations had been consolidated in one country for them.

Essentially, the huge demand for cocaine and heroin in North America and Europe dooms any campaign against the source of drugs. As long as there is demand in the developed world, there will be poor farmers willing to turn to poppy and coca cultivation in order to survive.

The USA has tried to cut off the supply of drugs – with strictly limited success, as for each cartel brought down, another, or several, have risen up to take its place. A second strategy of telling Americans that drugs are bad seems to have achieved even less, though, to be fair, much less money has been spent on this aspect of the strategy than on the war agains production and trafficking. Meanwhile, the number of Americans behind bars for drugs-related offences has swelled exponentially, another expensive by-product of the 'War on Drugs'. While other governments have attempted different strategies, none has quite the problem that the USA faces, though that may well change with increased prosperity in those countries in the future.

It was reported in August 2006 that Barclays Bank, one of the cornerstones of banking in the UK, had been involved in handling drug money. A subsidiary of Barclays Bank, Barclays Private Bank (BPB), had been used to launder drug money, according to an undercover sting operation by agencies in the USA and Canada. At one stage, at the request of the US government, the British government froze $54 million held with BPB. Internal BPB memos apparently showed that one of the bank's officers who had expressed concern over the source of the money was overruled. BPB continued to allow the accounts to operate while two other leading banks used by the same customer – HSBC and ABN Amro – tipped off the British police. Investigators had begun to follow the money trail that led to BPB during 2001 when agents from America's Drug Enforcement Administration (DEA) managed to turn a money launderer in Medellín, Colombia, into an informant. British investigators also linked deposits of more than ££8 million into the BPB accounts to two other Colombian laundering suspects. In the end thirty-four people were arrested in New York on charges of drug trafficking and money laundering, of whom twenty were convicted or pleaded guilty.

Juan David Ochoa, one of the leading members of the Medellín cartel in the Colombian drug trade who turned himself in in 1991, has revealed something of his life through being interviewed. He and his brother Jorge got involved in the drug trade almost by accident, he claims, when Jorge met someone on a trip to the USA in the late 1970s. His first transactions were carried out while living in Bogota. At that time he did not set much store by the fact that he was trafficking in something that was highly illegal because no one spoke much about that and, besides, it was all so easy. Apparently, while it wasn't seen as entirely acceptable for Colombians to be selling cocaine to the United States, at the same time no one said anything about it, and since there were no repercussions, it was very easy to get deeper in. Suppliers would bring coca from Peru and Bolivia and it would be processed in Colombian drug laboratories. The labs the Medellín used could produce a thousand kilograms of cocaine or perhaps more every two weeks, depending on demand. He and his brothers would buy the drug from the labs and arrange for someone to transport it to the USA, by air or sea, where someone would be ready to receive it. That person would then send it on to clients in California, New York and elsewhere. The same person would also be responsible for receiving the money and sending it back to Colombia.

Ochoa had two basic business models: one as described above, involving the contracting of other people, and another in which he had his own lab and means of transporting the drug which would be sent at his own cost. In terms of profit, in the early days, the drug cost 800 to 1 million pesos a kilogram and could be sold for between $30,000 and $40,000. Taking into account the cost of transportation (about $10,000) left a profit of about 50 per cent, though that depended very much both on supply and demand. After a while, there was still demand, but the profit was squeezed as many more people became involved in the business.

According to Ochoa, though, the media exaggerate the profits to be made in the drugs trade. He acknowledges that sometimes the deals would go well and there would be huge profits, but sometimes deals would be much more difficult – planes might have to be diverted, or someone might be arrested and the whole organization would have to be changed. Ochoa can't really say how much money he made from trafficking cocaine, but estimates it to be somwhere around $20 million to $25 million.

In the early days of the drug trade, apparently, US law enforcement agencies used to intercept no shipments of drugs at all, and even later on only 20 to 30 per cent of shipments would be intercepted. The early days, according to Ochoa, when only fifty to sixty people were involved in the drug trade were the best; things became much harder when many more people became involved.

Asked if he remembered seeing headlines calling cocaine the 'champagne of drugs' and what he had thought of that, Ochoa claimed not to have paid too much attention, but that it didn't seem to make too much sense to him – that drugs may have different effects on different people, but that there's nothing good about them. He was always grateful for the free advertising, though. The articles showing that cocaine was consumed by people of high status in society did make the drug sell in greater quantities.

Carlos Lehder was an important member of the Medellín cartel as he was 'a boy from high society'. He was also one of the pioneers of drug trafficking and a kind of leader; he had his own planes and very sophisticated ways of trafficking. He had also bought an island in the Bahamas called Norman's Cay which served as a bridge for planes trafficking the drugs, with large planes coming in and a number of smaller planes flying out again to deliver the cocaine to the USA.

Ochoa met Pablo Escobar in Bogota, where they both lived, through a shared love of car racing. Ochoa would go to the races and then to his restaurant which is where the two men met. Later on, when Ochoa went to live in Medellín, he saw Escobar a few times there, but although his brother Jorge did a few deals with Escobar, Ochoa never dealt with him directly. Escobar was the one with the ambition, with the desire to dominate and to be involved in politics. Jorge was closer to Escobar, often intervening in an attempt to have things done in a non-violent way, though Pablo was not often amenable to that. None of the Ochoa brothers was that close to Escobar, though; Jorge would try simply to mediate, for example when there was a war with the Cali cartel, to bring an end to the violence. It was Jorge in the end who managed to convince Escobar to give himself up.

The drug business undoubtedly brought a lot of money to Colombia, but its ramifications – the violence and terrorism – have been severe. Ochoa and his brothers saw extradition as something very severe, 'like being buried alive'. Their hope that the end of drug trafficking might bring the end of the possibility of extradition was disappointed. They had appointed lawyers to work to block their extradition, but that too failed. Ochoa feels that prejudice against Colombians means that extradition violates their human rights, that to serve four or five years in prison in a dignified manner would be fine, but to spend life, chained up, in a high security prison is inhumane.

The brothers did apparently think of separating from Pablo Escobar, but it was not 'convenient' for a number of reasons which he prefers not to discuss. Ochoa claims that Barry Seal never flew his cocaine, though he did for Escobar and his brother Jorge. Mexico was important to the Medellín cartel because of its extensive border with the USA, one which he suggests it is probably impossible to police effectively. Ochoa sees the war on drugs as being very unequal because as long as there is demand he believes there will always be a supply. He believes that the only way forward is to to legalize drugs in the same way that liquor is legal.

Ludwig 'Tarzan' Fainberg

The city of Odessa, situated in the south-western corner of Ukraine on the shores of the Black Sea, has had a tremendously rich and colourful past. It was a free port from 1819 to 1858 and from the early part of the twentieth century it became one of the most important naval bases of the USSR. It was the site of an ancient Greek colony and the city is full of monuments of great antiquity to civilizations now long since extinct.

In the era of modern crime it has some notoriety as the birthplace of Ludwig Fainberg, also known as 'Tarzan' Fainberg. At the age of three, following the divorce of his parents, he and his mother moved to Czernowitz, a small, remote, inland town where Ludwig, who was a bright boy, sang in the choir and also learnt to box. His step-father worked in a factory producing rugs and fur, often trading these items on the black market for theatre tickets, good clothing and fine foods. Just ten years later, they were all to be uprooted again, and transplanted, this time to Israel. The family converted all their wealth into diamonds and gold, hiding the precious cargo in secret compartments built into tables and chairs, which they had shipped with them. Some of the valuables were even carried in secret compartments in the heels of their shoes.

Ludwig was a strong and boisterous child, always wanting attention, which is where his nickname came from: one day he leapt from one high building to another to get the attention of a small gang thereby earning himself the nickname 'Tarzan'. There is another story, which Fainberg himself tells, that he received his nickname because his hair was once a wild mane and he used to act as if he had come straight from the jungle. As a child, he showed no fear and had quite a reputation on the streets of his new home town. Ludwig joined the Israeli Marine Corps and after a period of service was keen to move onwards and upwards. He struggled with the necessary exams, however, and was eventually discharged.

Fainberg had made many friends in the forces, though, and a contact provided him with a possible opportunity in East Berlin. He was to join a gang led by Efim Laskin, who sold weapons, ran a large extortion racket and was involved in many kinds of fraud. As the size of the operation and the scope of the criminal activities grew, Tarzan was offered bigger and better assignments to handle. He was given the job of putting the frighteners on a very successful Berlin banker, which he and two of his colleagues did. They kidnapped the banker and held him until he was able to arrange payment. They had to let him go so he could organize the funds and while he was away all the young men could do was wait at the arranged place. Ludwig was nervous and went for a smoke and, in the meantime, four large Mercedes cars drove up and cornered the two unsuspecting criminals, who were beaten practically to death. As he walked back towards the car, Ludwig saw what was happening and feared for his life. He lay low and got some money together before buying a ticket to the USA. His destination was the Russian enclave of Brighton Beach in New York.

In the late 1970s, Russia was put under tremendous pressure to let resident Jews emigrate freely and many found their way to Brighton Beach. It was called 'Little Odessa' by many Russians, which suited Fainberg as the real Odessa was his home town. Over a period of three to four years, almost forty thousand Russian Jews found their way to this part of the world; many of them were convicted criminals who had spent long, hard time in the gulags. The streets of 'Little Odessa' became virtual 'no go' areas for many and most of the Russians carried guns as any sort of business or factory needed protection. Many of the newcomers had a very different set of values and beliefs from the native New Yorkers. For example, the ways in which men and women interacted was very different – for many of the new immigrants, for a man to slap a woman was nothing out of the ordinary and part of a normal relationship, yet this was something that one could get arrested for in the USA. This was just one of many things that the Russians newcomers had to learn to fit in in their new surroundings. Many accounts of Fainberg's early years in the USA indicate that he degraded women of all nationalities and backgrounds, something that did little to advance him in the new multi-cultural society in which he found himself.

This was until he met a girl – not just any ordinary girl but the daughter of a Russian Mafia boss. Fainberg was to hold the same views of women his entire life, once chasing a stripper down the road, beating her and making her eat gravel as she lay on the road, but the reprisals for mistreating this particular woman would be very severe indeed. 'Tarzan' had to put a temporary halt to his criminal activities as he got married and lived life on 'easy street'. His wife was able to support them and she didn't want him caught up in crime like her father. The other men in the family were all deeply involved in extortion rackets, robbery, drugs and running whorehouses but he had to stay at home with his wife. In the evenings they would go out to expensive restaurants where she would pay for everything. Fainberg was just not that kind of guy and soon joined forces with a gangster called Grecia Roizes, who owned a string of furniture stores across New York which were, in fact, fronts for an elaborate heroin-selling network. Fainberg went to work in one of the shops from where he handled a growing number of drug deals. One day an old woman came into the shop in which

Fainberg was working, to buy some furniture. A new, young assistant was treating her disrespectfully at which point 'Tarzan' stepped in and, in a very rare act of compassion towards any female, he sorted out the problem and let her have the goods she wanted free of charge. Good fortune was shining on Fainberg that day as the old woman was, in fact, the mother of Frankie Santoro, a leading member of the Colombo Mafia family. The following day, Santoro came into the store and asked for Fainberg. He said if there was ever anything he needed, Fainberg should just call him. Santoro subsequently helped Fainberg on many different occasions until he was shot and killed in a gangland hit.

In 1990, Fainberg decided it was time to move his operation, feeling New York was too hot for him and that he would have a better chance of controlling the flow of his ever-increasing drugs business from Florida. His marriage was also on the rocks and he felt space between him and his wife's family would be no bad thing. He needed a front so he opened a nightclub called Porky's, a pink neon beacon on the outskirts of Miami International Airport, which soon became a meeting place for just about every ex-Soviet official, agent and Russian gangster living for miles around. It was also a magnet for Eastern Bloc criminals wanting to do business in the USA or with US-based hoods. Information would be traded and 'Tarzan' became the lynchpin in an explosion of drug smuggling. Contacts were made with the big Colombian drug cartels, in particular the Cali organization. Fainberg was in the right place at the right time – all the cartels needed weapons, not just a few high-precision rifles and the odd load of explosives. They had a war to fight and the demand for up-to-the-minute weaponry was extraordinary. Using his extensive Russian connections, 'Tarzan' traded heavy-duty weapons such as assault guns, automatic long-range rifles and rocket launchers in exchange for heroin and cocaine. It was a trade that worked for both sides and no money was changing hands – another factor of great benefit to both sides. Fainberg then set up an elaborate street-level distribution network for these highly sought-after substances, sending packages right across Europe to Russia and beyond. Very few of his shipments were bound for US cities, which had the advantage of keeping him beneath the FBI radar for some time. It was rumoured that Fainberg had traded military aircraft and helicopters, but probably his most notorious exploit was his attempt, in the mid-1990s, to negotiate the sale of a Russian diesel sumbarine, complete with retired naval captain and a twenty-five man crew, to a Colombian cartel for $5.5 million. The submarine was to be used to smuggle cocaine into the USA along the Californian coast, but the deal fell through.

With the increasing scale and success of Fainberg's operation, the attention of the FBI and DEA was not far behind. He had always travelled extensively, laundering money through a maze of accounts that were virtually impossible to trace back to him. Many Russians with links to organized crime have offshore bank accounts on Caribbean islands and have spent millions on the most expensive strip joints in southern Florida. According to federal officials, both the banks and the clubs are used to launder drug money. The whole set-up gives both the Russians and the Colombians access to new markets and new ways to launder money, just as the USA, European countries and some South American countries are moving to seize drug-trafficking profits.

Felix Jimenez is the DEA's special agent in charge of the Caribbean, based in San Juan, Puerto Rico. He has noticed a dramatic increase in Russian investment in hotels and gambling in the Caribbean. The Russian organized crime 'families' based in Miami and New York with strong ties to Puerto Rico are very tight organizations, difficult to penetrate with the added difficulty of presenting language barriers to most US law enforcement officers. All of this makes gathering intelligence on these gangs extremely difficult.

As well as involving himself in drug smuggling, Fainberg turned to prostitution to expand his business empire. He was a natural born organizer and set about importing women from all over the world, though mostly from Eastern Europe. He had a girlfriend by the name of Faina Tennanbaum who, in line with Fainberg's previous known behaviour, was regularly beaten; the police were often called to deal with domestic disturbances. At Porky's he was even more violent towards women, once chasing a stripper from the club and beating her head against the door of his Mercedes until the car was covered with blood. Louis J. Freeh, a director of the FBI in the mid-1990s who was tracking the alarming rise of Russian organized crime in the southern States of America, stated that these gangs pose a significant threat to the United States. Fainberg was acting as a kind of magnet, drawing Russian criminals to the USA. There were plenty of crooks who had made tremendous profits from the fall of the Soviet Union, who wanted to start new lives with their ill-gotten gains. The US authorities were having problems getting reliable and damning evidence on Fainberg, but they made a breakthrough while investigating Grecia Roizes, a close ally of Fainberg's in New York. Roizes was a trusted friend and, as always, Fainberg had had difficulty keeping quiet about all the great deals he had going down and all the 'new friends' that he had made. The FBI had a growing mountain of information on Roizes and put huge pressure on him to become an informant. Eventually he did and the floodgates were opened. Fainberg was arrested and on 17 October 1999 he was convicted on drug-smuggling charges. After spending just a short time behind bars in the USA he was deported to Israel.

Fainberg has not been idle since his deportation from the USA. Only a year after having been deported he turned up in Canada, calling himself Alon Bar (at least for travel and immigration purposes), with plans to make a new fortune through prostitution. He settled on the banks of the Ottawa River with his new Canadian wife and a young child from a previous relationship. Well known for his readiness to lose his temper and to resort to extreme violence, his first organized crime exploits in the USA had involved arson attacks on businesses in competition with those that were Russian-owned.

In Canada, though, his plan was to open a strip club in Gatineau, Quebec, which would feature Russian and Ukrainian strippers and lap-dancers. He claimed to be able to bring women in from Russia, Ukraine, Romania and the Czech Republic for $10,000 each. He knew the 'brokers' in Moscow and claimed he could give them a call and have fifteen to twenty women shipped within a week.

Fainberg was also known to be interested in exploring 'business possibilities' right on the doorstep of the USA, in Cuba.

John Gotti

The streets of New York in the 1960s and 1970s saw plenty of changes within the murky criminal underworld – the proliferation of supergrasses, mob bosses being put behind bars, assassinations and polarisation of power bases within the Mafia. At that time, five families ruled much of the city and although there were the usual turf battles from time to time, the gangs were mostly preoccupied with the expansion of their business empires and keeping under the radar of the increasingly emboldened law enforcement agencies. The families were the Bonanno, Colombo, Gambino, Genovese and Lucchese clans and changes in law enforcement meant that the gangs' tried and trusted ways of working were now simply not good enough. In this environment, one man rose to public infamy, someone whose name alone was to strike fear into his adversaries – John Joseph Gotti Jr, who would become known as 'The Teflon Don'.

John Gotti Sr and Philomena (usually called Fannie) Gotti had five sons and spent much of their early life in the Bronx, New York, before moving to the equally tough neighbourhood of Brooklyn. John Gotti Jr is alleged to have started on his career in crime as a gun for hire, a hitman. He was employed by many of the big gangs, but he became closest to the Gambino family. He was to become a powerful influence on his family and friends as each of his brothers – Peter, Gene, Richard and Vincent – became involved in mob activities, joining the Gambino clan. John Gotti was to become a natural leader, a strong man with great drive and ambition from a young age. He was also someone with a very short fuse who had absolutely no compunction about using violence to get what he wanted. He was born on 27 October 1940, the fifth child in his family, and learnt to use his fists from the moment the first argument broke out at his school. Gotti was drawn not to the high-rolling legitimate businessmen in Manhattan, but to the activities of the street guys, and he was running errands for them from the age of just twelve. He didn't seem interested in a proper education, but he learnt the tricks of the trade from the older boys and by hanging around various gangs. He was a bully by nature, wanting his own way the whole time, and he became more involved in gang operations as he reached his teens. At the age of fourteen, he took part in the theft of a cement mixer from a local building site and was injured when the heavy piece of machinery toppled over and landed on his toes, crushing them. He was confined to hospital for most of the summer, plotting his departure from school and deciding which of the local gangs to join. In the end he ran with the Fulton-Rockaway Boys, rising rapidly to become leader of the gang, taking them on to bigger jobs such as stealing and fencing cars – and just about anything else they could lay their hands on. While a member of this gang, he was arrested five times, on a variety of charges, but each time he managed to get the charges dismissed or reduced – a valuable attribute that would serve him well over the years to come.

In 1960, Gotti met a small, pretty, raven-haired Jewish-Italian girl by the name of Victoria DiGiorgio and, although she was a couple of years younger than him, the two fell very much in love right away. Victoria soon became pregnant and gave birth to their first child, Angela. The two eventually got married on 6 March 1962 close to the date of their daughter's first birthday, although theirs would prove to be a stormy relationship. Victoria wanted her husband to hold down a proper job and John did try several, including working in a coat factory and as a truck driver, but he didn't apply himself with the same vigour as to his street activities. He returned swiftly to his life of crime, which he saw as offering much better prospects for his growing family. The young parents had two further children in quick succession, Victoria and John A. Gotti, who was to become known to close friends and family as 'Junior'. John Gotti was arrested in 1963 and was unable to avoid a jail sentence of twenty days, having been caught in a stolen rental car. Three years later he spent several months inside, having been caught attempting a theft. He had yet to learn the ropes, but he wasn't about to let a couple of bad breaks halt his criminal career.

When looking at the life and times of John Gotti, it is important to know how the underworld of New York was operating at that time and who the main players were. Vito Genovese was in control of his 'family', though he was finding conditions increasingly tough due to a spell behind bars. Geraldo Catena was the first man put in charge of the day-to-day affairs of the family but he retired to Florida due to ill health and Tony Bender was appointed in his place. Genovese was not entirely convinced that Bender was acting in his best interests; he was also receiving reports that suggested that Bender was acting out of motives not entirely in line with the requirements of a Mafia family. Genovese had been Bender's best man, but in later years Bender had changed allegiances in the course of several affairs – most notably in the course of the affair which lead to the shooting of Little Augie Pisano and the unsuccessful assassination attempt on the life of Vincent Gigante. Bender didn't seem like a man who could be trusted, but Genovese didn't have many alternatives. Finally, in the face of growing evidence, the imprisoned Genovese sent word that action needed to be taken.

On 8 April 1962 Bender kissed his wife goodbye on the steps of their palatial home and got into his car. He was never seen again. Tommy Eboli, who had limited relevant experience, took over, but he lacked the organizational abilities of even his predecessor. The Genovese family were beginning to lose out on key opportunities, and their power on the streets of New York was waning.

The ever-expanding Gambino family was the main benefactor of these troubles experienced by the Genovese gang, as they moved in on several drug, prostitution and racketeering opportunities. In 1972, a large drug deal was being put together by Eboli with an associate by the name of Louis Cirollo, but Eboli couldn't raise the entire capital sum required, so he went to Carlo Gambino (the head of the Gambino family at that time) for assistance. A deal was brokered and the money transferred to Eboli. While trying to ship the goods, Cirollo was arrested, having already been under surveillance for many months, and the whole deal went bad. However, the loan was not repaid to Gambino and so late on the night of 1 July 1972, as Eboli left the Brooklyn flat of one of his mistresses, he was shot five times in the head and neck. His bodyguard took fright and never saw who fired the fatal shots. Carlo moved swiftly and placed Frank Tieri in charge of the Genovese operation, a man with strong loan-sharking, gambling and racketeering experience. Tieri proved a much more popular boss and brought greater stability to the streets and to the various families. He was to go down in history, however, as one of the first major underworld figures to be charged under new legislation brought in by the Racketeer Influence Corruption Organization Act (know as RICO).

The Gambino family were also having their rocky moments, but while Carlo Gambino was in charge, things were at least always going forwards. It is widely believed that Carlo Gambino was the figure on whom the central character in *The Godfather* was based. Much of his wealth dated from deals made during the Second World War, which proved very profitable for him indeed. Carlo set up a huge black market for ration books, produced by forgers who created exact replicas which were then reproduced on printing presses overnight. He also acquired the reputation on the streets of being a hard man. When he discovered that someone had been sleeping with several Mafia wives while their husbands were in jail, he allegedly fed the man, feet first, into an industrial meat grinder.

At around the same time, John Gotti joined the Bergin crew, a Mafia organization which operated out of the Bergin Club in the wonderfully named, Ozone Park, Queens. During the mid-1960s, this outfit had developed a number of highly lucrative hijacking scams. In one such operation, the men had hired a truck and, by forging the name of the company agent, managed to get into an airport cargo area filled with United Airlines property. They quickly filled their van with around $30,000 of exclusive women's fashion and drove off. When the same crew tried to mount a virtually identical operation four days later, they were watched by specially positioned FBI agents. Gotti pleaded guilty and was given four years in Lewisburg Federal Penitentiary, Pennsylvania, though he served fewer than three years before his release on parole. As part of his early release settlement, Gotti had to get a job and so he worked for the construction company belonging to the stepfather of his wife. Soon, though, he was spending more and more time back at the Bergin Club. He was finally made boss at the age of thirty-one.

Gotti reported to the number two in the Gambino organization, Aniello Dellacrose, who, in turn, reported to the boss Paul Castellano, a man with few allies who had been unexpectedly appointed when Carlo Gambino decided to retire. Castellano was Gambino's cousin and a trusted family friend, which might have influenced the ageing boss's decision. The family had, since the 1950s, been opposed to dealing in illegal substances, but increasingly the bosses were turning a blind eye as the money flowed in. With the proceeds from drug running, Gotti was becoming more powerful and struck up a close relationship with Dellacrose. The two men shared a love of smart clothes and fine food, and they both lost heavily and regularly when gambling. Dellacrose, who was being secretly investigated by the IRS, was finally indicted for income tax evasion after reporting an annual income of only $10,400 in 1968. To put that claim in perspective, Dellacrosse once managed to lose more than that sum in just one night gambling in Puerto Rico. With Dellacrose in prison, Gotti spotted his chance to move up in the organization.

In the early 1970s, a wave of kidnappings swept New York gangland. Many of those affected were Mafia families themselves who seemed willing to pay ransom money for the return of relatives. On a bitterly cold winter morning in 1972, one gang who had already benefited from several successful kidnappings, decided to snatch Manny Gambino, the son of Carlo's brother Joseph. The gang, run by Eddie Maloney and Jimmy McBratney, pulled Manny from the street at gunpoint and beat him several times over the head. The act was watched by two young boys who got the number plate of the getaway car and turned it over to a friend with suspected Mafia connections. A ransom of $21,000 was paid and mob henchmen were closing in on the hapless gang. They found the gang's hideout, but the victim had already been moved.

In the process of returning Manny, the kidnap victim made a run for it from the back of the car as it stopped. McBratney fired several shots at the partly bound man and killed him instantly. The body was later found dumped in the back of a car near a New Jersey dumpsite. Maloney suggested that McBratney leave the city – a piece of advice which the six-foot, three-inch, 250-pound McBratney ignored. Gotti was seen several times asking after the whereabouts of McBratney and eventually he caught up with him at Snoope's Bar, Staten Island. Gotti had several hoods in support and tried to convince McBratney that there were police officers present too, who would get him outside. McBratney would not move from the bar, believing he was safe as long as he was in public. A furious fight ensued before one of Gotti's men opened fire, shooting McBratney three times and killing him instantly.

On 17 October 1973 Gotti was indicted to appear before a

grand jury, charged with murder. Although he went into hiding, Gotti was later arrested by FBI agents during the following summer and court proceedings began almost immediately. The defence lawyer acting for Gotti, Roy Cohn, had worked extensively on Mafia cases and managed to strike a deal. Gotti would plead guilty to manslaughter and get only four years in Green Haven Correctional Facility. He was released after less than two years, having spent a great deal of his time playing cards, lifting weights and orchestrating gang business virtually uninterrupted.

When Gotti was released he took part in the full induction ceremony into the Mafia family – the oath of *omerta*. He was now a full member of the Gambino family. This official status carried huge respect among his peers and things would be done differently from now onwards including keeping him personally well clear of the riskier crimes. The entire Bergin crew were told to keep the heat off Gotti and maintain a lower profile than usual. They had moved up a step in the crime underworld – a very big step. With this greater notoriety came more attention from the FBI and other law enforcement agencies. Gotti was a bigger fish and quite a prize to anyone who could nail him. Gotti was advised to built an inner circle, which he did. This included his long-time friend Angelo Ruggiero as second in command, brother Gene, John Carneglia, Tony Rampino and Willie Johnson as cash collectors. Other brothers Peter and Richard were also employed but in more junior and peripheral positions. All the men had to come to the Bergin Club at least every other day to check in. They had to bring with them full reports of all activities and deals. A previously rather disorganized bunch of everyday hoods was beginning to look like a formidable gang, capable of taking on just about anything.

John and Victoria Gotti's forth child was Frank, a good student who excelled in sports and who didn't seem to share the family's appetite for crime. One afternoon, the twelve-year-old Frank was riding his small motorbike around the streets outside the family home, much like any other kid on the block. One of Gotti's neighbours, John Favara, was driving his car and didn't see the boy come out from behind a large parked truck. The car hit Frank and killed him outright. Victoria lived for her children and this was a devastating blow. She became so distraught that one day she attacked the man with a baseball bat. Favara had to be treated in a local hospital but decided not to press charges. He was also advised by the police, and just about everyone who knew him, to sell his house and to move away. John Gotti's reputation was well known. The man eventually heeded the advice, but continued to live in his home until the sale went through. Just three days before he was due to move out, he was abducted while leaving work, clubbed over the head and dragged into an waiting van. He was never seen again. John and Victoria were away on a trip in Florida and no one has ever been charged with the abduction. Victoria stated, 'I don't know what happened to him. I am not sorry if something did. He never sent me a card. He never apologized. He never even got his car fixed.'

Since being 'made up', Gotti had been connected to a string of murders and new deals. The authorities put him high on their priority list and additional legal powers were granted to gather intelligence on his activities. The Bergin crew were being bugged and many telephone calls were being monitored twenty-four hours a day. Gotti knew about much of this, but couldn't get close enough to whoever was providing information to the chasing pack of FBI officers. Many of the gang were heavily involved in drug trafficking and distribution, but Gotti remained publicly against the practice. He did, however, benefit greatly from his share of the revenue. In the early 1980s Special FBI Agent Bruce Mouw was chosen to head up a task force to break the Gambino family – he was told to cultivate a number of informants, to bug premises and to tap phone lines as well as to keep track of every movement of all the gang leaders. On 8 August 1993, five members of Gotti's inner sanctum were arrested – Angelo Ruggiero, Gene Gotti, John Carneglia, Michael Coiro and Mark Reiter. Along with plenty of evidence of drug dealing and many other illegal activities, it was leaked that there were disparaging remarks made on the tapes about the head of the family, Paul Castellano. Gotti and Castellano both became obsessed with getting these tapes and discovering what had been said on them.

By the mid-1980s, the ageing Castellano's problems were beginning to mount – Ruggiero had talked about the boss's operation and activities over phone lines that he knew were being recorded by the FBI. This would give them valuable information about where to look for further evidence. In addition, other close associates were being indicted and tracked down, closing the circle around the boss. During the summer of 1985, Castellano finally got his wish to hear the tapes after they had become available as part of the court case and he soon put a plan of action in place to shake things up. Expecting to be the target of attacks, Gotti and Ruggiero made their own plans, gathering support from other families and interested parties. The strike was to be audacious – in a busy area of Manhattan, outside a well-known restaurant, Sparks Steak House on East 46th Street. Eleven men took part in the conspiracy and four designated shooters were placed at the best vantage points along with armed men as back-up and those involved in the planned getaway. Tony Bilotti drove Castellano's spotless black Lincoln into an available space almost right in front of the restaurant and Castellano stepped out. Before he had moved more than a couple of paces, however, the four gunmen had put six bullets into his head, neck and chest. He died instantly and as Bilotti froze to the spot he was also sprayed with a number of fatal bullets. The firing squad merged into the streaming crowds, all moving rapidly and looking for cover. They made their way back to Second Avenue and the safety of their waiting vehicles unchallenged. Gotti was crowned boss of the Gambino family that very evening.

However, life wasn't quite the bed of roses that Gotti had

envisaged on becoming the big boss. Several lawyers were preparing defence cases for two separate trials against the 'Don', as he liked to be called. The first was against a refrigerator repairman, a six-foot, two-inch man by the name of Romual Piecyk. One day he found his car blocked outside a Queens bar and wasn't happy. After pushing on the horn for several minutes, the owner, Frank Colletta, came out and a brawl broke out between the two men. Gotti was inside and hearing the ruckus, went to investigate. Colletta was an associate of Gotti and walked right up to Piecyk, slapping the man across the face. Piecyk had been robbed of over $300 and had been badly beaten. Not knowing who he was up against, he went to the police who promptly charged Gotti and Colletta with assault and theft. Piecyk had testified against both men and during the time leading up to the trial, he became increasingly concerned about his own well-being. As the trial date came closer, Gotti's men threatened the repairman over the phone and cut his brake leads, all of which culminated in Piecyk not showing up for the trial. Eventually the police tracked him down and forced him onto the witness stand, where he famously couldn't remember the two men who had assaulted him. Gotti was free again and the headline of the *New York Daily News* the following morning read, 'I forgotti'.

No sooner were the celebrations over than Gotti and six other members of the Gambino family were served with indictments on racketeering charges spanning a full eighteen months. If found guilty, all the men involved were looking at long spells in prison of up to twenty years each. Gotti's first reaction was to use similar intimidation tactics; they had worked in the past, and he felt sure they could work again. Federal Judge Eugene Nickerson was ahead of the game on this occasion and withheld the names of the witnesses to try to prevent any contact or tampering. However, the reach of the Mafia had been grossly underestimated; before the trial had been going on for six weeks, one associate of the group had been murdered in a car bombing, a string of defendants had gone missing, there had been a bomb scare and widespread intimidation of witnesses. On 28 April 1986, the judge postponed the entire hearing for four months. The following month saw Nickerson rescind bail for Gotti only, citing him as a potentially dangerous and reckless man, who was worthy of detention. On 19 May he arrived at the courthouse in a large black Mercedes, but left using very different transportation bound for the Metropolitan Correctional Center in New York.

All the big New York Mafia families seemed satisfied with Gotti's actions in removing Castellano, except one. Vincent Gigante, also known as 'the Chin', was the head of the Genovese gang, and had enjoyed a close working relationship with Castellano for a number of years. The assassination of Frank DeCicco, which had interrupted the latest trial, had been planned by Gigante and was supposed to have removed Gotti as well. Gotti was still unaware that Gigante was gunning for him when one morning he received a strange phone call from an FBI agent. The FBI had planted bugs and had phone taps in a number of Gigante's known offices and had overheard a plot to kill Gotti. In a curious twist of fate, the FBI were legally bound to inform him of what they had heard. Three men working for Gigante were arrested and subsequently convicted of putting together a murder plot and sent to jail. Gotti now seemed to have the law working for him. To many people he seemed untouchable, completely above the law, which led to his acquiring a new nickname from one of New York's newspapers; from this point onwards Gotti would be known as 'The Teflon Don'.

The adjournment in Gotti's racketeering case had come to an end and on 25 September a packed federal court in Brooklyn, New York, heard the opening statements from lawyers on both sides. Many of the spectators were newspaper journalists, television reporters, photographers and other broadcasting groupies who knew the media value of these proceedings. The case for the prosecution did not get off to a fast start – their initial witness was Salvatore Polisi but his evidence had to be delayed as he had given an interview to an author who was writing a book about his life. The court ruled that the defence was entitled to have at least the same information about a witness that the prosecution had. The government had another setback when the testimony from Eddie Maloney could not be presented to the jury because the evidence was too thin and circumstantial. Maloney was an informant who had gone into the government witness protection programme and he had now diappeared without providing the crucial help which the government had hoped that he would. Polisi was eventually called back and cross-examined, but racist remarks that he had made in public several years ago were to count against him, especially as the jury contained a number of black Americans. A former police detective was next in line, providing information about the surveillance operation – he was far from convincing. Gotti gave statements to the press, taking great delight in trashing the proceedings and the prosecution's whole case – these statements made great headlines and the trial was turning into a circus.

Gotti had another card up his sleeve. One of the jury was a hard-drinking, middle-aged New Yorker called George Pape. This man was short of cash and wanted to profit financially from the proceedings. He had contacted a gang who had got in touch with the Gambino family to set up a meeting. A sum of $60,000 was allegedly paid to him, which meant the worst that Gotti could expect would be a hung jury. James Cardinali, a man who had served time with Gotti and knew him well, took the stand in December. He had previously worked for the Bergin Club crew running errands and robbing drug dealers. Cardinali had turned informant in an attempt to reduce his current sentence, which weakened the prosecution's case when he revealed that he had been paid $10,000 to appear as a witness. Witness after witness came and went until, finally, after more than six months of evidence had been heard, the jury was sent away to deliberate. After seven days, a spokesman for the jury handed the verdicts to the judge – a raucous courtroom heard the non-guilty verdicts ring out.

Gotti was a free man and for the first time in a number of years, he had no law suit or court case hanging over him. He was to turn his attention fully to growing the family business and broadening the activities of his illegal empire. As ever with Gotti, trouble seemed to lie in wait on every corner. A suspected Gambino family member by the name of Philip Modica was building a new restaurant near the tip of Manhattan Island in early 1986. For the construction work, he decided to use his own contacts and not to use union representatives. New York at that time was heavily unionized and the carpenters' union in particular was one of the strongest. The local branch of the United Brotherhood of Carpenters and Joiners was run by John O'Connor and he had a number of his boys pay a visit to the restaurant which incurred tremendous damages for not using his men. Modica turned up in the morning and immediately contacted Gotti, who acted swiftly. This wasn't a simple one-off incident to Gotti, it was Mafia power against union power. He had to be seen from both sides to take charge if he was to retain his reputation. A gang of hoods were despatched and O'Connor was shot four times in the leg and hip, putting him in nearby St Clare's Hospital. The second in command of this gang was to turn state witness and over two years later Gotti was charged with first degree murder and conspiracy to commit murder. Officer Joseph Coffey arrested Gotti along with Angelo Ruggiero and Tony Guerrieri. The prosecution had plentiful incriminating tapes from bugs and phone taps and two main witnesses who had allegedly heard Gotti say 'bust him up'. Many of the important conversations on the tapes used much of Gambino's peculiar vernacular and a lot of slang. It was proving difficult to decipher exactly what was being said and what it was supposed to mean. The key witness, James McElroy, was a former member of the gang who had carried out the job, and was already serving time and wanted to reduce his sentence. The cross-examination was determined and prolonged, but Gotti was clearly heard on the tapes stating, '. . . gonna bust him up'. The twelve jurors and four alternates were confined to a specially prepared hotel and were allowed no contact with friends, family or anyone in the outside world. On 9 February 1990 the jury finally returned a verdict of not guilty on all charges, stating that the taped evidence carried insufficient weight. As it turned out, O'Connor spent over a year in jail for his part in the attack while Gotti walked free.

Gotti's inner sanctum of people was getting smaller – brother Gene and John Carneglia were behind bars on drug-trafficking charges, Joseph Gallo and Joseph Armone had also been sentenced to long prison sentences and Robert DiBernardo had been assassinated. Then, his long-time friend and confidant Angelo Ruggiero died of cancer. The FBI, in association with the New York Police Force, had mobilized a full-time task force which continued to gather evidence, pay informants and bug homes and offices in an effort to put together a watertight case against the most visible and most powerful mob boss of the modern era. Gotti seemed to believe that while new charges were bound to be brought, he would always be able to find a way out or negotiate some kind of deal. On the evening of 11 December 1990, Gotti's movements were being tracked every step of the way and when he went into the Ravenite Club, the orders were given to arrest him. In a well-planned and well-executed operation, many police officers and FBI agents converged on the club from all sides and arrested John Gotti, Sammy Gravano and Frank Locascio. Thomas Gambino was also arrested that same evening but at a different location.

This case was different from the very start. The various law enforcement agencies worked together more closely and they had learnt from the mistakes made in the previous three court cases. Gotti was also charged with the murder of Castellano and Bilotti, much more serious charges than he had faced to date. The prosecution team won an important battle at the outset; Judge Glasser moved to disqualify lawyers Cutler, Shargel and Pollock from representing Gotti because they were mentioned in the recording tapes. The names of the entire jury were kept secret under strict supervision. This would be the least of Gotti's worries, however, as Sammy Gravano had decided to defect and give evidence for the prosecution. It can only be imagined what 'the Don' thought of this and what he would have done if he had got his hands on this one-time close associate. The initial weeks of the trial were relatively uneventful, with testimony from FBI agents George Gabriel and Lewis Schiliro about how the bugging and information-gathering had taken place. Tape after tape revealed Gotti giving orders for men to be murdered, drug deals to be done and demanding to know how rackets were performing. Much of this seemed to be low-key; it was as if everyone connected with the trial was waiting for a climactic event to turn the trial on its head. This was to come when Salvatore Gravano took the stand on 2 March 1992.

Videos were shown and tapes played to back up much of Gravano's testimony. Other witnesses from the mob world, especially from the Genovese family, were called and provided further information for the judge and jury. An IRS inspector was called and confirmed that Gotti hadn't filed a tax return for six years. Gotti's defence, without its usual personnel and their skills, started to look hopelessly out of its depth. They called five witnesses who were deemed ineligible and not even the usual bomb threats against the courtroom could prevent the onward march of justice. The jury took just thirteen hours to come to a decision and on 2 April they found Gotti guilty of all charges. Just over two months later. Gotti stood in front of Judge Glasser to receive his sentence – life in prison without the option of parole. Gotti was expected to be transported to a new, state-of-the-art, maximum-security prison in Florence, Colorado, but instead he was taken to the Marion Federal Penitentiary in Illinois where he was reportedly kept in solitary confinement for twenty-three hours a day. He was subsequently diagnosed as having throat cancer and moved to a specialist facility in Springfield, Missouri, where he died on 10 June 2002.

For many people, this was the end of a significant chapter in modern Mafia power. The undisputed boss of New York was gone and if the Mafia was to prosper again, things would need to change radically. Only time will tell if the Mafia will be able to achieve a position of strength once again.

The Russian Mafia

The Russian Mafia is a very broad term used to describe often highly organized gangs of criminals from various disparate parts of the former Soviet Union. They are also referred to as the Red Mafia or even the Organisatsiya, although this latter description is also sometimes used for the American arm of the Russian Mafia. Members of the Russian Mafia originate from as far and wide as Ukraine, Armenia, Kazhakstan, Chechnya, Moldova, Belarus, Estonia, Lithuania and Russia itself. Political instability in the region has given rise to many new republics and to great economic uncertainty. One thing that has remained constant, however, is the power and influence of the large Russian Mafia groups. It is estimated that the total membership of the Russian Mafia is well over 100,000 people, in around 8,000 gangs which control no less than a staggering 40 per cent of the various nations' total wealth. At the heart of the Russian Mafia's power lies their ownership of the banking system – fragile and remarkably simplistic by Western standards, it remains at the centre of commerce and trading. This gives the major gangs a stake in just about anything they wish to get involved in. To achieve this position by moving their own people into positions of power, they have had to threaten and assassinate leading bankers and businessmen. The underpaid and poorly equipped law enforcement agencies have been able to do little but stand back and watch this state of affairs unfold.

To fully understand the environment for organized crime in and around Russia, we need to look at some of the cataclysmic changes that have occurred in that part of the world. In 1989, the Berlin Wall fell and East Germany, as it was, ceased to exist. The reunification of Germany initiated a stampede of other countries looking for democracy and reform. President Gorbachev's plan was to preside over a slow and orderly transition to independence in the Eastern Bloc states and the western Soviet republics, but once Russia's grip had been relaxed, there was no going back. Many Eastern European states overthrew their dictatorial regimes, declaring themselves independent from Russia. Uprisings in Poland, Romania, Hungary and Czechoslovakia all led to the establishment of sovereign states and with the changes in their political systems came enormous opportunities for companies, individuals and gangs who had money and influence. State assets could be purchased for a fraction of their value and whole areas of commerce were opening up. This was, indeed, the perfect breeding ground for the major criminal gangs and they took full advantage.

Any foreign company wishing to do business in Russia ends up paying around 20 per cent of their proceeds to the Russian Mafia, such is their stranglehold. Even when this is done, leading Western businessmen often feel the need to hire bodyguards and security firms to keep themselves safe. Often these services too are owned by the Mafia. Several foreign companies have attempted high-profile joint ventures with established Russian companies, but rarely has this proved fruitful for outsiders – doing business in the ex-Soviet Union is very different from doing business in most other parts of the world. The whole system is both self-defeating and highly unpredictable – it has all the hallmarks of an economy in a massive downward spiral, with no end in sight. Many of the leading gangs operate in a similar way to the Italian Mafia families – a strict hierarchy is established under a leader who gives orders to a series of group leaders below him who have control over specific activities or regions. Secrecy, brutal killings and black marketeering are all by-products of the current regime.

Organized crime is seen by many in Russia to be a rebellion against the inefficient and corrupt political system and those who enforce it. Despite attempts to curb the power of the gangsters by the Kremlin, lack of resources and inadequate legislation have meant that these efforts have been ineffectual. In many ways, the government policy of declaring many products illegal simply stimulates black markets overnight and plays directly into the hands of the Mafia groups. They know that a large domestic market exists for many goods so they simply open up illicit trade links with Western companies to import those goods on a massive scale. Getting produce into Russian states is only a matter of money, through bribery or influence in the right places. Also, due to price controls on many Russian goods, a higher price can often be gained overseas, which again leads to illegal trading. Poor legislation has resulted in Russian raw materials being exported and sold at low prices in the West. In addition, many government and army officials have strong Mafia connections or are paid by them for turning a blind eye to much of what goes on. Since the 1990s many of the richest gangs in Russia have set up operations around the world, using their tremendous wealth and power to make inroads into illegal operations especially in America, but also in the Far East, South Africa and Australia. Much of this trade was opened up through drug trafficking and the sale of weapons. Soho, in London, has become a focus for much Russian Mafia money and attention, along with Brighton Beach in New York. From Brighton Beach, many Russian gangsters do deals which impact negatively on the American markets for goods and services. The FBI and Russia's security forces have tried to co-operate, but there is perhaps too much distrust and secrecy on both sides, and the two organizations have very different procedures and approaches.

The steady flow of gangsters leaving Russia is almost

matched by optimistic individuals and businessmen moving in, wanting to take advantage of the transition from 'pure' Communism to a freer, more market-driven economy. The opportunities available to be exploited are often referred to as 'the second gold rush', although, as we have seen, much of the gold ends up in the already swollen coffers of the Russian gangs rather than in the hands of the foreign entrepreneurs, who can be either lucky, or unlucky. Many have tried to buy local goods using near worthless roubles and holding them for a while until they could exchange them for dollars. Others put money into Russian banks as, for a time, they were paying very high interest rates. However, what looked like a foolproof plan on paper came unstuck as many Russian banks went to the wall taking these investments with them. This not only put a swift stop to this investment strategy, but also undermined the whole economy – if people couldn't rely on banks, what could they rely on and how could they conduct business? The unluckier investors either lost enormous sums of money to corrupt officials or the Russian Mafia, or they were shot. Russia has never been, and is still not, a place for the faint-hearted to do business.

The Russian Mafia have generally taken a dim view of any outsiders attempting to do business on their turf. Many businessmen have suffered at their hands for having the temerity to attempt to go up against them. In February 1997, a Chinese businessman and fast food-chain owner, Lee Wong, was shot in the face at Ploschad Revolutsi metro station in central Moscow for having complained to the police about Mafia harassment.

Paul Tatum, the American co-owner of the Radisson-Slavanskaya Hotel in Moscow, was shot eleven times in the head and neck (his attacker knew that he was wearing a bullet-proof vest) and killed in a metro station in November 1996 for refusing to pay *krysha* (literally 'roof', which is Russian gangster slang for 'protection'). Tatum was surrounded by bodyguards when attacked, but they made no attempt to save him and allowed his attacker to escape unharmed. Only weeks beforehand, Tatum had taken out a full-page advertisement in a local newspaper to denounce his Chechen partner Umar Dzhabrailov for trying to squeeze him out of their joint venture. Although Tatum was a multi-millionaire investor with connections both to then US President Bill Clinton and to many high-ranking Moscow politicians, his murder has never been solved.

A Canadian businessman, Ken Rowe, the joint owner of the Moscow Aerostar Hotel, was threatened by the Russian Mafia in an attempt to force him out of a joint hotel-airline venture. At one stage Mafia gangsters entered the hotel and forced all the employees to leave. Rowe later retaliated by having an Aeroflot plane seized in Montreal in order to recover his award in a Russian court.

In 1998, Australian businessman Richard F. Hollington, owner of a Moscow disco, was killed for control of his business. A year earlier, John Tillmann, a Canadian who owned some Moscow street vendor kiosks, had been shot and wounded on Sirenevy Boulevard in the east of Moscow for not paying *krysha*. A Mafia hitman Sergei Nechayev was killed during the shootout with Tillmann, who had always taken the precaution of being armed since the killing of Tatum. After his recovery, with a price on his head, Tillmann sold up and left Moscow; he lived for a while in Sochi on the Black Sea, but left in the end for Switzerland.

Other foreign investors who have been killed in Russia, either for control of their businesses or for not paying *krysha*, include: Briton, Christopher Kline, who owned a Moscow department store and was killed by an explosive device for control of his business; Jan Praamsma, a Dutch cheese distributor, drowned in the Moskva River for not paying *krysha*; Ariel 'The Spider' Abramson, a well-known Israeli businessman who was lured into a St Petersburg subway and killed in September 1998 for not paying *krysha*.

In the same way that the bosses of the Italian Mafia and the Colombian drug cartels exercise great power and influence over vast areas of land and commerce, so too do the leaders of the various Russian Mafia groups.

One of the best known and most feared Russian Mafia leaders is Semyon Yukovich Mogilevich. In the late 1990s, British intelligence agents and other international law enforcement agencies began an investigation into money laundering activities being co-ordinated by Russian gangs in the UK. A report published by the *New York Times* in July 1999 showed that the British believed that at the heart of the scam was Mogilevich, a man estimated to be worth over $100 million which had come from extortion, prostitution, arms dealing and drug trafficking. Much of the money was laundered through a London-based bank. After this had been shut down by the authorities, Mogilevich was believed to have moved on to purchasing stocks in legitimate businesses in Canada and America. Traditionally, drug runners have pushed their cash through smaller, private companies, which makes it harder to track. Mogilevich purchased a significant shareholding in a Philadelphia company called YBM Magnex, which had factory premises in Yugoslavia and Kentucky. After an investigations by the FBI, several managers of this company pleaded guilty to securities fraud in a federal district court and were duly sentenced before going to jail. It was suspected that the money used by the company came from Mogilevich, and although he is not allowed into the USA, he is clearly able to exert his influence anywhere in the world. Before prosecutors moved in, YBM Magnex had used the illegal cash to raise more finance, to the tune of $114 million via the Canadian stock market. When the government went through the books, they found vast sums of money moving in and out of the company – on one occasion $3.2 million was transferred from a bank in Lithuania to a trade account in Hungary, then on to the Chemical Bank in Buffalo, indicative of money laundering on a grand scale.

Mogilevich was born on 20 June 1946 in Kiev, where for much of his early life he learnt the ropes as a small-time crook, sourcing and supplying black market goods and laundering money. He spent two spells in jail in the 1970s before setting up a company that transported the possessions of Russian Jews heading to Israel or the USA. The fee would often simply be pocketed, and the goods would never arrive at the other end, remaining behind to be sold for a tidy profit. With the cash proceeds, Mogilevich got into serious criminal businesses: buying and selling weapons and drugs and setting up prostitution rings. During the politically turbulent 1990s, he decided to leave Russia for Israel, where he bought nightclubs and factories, as well as art from all over the world. He also expanded his arms trading business. In 1991, he married a Hungarian woman which enabled him to set up a base in Budapest, which soon grew and served as a front for a whole range of similar legal and illegal activities. Within two years, he had 250 people working for him in his Hungarian businesses alone. His premises were raided in May 1995 and many people were arrested, although virtually everyone was released without having been charged. It was a bold attempt by the police to find out more about his empire, but in the bigger scheme of things caused only minor disruption to his ever-expanding operations. The Hungarian police are working with the FBI on tracking a number of leading European criminals and Mogilevich is on that list. Catching and convicting him, however, will not be easy as he has proved a very slippery character.

Another big Russian gangster is Aleksandr Solonik, who, after completing basic training in the Russian military, went into special operations. He was sent to the gulag for eight years for rape offences, but managed to escape by jumping from a second-storey window during a hospital visit and was employed as a hitman by a gang of criminals near his home town of Kurgan. After several successful hits he and other members of his gang moved to Moscow to expand their business; he soon became one of the most prolific killers in the Russian underworld. Viktor Nikiforov, Valeri Dlugatsj, Valdislav Vinner and Otari Kvantrishvili were all big names killed by Solonik. Several gangsters were concerned that they were next and an informant called the Moscow militia after Solonik was spotted entering a bar. The gun battle that ensued saw Solonik shoot four men in the bar and another two as he escaped at speed. He was hit and eventually captured, the bullet being removed the following day in the prison hospital. After serving less than one year of a very long sentence, he managed to escape again and with Russia being far too hot for him, he made his way to Greece, where he set up a drug business. For Solonik it was difficult to hide as he was extremely well known to both law enforcement agencies and many criminal gangs and in 1997 the police and other gangs were closing in on him. He had made a lot of friends, but even more enemies. The police found a body which they believed to be his, strangled to death. No one was ever charged with the killing, but it is widely believed that one of the largest Moscow-based gangs put out a contract on his life.

Another Russian gangster is Vyacheslav Ivankov, known in gangland circles as 'the father of extortion' or 'the Red Godfather'. Ivankov was born in the Soviet Republic of Georgia, brought up in Moscow and was a champion wrestler in his youth. He formed a gang called Solnntsevskaya, whose initial focus was supplying stolen goods to the black market. However, in 1982 he was arrested for drug trafficking, possession of firearms and robbery, receiving fourteen years behind bars. He served ten years in Siberia, before resurfacing as 'a movie executive' and moving to the USA, or at least that was the profession attested to on his visa application. The real story of how this ruthless convicted criminal and murderer was released early from prison and then given permission to enter the USA will probably never be fully known. Russian internal affairs departments stood accused of bribery, corruption and a lack of proper information, but considerable pressure had also been brought to bear on a highly successful New York-based American company. It later turned out that Ivankov controlled the company. He was arrested by the FBI in the summer of 1995 on extortion charges, but even this seemed suspicious as most of the big bosses were usually safely distant from the day-to-day running of extortion rackets. However, he was sentenced to over nine years in prison.

In the second half of 1975, over 5,000 Russian Jews left Russia for the USA. Many of these immigrants were hard-working tradesmen who happened to get on the wrong side of the authorities, but in among the new arrivals were some hardened criminals. One such man was Evsei Agron. He had already served seven years in the gulag for running one of the largest prostitution and illegal gambling operations in Europe. He set up shop in New York's Brighton Beach area, developing the same business activities as he had in his homeland. Agron had a fearsome reputation and was paid extortion money by many Russian immigrants – in one notorious case by the father of a woman who had received death threats on her wedding day. Carrying out orders, one of Agron's hoods, a former Russian weightlifter, reportedly killed a man in a New York parking lot. In front of several law-abiding Russian immigrants, he picked the victim up with one hand and stuck a knife in his stomach with the other. In the spring of 1980, while walking with some colleagues through Coney Island, Agron was shot. He was looked after by the Genovese family with whom he had been doing business for some time. There were many people who wanted to see the back of Agron and although no one was charged with his attempted murder, the news on the street was that someone had paid with his life for his attempted assassination.

Agron made a full recovery and saw his profile rise higher. His empire had now expanded to include five other American cities, but he faced a big problem. Unlike the faithful Italians who worked for any of the American gangs, the Russians who worked for Agron all seemed to be loose cannons. They tried to extend their activities into the turf of other gangs, they tried to rip off the wrong people or to hijack other criminal operations. The underworld was beginning to think that Agron didn't exert the level of control required for such a business. In the winter of 1984 he was shot twice as he entered his home, one bullet entering the side of his face and the other his neck. He recovered very quickly again, but his face would always be marked with the scars of this attack. The prime suspect was Boris Goldberg, a Russian Jew who traded in illegal weapons and had a drug supply network. The two subsequently had a major face-to-face stand-off at a country club, but no blood was spilt. An uneasy peace settled between the two, but no one involved thought it would last. However, Agron had plenty of other enemies and on the morning of 4 May 1985 he was assassinated with two bullets to the head right outside his house. He was fifty-three years old and the first of the big Russian gangsters to set up an empire in the USA. He was not to be the last.

A fifth noteworthy Russian gangster is Victor Anatoliyevich Bout who came from the small province of Tajikistan. Like most young men, he went into the army, but he stayed longer than most, training in the commandos and in the air force. He graduated in 1991 from Moscow's prestigious Military Institute with six languages and a huge network of useful contacts. After the break-up of the old Soviet Bloc, Bout was out of a job so he got together with several ex-army colleagues to start a company called Transavia Export Cargo, an arms dealer. Several high-profile deals helped to propel these individuals to global gangland recognition – they supplied the Belgian peace-keeping forces in Somalia and the Afghani North Alliance with virtually all their weapons. He moved the hub of his business to the Middle East, opening premises in Sharjah in the United Arab Emirates, operating Air Cess in Liberia and several other businesses too. Working in that part of the world proved easier for Bout in terms of banking, transporting goods and staying out of sight of the major international law enforcement agencies. Bout has also been able to corner the massive market for supplying arms to Africa, including assault rifles, missile launchers, explosives and sufficient ammunition to provide for several wars simultaneously and continuously. Much of this was coming initially from Russia but subsequently from his own factories in the desert. Bout has managed to use a string of different companies, none of them directly linked with him; he has also built strong political allies in the Middle East, which have made him very difficult to track and convict. Things did change considerably after the attack on the World Trade Center on 11 September 2001, with many of Bout's clients, such as the Taliban, being actively pursued by the FBI, Interpol and other law enforcement agencies. Bout's name also came up on their wanted lists and he has been forced to go underground though he is still believed to be alive and operating as an international arms merchant on a large scale.

A sixth and final Russian gangster worthy of consideration is Alimzhan Tokhtakhounov, who was born in 1949. As a youngster he enjoyed football and playing cards – he was good at both, but gambling proved much more lucrative. His first big move was from his home town of Tashkent in Uzbekistan to the bustling streets of Moscow, where he joined the Izmaylovo gang. From then on he led the life of a full-time crook. His physical attributes made him perfect for debt collection, which opened many opportunities to him in East Germany, although his stay was a brief one because the police were getting too close to his colleagues and to his business dealings. He then moved to France where he was involved in one of the largest money laundering cases in French history up to that point. The sum involved was reputedly in excess of $70 million, which had the local authorities on his tail once again. Tokhtakhounov then moved from Italy to Israel in search of new criminal avenues to explore – with his sporting contacts, he set up an elaborate bribery scam involving the ice-skating at the 2002 Salt Lake City Winter Olympics. This amazing incident reveals the extent of Tokhtakhounov's influence and how, by moving from country to country, he has managed to keep the authorities guessing as to his activities. He was finally arrested in Italy under charges of affecting the outcome of the pairs figure skating in the Winter Olympics through manipulating the scores of the Russian judges. He is currently in prison but is understood to be able to direct many aspects of his operations from inside.

The reach of many members of the Russian Mafia is extraordinary – practically nothing is beyond them, if the money is right. Sergei 'Mikhas' Mikhailov continues to live at large, running his global criminal business activities from one or other of his secret hideouts. The Organizatsiya has been linked to Osama Bin Laden and Al Qaeda as well as a string of South American drug cartels. There are also some who think that leading Russian statesmen condone and may even facilitate some of the weapons deals being done by the Russian Mafia. These provide a welcome influx of cash, as well as providing much-needed employment opportunities. Russia also benefits from inside intelligence on what other countries and major crime groups are using. So is the Russian government losing the fight against crime or are they simply taking a different approach to tackling it?

Many people in the USA are concerned about the amount of influence that leading Russian criminal figures have in the USA, but, in the following open letter to the FBI, George B. Avisov, President of the Congress on Russian Americans, California Chapter, disapproves of the term 'Russian' in describing such criminals and argues that it is an unfair and harmful misnomer.

March 29 1998

Mr George Grotz
FBI SF Field Office
450 Golden Gate Avenue
San Francisco, CA, 94102

Dear Mr Grotz,

We are contacting you in connection with recent media reports of FBI sting operations involving San Francisco businesses owned apparently by ethnic Jewish and other refugees from the former Soviet

Union. We support and commend your efforts in tracking down any and all criminal activity in our city.

Unfortunately, the media (i.e. KGO TV, *San Francisco Chronicle*) continues to mislead the public by continuously referring to these alleged criminals as 'Russians', 'Russian Mafia', 'Russian businesses', occurring in 'Russian neighbourhoods', etc. The media also makes reference to the FBI, saying that your organization is using terms like 'Russian Mafia' and, accordingly, it is, in effect, proper for them to follow suit. In the *San Francisco Chronicle*, dated March 21, you are quoted as stating that 'The case involves allegations of health care fraud and money laundering. We believe Russian organized crime is involved.' Furthermore, the *Chronicle* states that you indicated that investigators believe a combination of gangsters inside the former Soviet Union and ethnic-Russian gangsters in the United States were involved. A similar story was printed in the *San Francisco Examiner* of March 29, 1998.

The Russian-American community and our national organization continue to be very concerned about the serious negative 'Russian bashing' that the media is propagating every time some adverse political or criminal events take place. During the 'Cold War', the media continuously equated the term 'Russians' with 'Communist'. During periods of very high tension (i.e. after flight KAL 007 was shot down by a Soviet fighter), and as a result of extensive and continuous anti-Russian propaganda by the media and even by some elected officials, the Russian-American community endured severe hardships. For example, on October 24, 1983, Tanya Zelensky (born in the US), a resident of Pittsfield, Vermont, was shot to death by an individual who ran into her store. In his confession, the assailant, Harvey, said he killed Ms Zelensky because she was a 'Russian spy' and that the earlier downing of the KAL plane and the bombing of US marines in Beirut had convinced him that there was a severe threat from the 'Russians', etc. While William Harvey did the actual killing, the real murderers were those who polluted his mind with the notion that 'Communist' equals 'Russian'. The night before Tanya's murder, a senator from New York spoke about the 'Russian dynamite' that murdered US marines in Beirut on national TV. Perhaps this helped William Harvey make up his mind and do away with the 'Russian spy'.

Today, as the Soviet Union no longer exists, the media has conveniently substituted 'Russian Mafia' for the former Soviet Union's criminal element that was able to slip into the US under the special 'Refugee Act'. (This legislature allows annually up to 50,000 refugees, predominantly ethnic Jews, to enter this country under very favourable conditions.)

Earlier, when FBI Assistant Special Agent in Charge, Edward Appel, spoke at a speaker's forum at the Russian-American Chamber of Commerce in San Francisco (now known as Russian American Trade & Commerce), he noted correctly that 'Russian Organized Crime is a misnomer: many organized crime members are from Uzbekistan, Kazakhstan, Georgia, Armenia, Azerbaijan. Many Russian organized crime members have emigrated to Finland, Germany, Israel and Italy, as well as the US.' Not once did he refer to all this criminal element as the 'Russian Mafia'. Similarly, at the earlier congressional hearing in Washington, senior FBI and other speakers referred to the above criminals as belonging to 'Euro-Asian' organized crime.

In spite of the above efforts to describe more accurately the criminals from the former Soviet Union, the media continues to mislead the general public with the above-described Russophobic name tag – propaganda that, today, is nothing short of a 'Hate Crime' when one considers where this anti-Russian media blitz can lead to.

To conclude, as stated above, we appreciate and support the efforts of the FBI to rid our society of all criminal activity. Yet we deplore the fact that the media and even some members of the FBI continue to utilize the term 'Russian Mafia' – a cliché that the media exploits at every opportunity and, indeed, cites the FBI as a source utilizing the term.

We shall be pleased to meet with you and or/your representatives to discuss the above matter which continues to be a serious threat to the well-being of our community here, as well as elsewhere in the country. It spreads the wrong message to people, at large, and defames the character and well-being of all law-abiding members of the Russian-American community.

Sincerely,
George B. Avisov, President
Congress on Russian Americans, California Chapter

Many global economists like to describe Russia as being run and ordered by thieves. Despite the incredible cash proceeds made by the few, the majority of ordinary Russians are certainly no better off. Just about everything has been privatized to a certain degree, even law and order. The government often has to turn to major gangs for protection and in some areas, such as Rostov, the state's ability to enforce the law has been broken. A senior British Special Branch officer has said in an interview that he thinks that of the gangs on the streets of the UK, the Russians are the most violent, with the Chechen Mafia being the most ruthless of all. It is not just countries that have felt the impact of Russian gangsters; major multinational corporations have also been affected. The most high-profile case in recent times was the illegal movement of money from Citibank accounts which was traced back to hackers in Russia. Russian mobsters have embraced the technological revolution and expanded their turf into cyberspace; they were among the first to see the opportunities in this sector of rapidly evolving technology. In May 2004, Australian businessman Hamish Davidson, the owner of Wollongong based Sportsbetting, received a demand for $30,000 via email. If he did not pay, the email threatened, his betting website multibet.com would be attacked. Davidson ignored the email. Quickly his website became slow, then crashed entirely. Then the entire local network for Alice Springs crashed, leaving the whole area without a connection to the internet. Telstra, the Australian telecommunications firm who provided Davidson with his internet connection, soon managed to get their service working again, but Davidson's website stayed down for four days, costing him millions of dollars.

The Crips and the Bloods

When many of the great American cities like Chicago, New York and Boston were incubating great crime barons and famous gangsters, Los Angeles was still on the starting blocks. During the 1920s and 1930s, it was still, in terms of organized crime, a dusty, parochial backwater, with very little going on in the way of activity by large criminal gangs. During the Great Depression, gambling was illegal, as it was in most states at that time, but California had a novel way of overcoming that particular stumbling block. Boats would moor themselves off the coast near Santa Monica and players would be ferried from small platforms or piers. It must have seemed very glamorous in those days to be rowed out towards a brightly lit vessel with a band onboard playing a welcoming tune. Another pleasure trip for the residents of southern California was to the race track and the casinos of Tijuana on the border with New Mexico. However, this was more popular with the citizens of San Diego, which was closer to Tijuana, than it was with the citizens of Los Angeles for whom the journey either overland or by sea was quite long.

In the years after the Second World War, Los Angeles grew rapidly in size and wealth; the movie business had grown beyond all recognition from the early days of silent films and had spawned a whole raft of associated industries. Many leading gangs now wanted a west coast base and LA was the favourite choice for many. The links between the big gangs and the entertainment business have been well documented; the bright lights of Tinseltown were extremely attractive to many hardened criminals, just as, in more recent times, criminals have been attracted to the music, internet and computer gaming industries. Each of these industries has a glamorous appeal far removed from the conventional day-to-day gangster pursuits of drug running, extortion, smuggling and prostitution. A number of the big Mafia families were beginning to buy homes in California and move their families down to the west coast to enjoy the weather, the Californian lifestyle and, of course, to develop their illegal networks further.

Many African-Americans and Asian, Mexican and other immigrants, both legal and illegal, from all over the world were making their way towards Los Angeles and its surrounding towns and cities. LA became a mecca for those searching for the American dream and a new beginning. This massive multicultural influx brought its own difficulties and soon Los Angeles became a city of enclaves and pockets of different ethnic groups. The Watts riots of 1965 in the suburbs of LA saw principally young, black Americans taking to the streets, something that was mirrored in over a hundred other US cities, resulting in civil disturbances and the deaths of forty-three people. In general, minorities were looking for ways to express their feelings, and one of the ways in which a sense of alienation and oppression could be expressed was through crime. The Bloods and the Crips, with a membership that is predominantly African-American and male, are the best-known street gang in the Los Angeles area. In addition, there are estimated to be over 600 Hispanic-American groups. As well as these gangs, other major forces were taking shape, including Asian gangs comprising approximately 20,000 members with links to China, Korea, the Philippines, Cambodia and Laos. There are many other African-American gangs, most notably the Dragnet and Hoover groups, all of which add to a heady mix of multicultural tension, anger and violence.

The Crips are one of the oldest and most violent gangs in the United States. They have been linked to and allegedly involved in an enormous range of robberies, drug deals, extortion rackets and murders. Identified by their distinctive blue-coloured accessories, they do not operate as one unitary gang, but more as a series of loosely associated franchises. The Crips gang was formed by Raymond Washington and Stanley Tookie Williams in 1969. They were young men, concerned, ironically, to protect themselves against gangs. There are different views as to how the name came into being, one theory being that it is derived from 'crippin' which on the streets meant to steal or rob, although the most likely explanation is that the name is derived from an earlier name, Baby Avenue, which became Avenue Crib (a street that many gang members lived on), then Avenue Crip, and, finally, simply, Crips.

The Crips grew swiftly in the early 1970s as many small groups from the southern suburbs of Los Angeles joined in, although this sparked numerous disputes with rival gangs such as the Athens Park Boys, the Bishops, the Pirus and the LA Brims. The major expansion of the Crips' activities came with the arrival of a highly addictive substance called crack, a chemical derivative from cocaine but cheaper to make and therefore cheaper on the streets. The 1980s and 1990s saw the Crips use the vast amount of cash generated from the sale of crack to fund a growing range of illegal activities, although distributing and selling drugs remains their primary business. Gangland killings have became commonplace as gangs use more guns and greater violence, even though Williams and several other leaders have tried to broker peace between the various factions. Several years earlier, a feud had broken out between two rival Crips gangs and the Piru Street Boys decided that being part of the Crips was not for them. After long discussions, the Piru gang broke away from the Crips and started a new organization, which was to be called the Bloods. Rivalry between these two criminal enterprises has terrorized the streets of Los Angeles ever since.

Many popular west coast rappers have had close links with the various organized criminal outfits and especially the Crips gangs. The best known is probably Snoop Dogg who was formerly a member of the Rollin 20 Crips from Long Beach. Others include Daz Dillinger, MC Eiht and Jayo Felony, and now many young rappers, who have never set foot in Los Angeles, write lyrics claiming to be Crips members or use much of the vocabulary of the gangsters. Some of these lyrics use abbreviations and street talk to get messages across, an example being the reference to 'C', which is short for Crips. On WC's song 'The Street', he and Snoop Dogg rap about the C-walk's popularity in the mainstream, outlining the fact that this is a dance for Crips members only. On the business side, several Crips gangs have also developed relationships with other gangsters in the South American country of Belize. They had been using middle-men for their drug shipments, but wanted greater control over the timing, quantity and quality of the illegal substances concerned. It was to become a highly and mutually beneficial relationship as Belize was a very poor country, but had easy access to opium and other raw ingredients essential for the production of heroin, cocaine, crack and other drugs. The groups working in Belize could not grow enough to meet the demand from the Crips and soon they started importing from Colombia, Panama, Venezuela and other neighbouring countries. Drugs ready for the street would be shipped across the Mexican border into Texas, California and Florida, or be placed on boats for the relatively short trip. Some even went via Cuba and the West Indies. After several years many of those involved in Belize used their cash reserves to set up their own operations in Los Angeles, New York and other cities, further adding to the cultural mix of the drug trade.

The initiation ceremony to become a fully fledged member varied from gang to gang and is certainly not like the formal, quiet Mafia version. The most usual is for the new entrant to have to commit a crime, while being watched by other members of the gang – the more serious or clever the undertaking, the higher standing that individual will gain at the outset. Many gang are nervous of new members as the police authorities right across America have tried to infiltrate the gangs in this way – but to date without much success. New members usually have a six-month vetting process, where they only get involved in minor activities and see very little of the enterprise or the bosses. This is clearly an apprenticeship by any other name. Many gangs have no female members at all; those that do usually have similar initiation ceremonies, or, it is rumoured, new female members have to have sex with several of the gang's leaders. For the most part, women are kept on the periphery of decision-making and of the organization generally, although many turn out to be highly successful on the streets, dealing drugs.

Born in New Orleans, Louisiana, Stanley Williams moved to a poor Los Angeles suburb when he was six years old, getting into scrapes from the word go. Many have taken Tookie to be a nickname, but it is, in fact, his real middle name. He was sometimes given the nickname 'Big Took' by close associates. Certainly, he was big for his age growing up and he matured physically very early in his teens, becoming very well built indeed by the time he left school. He was suspected of many murders and of co-ordinating drug trafficking for many years, but nothing would stick. However, he was arrested for the murder of Albert Owens, Yen-Yi Yang, Tsai-Shai Lin and Yee-Chen Lin and received the death penalty in 2005. The last three were killed in the notorious Brookhaven Motel incident. At 5.00 a.m. on 11 March 1979 Stanley Williams entered the motel lobby and broke down the door to the office. The Yang family, seventy-six-year-old Yen-Yi Yang and his wife, Tsai-Shai Yang, immigrants from Taiwan, were asleep in bed. They ran the motel along with their forty-three-year-old daughter, Yu-Chin Yang Lin. Williams ripped open the cash register but was interrupted in the robbery. He shot all three people and got away with the contents – the princely sum of one hundred dollars.

The prosecution in the case removed three African-Americans from the jury and there were claims that the trial was grossly unfair. The District Attorney held firm and Williams was convicted on all counts. The case went to the appeal court but they too, returned a guilty verdict. As inmate number C29300, Williams spent much of his time in solitary confinement for many assaults on guards and fellow inmates. There were many signatories to a petition for clemency, which eventually received a hearing from California Governor Arnold Schwarzenеggar, who denied the plea stating that this was based on the 'totality of circumstances'. At San Quentin State Prison, Tookie Williams was executed by lethal injection on 13 December amid a great debate over the whole issue of California's controversial stance on capital punishment and whether his anti-gang stance while in prison should have been acknowledged with a reduced sentence. Williams, though, to his dying day continued to refuse to help the authorities with their investigations into Los Angeles gangland.

The other co-founder of the Crips was Raymond 'Truck' Washington, who came from the eastern side of Los Angeles and was just fifteen years old when the gang was formed. He had been part of a group calling themselves the 'Baby Avenues' for several years but now wanted to emulate his older colleagues. This gang merged with some new people and became the Avenue Boys, since they claimed their turf was the bustling Central Avenue in East Los Angeles. This is where Washington first met Stanley Williams as they did work for several other bigger gangs, most notably the influential Black Panthers. The men had a strong understanding from the start and would soon persuade many others to join them. However, it was also a highly destructive relationship, which did not meet with much success on the street. In the autumn of 1971, the Avalon Garden Crips and the Ingelwood Crips joined forces with the aim of expanding into new areas – non-Crips areas. The LA Brims from the west side of the city were powerful but were not part of the Crips empire, so the other gangs were reserved about asking them to a planned meeting. However, they knew if these individuals were going to expand into new things, they would need a strong network to fight the other gangs. The Pirus also had a history and good contacts. They had had a major falling out with the Crips from Compton but managed to survive with most of their gang intact. At the discussion, held on Pirus Street, the numbers were swelled by other gangs including the Athens Park Boys, the Pueblos and the Denver Lanes. A common theme was that the Crips organization had too much power and too great a say over how they ran their gangs and the drug business in California. At the time, the colour adopted by their gang did not seem important but they decided they needed to differentiate themselves from the Crips in public. They would wear red and create a united front called the Bloods, a strong group where all individual gangs would share information, protect each other and come together to form a drug dealing network from new sources.

The Bloods can usually be identified by their red-coloured garments, bandanas and 'chucks' (sneakers or training shoes) worn by gang members. The Bloods are more racially mixed than the Crips and have also branched out right across America. Much like their rivals, they are strongly dependent on drugs for much of their revenue although they are known also to be heavily involved in smuggling, extortion and prostitution as well. They also have a strong affinity with the music business – Death Row Records has employed a number of known Bloods members and it is thought that it has strong ties with the gang. The Bloods flatly refuse to use the letter 'C' in names, especially when it is a capital due to the use of that letter by the Crips. Instead, they insert a 'K' after the 'C' to create a distinction. Formed in 1993, the United Blood Nation, often known as the East Coast Bloods, have attracted some of the most violent and charismatic villains from New York and surrounding areas in particular. This offshoot started life in the New York City penal system as a prison gang and its trademark tactic was to slash the face of anyone who gets in their way with a knife or razor blade. Within a few years eight different gangs were created within the Bloods network across New York alone: the Mad Stone Villains (MSV); the Valentine Bloods (VB); the Blood Stone Villains (BSV); Sex, Money and Murder (SMM); the Hit Squad Brims (HSB); the Nine Trey Gangsters (NTG); the Gangster Killer Bloods (GKB); and, the One Eight Trey (183) Bloods. Much of their supply of illegal substances came from their affiliation with the Los Angeles gangs and their number has grown to rival some of the traditional Italian families in that part of the world.

By the latter stages of the 1990s, thousands of new members had been recruited and a formidable street-fighting force had been established. One of their major problems, a result of their loose structure, was that there was little or no co-operation between the rival east and west coast groups. The Bloods had become a favourite target for law enforcement officials because of their new-found strength in numbers and their ultra-violent behaviour. As a result many of the individual gang leaders called for a meeting. This took place in 1999 and a new bond was formed between the operations, called the United Blood Nation. They also used the term 'Damu' for their new alliance, which means blood in the Swahili language. Blood members often refer to themselves as 'dawgs' (dogs), and burn a triangular shape on their upper arm, which can look a bit like the outline of a dog's paw. Some new members create three circular burns on their arm with a cigarette or have a tattoo created of a dog with the acronym MOB – Member of Blood or Money Over Bitches.

Los Angeles and New York were typical in many ways of other major cities across the length and breadth of the American criminal landscape. One thing that was similar was that law enforcement officials were getting smarter and the big drug gangs relied on their network of street dealers to sell their expensive and highly dangerous goods. One novel approach was taken by the Chambers Brothers, who, having grown up in Arkansas, moved to Detroit, where they made sure that their dealers' network was much lower key. The four brothers, Billie Joe, Willie, Otis and Larry, realized that the less conspicuous the dealer the better, and that they should not try to draw attention to themselves with flashy jewellery, distinctive clothes or load music. The other interesting part was recruitment – they would go down to small towns, often in the Mississippi delta, and employ typically sixteen- to eighteen-year-old boys for a month. The boys would be told what they were selling and what they would be paid for four weeks work – often more than they could make in six months in local employment. They were then shipped up to Detroit and were made to live in squalid conditions and often work round the clock to meet their targets. Once a month-long tour of duty had been completed, the boys would usually be told to head back south with their cash. This would help to ensure that 'fresh' faces were on the front line at all times.

While exanding their operations, the focus of drug-related criminal gangs in the USA had been the inner cities. However, the most recent trend and something that is perhaps even more dangerous is that gangs have now shifted some of their network to rural suburbs and small towns. Although the potential market is much smaller, the fight against the local police force, often poorly trained in this field, is much easier. One of the very disturbing consequences is the associated violence that comes with this shift – nowhere now seems truly safe from the tentacles of drug-related crime. In a survey carried out by the US Department of Justice in 2001, 20 per cent of students aged between twelve and eighteen reported that street gangs had been present at their school during the past six months. Recruiting teenage dealers also seems to be straightforward – many street traders in crack alone can make $500 a day, which is a lot more than they could ever make in a regular job.

The Bloods and the Crips don't have things all their own way on the streets of Los Angeles or of other major cities, and gang-on-gang violence remains at high levels. In the mid-1980s, a Latino student threw a punch at a newly arrived Cambodian immigrant. This fairly innocuous incident led to the growing number of Cambodians forming their first LA-based gang, which was called the Tiny Rascal Gang (often referred to as TRG). They are generally small in stature and the benefits of a tight-knit gang have helped them to develop illegal activities such as extortion, home invasion robberies, burglaries, car theft, drug dealing, and murder. The TRG are generally less mobile it terms of where they operate than other gangs and focus very much on their small patch, but they have a fearsome reputation. There was another watershed moment in the late 1980s when a carload of TRG members pulled alongside a group of Latinos. There was a history of rivalry and the insults flew until one of the Asians pulled out a gun and opened fire into the crowd. Only one member of the opposing gang was killed, a sixteen-year-old by the name of Oswaldo Carbajal, but it was enough to spark a feud that would last for years and claim the lives of five young men the following year and twenty-one over the next three years. In a recruitment drive, the TRG now accepts non-Cambodians, usually local people needing protection, and mixed race Asian women, who often get late-night drug-selling duties.

The fight against drug-related crimes involves all law enforcement agencies, as drug dealing lies at the root of a great deal of violence and illegal activities. In February and March 2006, a two-week operation mounted by the Department of Homeland Security succeeded in arresting 375 men wanted in twenty-three different countries. Operation Community Shield, as it was called, differed from other crackdowns in that for the first time federal authorities made use of immigration and customs authorities in an attempt to dismantle what they call 'transnational, violent street gangs'. Although this was obviously good news, the number of arrests will have made barely a dent in the ranks of the estimated three-quarters of a million gang members involved in drug-dealing in the USA.

At the beginning of 2006, the FBI succeeded in breaking up part of the Crips drug distribution chain with the Medellín cartel in Colombia. Three people were arrested while a further three remain at large, but valuable information was gained in this undercover sting operation. It had been estimated that the Crips were importing 400 kilograms of cocaine a month from the Medellín cartel alone and much of it came in via Mexico. A police report from Trenton, New Jersey, on 21 June 2006 announced that a major manhunt was under way for the killer of an eleven-year-old boy. He had been shot in a drive-by shooting, allegedly the result of gangland tension between the Crips and the Bloods. Apparently feelings had been running high for several months following a confrontation in a Philadelphia nightclub and the drive-by was the most recent incident in an escalation of violence. Sadly, this is far from an isolated incident, or police report – it is something that has become part of the social fabric of US life.

Law Enforcement

In any examination of gangs and gangsters, it is important to consider the people who are trying to catch them: the police officers, both in uniform and undercover, and the special agents, all of whom risk their lives to uphold law and order. A tiny percentage of the police force actually get involved with major criminals and organized crime, as most officers are kept busy handling day-to-day neighbourhood issues, the bread-and-butter of law enforcement. However, most countries now have a law enforcement department which specializes in tracking and attempting to minimize organized crime. Given the international nature of organized crime, this has become a highly specialized task and one which requires constant international co-operation. What individual police forces are able to achieve is dependent on many factors: financial resources available for recruitment and special training, the political will to crack down on gang crime, and the quality of leadership – as anywhere, having strong, dependable and forthright leadership inspires confidence and the ability to achieve more.

Just as the development of the gangs themselves offers a fascinating history, so too has the development of attempts by law enforcement agencies to deal with the scourge of organized crime. The UK was the first country to have an official police force: the Peelers, named after Sir Robert Peel who had done so much to push for full-time, paid policemen. In 1829, the Metropolitan Police Act which provided for a permanent force of paid constables was passed by the House of Commons. The first 1,000 Peelers were dressed in blue tailcoats and top hats, so as not to look too different from ordinary citizens of the time. Each Peeler carried a wooden truncheon, a pair of handcuffs and a wooden rattle. A whistle eventually replaced the rattle for raising the alarm but not until the 1880s. Petty crime was rife on the streets of London at that time and the police force had an immediate impact.

In the 1920s and 1930s, during the era of the great American gangsters, fighting organized crime was made harder by severely limited resources. The Great Depression restricted the numbers of police officers that could be employed, it limited the equipment that they had access to, which meant that they were unable to respond swiftly when crimes had been committed. It must have been a tremendously difficult time to be a policeman in major cities like Chicago, New York and Boston, knowing that gangsters had the upper hand in the form of faster cars and better weapons.

One early policeman worthy of special note is Matthew Leach. He was a captain in the Indiana State Police during the heyday of the Dillinger gang. In the summer of 1933, with just about the entire state's police force, forty-two men in total, he set trap after trap to catch this much feared public enemy. Although coming close on three separate occasions, the police never succeeded in capturing Dillinger and his gang members. On one occasion John Dillinger even called Leach on the phone to taunt him about his failure to capture him. Radical action was required and 530 National Guard troops were mobilized and a volunteer posse formed to help track and capture the ruthless gang. Finally, Dillinger and his fellow gangsters were cornered and arrested in Tucson, Arizona, and Leach travelled there himself to oversee the extradition. On arrival, Dillinger greeted him politely, although Harry Pierpoint (who had, in fact, been the group's leader all along) personally threatened Leach because he had been responsible for putting Pierpoint's mother in jail. Leach told a horde of waiting reporters the news and this story, stating, 'There's a man who cares about his mother.'

The FBI grew in stature and its remit was expanded during this gangster heyday – a national police force had arguably never been more essential than during the interwar years in the USA. The FBI began life as the Bureau of Investigation, subsequently changed to the Division of Investigation, before settling on its current name in 1935. Its motto is 'Fidelity, Bravery, and Integrity' and, as an indication of its importance, its budget in the fiscal year 2003 totalled almost $4.3 billion. The political will to support a strong police presence has certainly been evident in America for virtually the entire twentieth century, but since recent developments in global terrorism, this has moved up a gear. It is difficult to know whether these terrorist acts have helped or hindered the major gangs, which carry out huge organized crimes – many people believe that perhaps the law enforcement agencies have had their hands full and have been forced to turn something of a blind eye towards organized crime.

The structure of British and American policing was sound from the outset, a credit to many of its early founders and visionaries. Japan, on the other hand, was a very different place and held very different views. The Ministry of Home Affairs created the *Keihoryo* (Police Bureau) in 1874, but it was not centralized and properly organized until after the Second World War. The role of the police encompassed a range of unusual services and extra duties, making them more like wardens. In the late 1940s, what were then seen as non-police functions such as fire-fighting and the upkeep of general health and sanitation services were moved to other administrative departments. Trying to battle the Yakuza while unblocking drains and carrying around the proverbial hosepipe must have been quite a challenge. In 1954, the law was reformed in several ways. While the Public Safety Commission aims and objectives were reinforced – protecting life, persons and property of the nation, investigating crimes, arresting suspects and maintaining public peace and order – a new chairman of the National Public Safety Commission was appointed, a Minister of State. This made public peace the responsibility of the national government. Many authorities have wrestled with the respective roles of state and local jurisdiction and, therefore, who should be responsible for which level of policing. History has shown us that there is probably no definitive right or wrong to this debate but what is important is that local and national forces communicate at every level to combat crime effectively.

The Russian political system and its various key figures over the years have had a very different attitude towards policing from most other places, some of them highly unusual.

For many years the Soviet KGB (the *Komitet Gosudarstvennoj Bezopasnosti* or Committee for State Security) kept a close eye on the whole population, especially those who had visitors 'from the West'. The supposed competence of the Soviet secret police is largely a myth; the KGB was incredibly incompetent even though it was so powerful. It must have spent inordinate amounts of money watching people to no good purpose – the wages of agents and informers; expensive, imported wire-tapping equipment; the analysis of data.

There was something almost comic about KGB activities, though the outcome of their activities was often tragic enough. One KGB informer by the name of Vladimir Lakeyev (which means 'lackey' in Russian) kindly offered himself to usher people in to the birthday party of a subject who was being observed, offering himself as a 'lackey', in fact. By ushering people in and announcing their names, he was able to compile a full list of all the guests at the party.

This had been a favourite method of the Czarist secret police, a hundred years before, who had assumed that only the closest of friends would come to a birthday party. And while the KGB were using laughably out-of-date methods, the manuscripts of dissident writers were being successfully smuggled out of the country and published in the West.

Perhaps the biggest difference between the various police authorities in Russia and many other forces around the world is secrecy. The former KGB is now known as the FSB, a throwback to the Soviet days in that it is able to operate under an official blanket whenever it wishes. In the 1990s, when General Vladimir Smirnov, a regional chief of the FSB, was asked about the organization, he stated, 'It is a special comradeship of people knowing about each other that they have devoted their best years to protecting the Motherland's security.'

In 1918, the jury system was all but abolished in the USSR and it was not until 1995 that any form of open trial process with judge and jury was seen again. This was an experimental phase and only a small number of regions were allowed to participate. The new system caused a number of difficulties as the protocol for judges was quite unusual compared with Western practices: before announcing a verdict and passing sentence, judges had still to consult political officials. In 1996, 99½ per cent of people tried under the old system were found guilty compared with around 80 per cent under the new dispensation.

According to Russian criminal procedure, capital punishment is restricted to only the most severe crimes, such as terrorism and murder, and no woman or child under the age of eighteen can be sentenced to death. The number of executions has dropped markedly in the recent past. A Pardons Commission was set up for the first time in 1991, although this was disbanded in 1996 despite the protests of many international human rights organizations and campaigners. Also Russia's membership in 1996 of the Council of Europe requires them to do away with the death penalty. Even if this is officially agreed it is impossible to be entirely sure that some of the old habits and practices of the USSR will not resurface at some point.

Law enforcement officers are generally only as good as

the law allows. The judicial process in most develops over time, which while it can offer measure of consistency, it can also leave gaps. On 2005 in a smart restaurant in Las Vegas, memb local police force assisted by FBI arrested former police detectives Louis Eppolito and Stephen Caracappa. They were both charged with murder, attempted murder, conspiracy, obstruction of justice, money laundering and drug distribution. According to the prosecution team, both men had been paid by the mob. This was no surprise to some as Eppolito's father was a life-long Mafia man. The time it had taken to assemble the evidence was not on the authorities' side as a statute of limitation of only five years was applicable in such a case. However, the federal prosecutors were not going to be easily deterred, and in February 2006 they filed new documents in court relating to a host of new charges. In Louis Eppolito's autobiography *Mafia Cops* he recalls, 'I kept a sawn-off shotgun in my locker for just such occasions. It fitted snugly under the folds of my trench coat. I spotted Frankie sitting at a card table, walked up behind him, stuck the barrel in his mouth and ordered him to his feet, "Bye motherfucker," was all I said. As I backed him into a wall I watched the stain in his pants get bigger and bigger. Suddenly I knew what it felt like to be my father. I was walking like a wiseguy, talking like a wiseguy . . . I cocked both barrels. "Please," he begged, "please." For one instant, I had this wonderful, heady urge to pull the trigger.'

There is a saying that where there is power, there is corruption and that absolute power corrupts absolutely. This is not always the case when it comes to law enforcement, but the US legal system is littered with cases of abuse and corruption. The USA is by no means the only place to have these problems; they appear to a greater or lesser extent all over the world. Some say we must expect this to happen, that it is just part of human nature. Others believe the better and more transparent the system, the less chance there is of injustice.

South Africa has had its share of scandals and court cases in its eventful history. The South African Police Service (SAPS) traces its roots back as far as the early Dutch settlers in the seventeenth century. The South African Police Force, the SAPS's forerunner, had close ties to the South African Army and would call on the military in emergencies. In most countries, the police are at pains to distance themselves from the military, but in South Africa prior to 1994 this was not the case. In 1948, when the National Party won a close-run election, the police were permitted to arm themselves to a greater extent than before, especially when facing hostile crowds. In 1965, the powers of the police were strengthened further when they were given the ability to stop and search any person, vehicle, aircraft, home or premises in certain regions without a warrant. They could also confiscate any belongings they wished without recourse.

In 1990, much changed in South Africa. The President Frederik Willem de Klerk rescinded the ban on political organizations representing black people and released from prison many leading black figures. A subsequent meeting of the regional heads of the police had the aim of reducing hostility towards the police by demonstrating greater tolerance; although this was accepted in theory, in practice things were slow to change. White police officers were, in general, ambivalent about how law and order would be maintained given the tremendous social changes taking place. Apartheid had been one of the cornerstones of the policing mentality and there had been little effective monitoring of police activities for years. For many of the rank and file of the law enforcement community, the end of apartheid had brought about an abrupt change. Black and white officers were now being trained alongside each other – a first in South Africa. In addition, outside police training experts were hired to increase the overall standard of service and, crucially, to improve race relations, both wit police service and in the police's dealings with th munity. New training regimes now included aspects defence, weapons handling, criminal investigation processes, inspections, law and public relations. More specialized areas, like riot control, management skills and detective work, were left to an elite within the police service. Police officers on duty carried, as a matter of course, a Z88 9mm pistol, a truncheon and often an R-5 rifle in their vehicle. In the face of hostile crowds, police would also have access to Browning semi-automatic and Beretta pump-action shotguns, semi-automatic rifles, water cannons, tear gas dispensers and barbed wire-laying vehicles. Many observers felt that these were a legacy from the past and that the police had at their disposal enough firepower to prosecute a small war, rather than disperse an unruly crowd. A complete rethink of the role of the police service in South Africa also considered its size. The 91,000 personnel, which included administrative and support staff in 1991, was increased by 1993 to 110,000 and 140,000 two years later. The Minister for Law and Order at that time, Hernus Kriel, also set up the first ever official ombudsman to investigate allegations of police misbehaviour and although this was completely inadequately resourced, it was a valuable step in the right direction. Things had changed and further changes, although not always easy to implement, accelerated the process of revising the whole remit of law enforcement. South Africa does have some unique policing issues but public confidence in the force is vital to the maintenance of law and order in a way which is just and equitable for all.

The Western Australian Police are responsible for an area of 2.5 million square kilometres (approximately 1.6 million square miles). This is the largest single police jurisdiction in the world apart from larger countries where a national police force is responsible for the entire country. With a current force level of around 5,000, this means that each officer has on average 500 square kilometres (over 300 square miles) to cover. This highlights the difficulty of policing such a large area, particularly given that in parts of Australia a high proportion of incidents happen in small, remote and inaccessible places. Beginning in 1894, the trickle of convicts deported from the UK to Australia became a steady flow. This forced migration lasted for a little over twenty years, but it planted the seed that grew to be modern Australia. The first big step in establishing a local police presence came in 1829 when Captain Stirling was appointed Sheriff. He had control over a newly established High Constable, constables in the field, bailiffs and surveyors of roadways. Early colonial policemen were recruited by magistrates only and worked part-time, getting paid for specific tasks such as serving a summons rather than being on hand to deal with problems as they arose. In a radical move at the time, the Criminal Investigation Department appointed its first female officer in 1921.

Citizens from many Far Eastern countries have been heading to Australia for many years and controlling illegal immigration remains a big issue for the authorities, especially as many leading gangs have sought to build a strong presence there. China and its Triad organizations represent a significant threat to many countries of the Pacific Rim, although the problems of law enforcement in China itself are quite different. The Republic of China's own police force has seen an interesting development, having for years not published a great deal about its organization. It is split into three parts, the first being the People's Armed Police forces (PAP), which is a paramilitary force primarily concerned with domestic security. The PAP was created in 1983, taking responsibility from the People's Liberation Army for internal security, border patrols, guarding prisons, executioners and a tactical counter-terrorism unit. The second is the Public Ministry of Security (MPS) which takes charge of day-to-day policing matters at a local level. Its criminal law activities cover investigation, apprehension, interrogation and detention and it boasts records of all people living in the country, split into regions. One section of the MPS is the secret police which employs agents, informants and a network of roving spies to gather information on suspicious people. It is difficult to know exactly how effective this force is and what exactly its aims are in relation to organized crime, but it is not generally viewed as having a major impact.

The third and last unit is the Hong Kong Police Force, which has for many years been considered excellent at keeping pace with modern criminal detection methods. Formed in 1844, the force has grown from those humble days of thirty-five full-timers and has for most of its life operated under British common law. Hong Kong is prone to natural disasters, suffering from high winds, rains and flooding, but these afflictions pale into insignificance against the effort required to maintain an effective force against organized gangs in that part of the world. Hong Kong is a major piece in the Far East crime jigsaw – many large, modern international gangsters need to operate in Hong Kong if they are to have a network in this part of the world. It is the gateway that provides access to a market greater than the seven million residents of Hong Kong itself. Two officials were needed to conduct a criminal investigation rather than a lone policeman or women as in many areas. They were required to show proper identification and inform the accused of the alleged crime or criminal act. Only in 1980 were these laws revised allowing the police to conduct an emergency search without a warrant. Also at this time, the police were able to intercept incoming and outgoing mail and order an autopsy when the cause of death was in doubt. Police officers were expected to act as role models and promote desirable behaviour while conducting their neighbourhood duties, something that must at times have been difficult to do while trying to uphold the law.

Law enforcement agencies and police forces clearly have different remits and requirements, different demands on their time and different tasks to perform. They are subject to political changes and fluctuations in funding, although with growing media attention and the evolving nature of many criminal acts, the resources brought to bear in fighting organized gang crime vary considerably from country to country, which brings its own problems as effective policing against major gangsters is now an international business. Gangs like the Yardies in the UK import drugs from a number of the Colombian cartels as well as from other places in the world. They use a whole host of contacts in different locations to source illegal substances, order and transport the finished goods. To provide a truly effective force against gangs like the Yardies, police forces need to co-operate to combat all aspects of this highly dangerous distribution chain. Interpol has a strong role to play but it is the police units within each country which need to work directly to try to reduce these kinds of crimes. It is unlikely that significant progress will be made in the fight against organized crime until a worldwide force is set up and funded by many countries, thereby harmonizing goals, objectives and methods.

Conclusion

Getting involved in organized crime is seen by some people as a way of escaping poverty and hardship, or it is seen as a glamorous road to a better life. In the same way that many sporting pastimes such as boxing, tennis, golf and baseball have helped people to amass great wealth and attain a lifestyle which they could not otherwise have hoped to achieve, so too can becoming a gangster. Far from making a hard and fast decision on a particular day, most gangsters seem to have got involved in gangs at an early age and then progressed, almost as if they were rising up through the ranks of an army. The question of what motivates people to become involved in gangs has been the stuff of many enquiring newspaper articles and much analysis, although less interest has been directed at the area of organized crime. So the question arises as to whether money is, in fact, the sole or primary reason for people to become gangsters. Research seems to suggest that money is far from being the only driving force as many criminals continue to kill, rob and carry out illegal activities long after they have more money than they can spend in their lifetime. There are other influences and factors at work and to understand these fully, we also need to look at other aspects of human behaviour.

Many leading businessmen, often seen by society as pillars of their communities, continue to work at a furious, occasionally life-threatening pace long after it is either good for them or necessary. They have already achieved great wealth, status and all the trappings of success. The power and personal esteem generated from heading up a division, series of companies or an international corporation is tremendous and successful gangsters go through a similar mental transformation. Their power is based on a more primal street recognition, but its genesis lies in the same human need to live in the spotlight and for adulation. For many gangsters, the need for personal justification or group reward often completely overshadows the value of their own lives or the lives of the people around them. Certainly, we have seen that it is not just the gangsters themselves who are at risk, but their families, friends, associates and, often enough, innocent bystanders. The further up in a gang that a gangster progresses, the greater the likelihood of his being maimed, seriously injured or having his life cut short violently. Many of the gangsters described in this book are here because they have managed a certain longevity, which has prolonged their ruthless and violent lives to the point that there is some kind of story to tell.

There are perhaps other reasons why people join gangs in the first place, and once they are established there, the gang seems to provide an invisible pull, often taking over their lives. Many of the toughest places in the world have spawned a large number of criminals and gangsters; poverty and deprivation have led many to reach out for things beyond the law. However, we have seen many gangsters come from both good backgrounds and bad backgrounds, or having had good relationships with their parents or bad ones, but the human desire to be part of a close-knit gang of peers remains true to this day. A group is also stronger once a common goal is established; gangsters will bond together in breaking the law, joined together sometimes partly by fear. Sports fans in large groups also often behave like warriors, rampaging along streets or banding together in stadiums, sometimes almost completely out of control. Many of the members of such a mob, taken individually, would not behave in the same way at all; many of them, when interviewed have said that they do not understand how they have ended up behaving in the way that they have done. Many gangsters believe that they are involved in some kind of war, fighting not only the people who want to lock them up, but also the rival groups who want to kill them. Anyone who has listened to soldiers who have fought together knows something of the special, close bond that they have for those who have fought alongside them in situations of great danger. Many gangsters have similar feelings for their comrades who have been through, in many cases, equally dangerous situations with them. This kind of fellow feeling, too, has helped to keep gangs together and further enhance their aims and objectives.

There have been some common themes over the last century within organized crime, with prostitution, smuggling, human trafficking and extortion all having remained standards of gang activities. But the largest single trend has been the increase in the size of the global drug trade. It now dwarfs all other criminal activities and is the fuel which drives much gangland activity all over the world. The profits of the drug trade are staggering and its impact on overall crime has not been equalled since the days of Prohibition in the USA. The US authorities have tried to lead the way in the fightback against drugs with a two-pronged strategy. Firstly, they have attempted to cut the supply of drugs; this has meant getting involved in those parts of the world where the raw materials for various drugs are grown and processed. The involvement of US officials in Mexico, Colombia and other central and South American countries angers many people, but many argue that it has had at least some success in reducing the flow of drugs to the USA. All countries face similar issues in terms of how big shipments get into their country, but those with longer or more porous borders do face a more significant problem. The second part of the US government strategy to tackle the drug problem has been a very public campaign to try to reduce the demand for illegal substances – arguably this has been less effective as the numbers of both the hard core of addicts and of recreational drug-users continues to rise. Tougher sentencing for street dealers and people trafficking drugs has been seen as a step in the right direction, though many point to the already overcrowded prisons as a deleterious consequence of this. Jamming them with yet more drug-related convictions will probably only mean that inmates guilty of other offences will be let out sooner. Perhaps special prisons need to be built just for drug criminals – institutions that provide a visible deterrent to getting involved in the drug trade. Certainly, it is essential that all governments should get on top of drug-related crime, and soon, because wherever drugs are bought and sold, violent, gun-related crime is never far behind.

All gangsters appear to be able to cope with danger, extreme violence, bloodshed and killing, seemingly without reservartion or remorse. Normal people, confronted with similar things, would experience emotional trauma and personal conflict, but somehow gangsters are able to carry on with everyday activities, bringing up children or going to the movies, knowing that they can face incredible atrocities and brutality within hours or even minutes. Perhaps many gangsters are able to put these things even further from their minds and to run their large empires as if nothing untoward were going on. Some gangs are more ferocious and brutal than others, but all gangsters seem to have the ability to resort to extreme violence when they deem it necessary. At some point in every gangster's life, he confronts a critical point, one which sorts the everyday criminals from the hardened gangsters. It is at that stage that the decision whether to use violence or even murder, becomes critical. This decision affects the status of that person in the gang, and often the whole gang's reputation as well as establishing which path the group will go down. Many gangsters have admitted that these situations of extreme danger and high levels of excitement act like a drug. If they perceive their normal life to be boring or mundane, then perhaps the incredible adrenaline rush of crime and violence acts as a fix for them.

High-tech crime has probably been the largest growth area since the start of the 1990s and many of the largest gangs in America, Europe, Russia and beyond employ some of the best minds in this field. The opportunities for gangsters to divert large sums of money into their own accounts, to order goods online without paying for them legitimately, to take part in internet gambling scams, to sell goods which they do not own by auction, to run pornographic websites are plentiful. The FBI and Pentagon have both suffered embarrassing lapses in computer security when potentially very sensitive information could have been accessed, stolen and sold on the open market. Large corporations are also becoming increasingly vulnerable to cybergangsters as the the business world becomes more and more closely intertwined with technology and the internet. The other key issue to do with organized crime in cyberspace has to do with the law – something created or transacted in a virtual world often falls between national jurisdictions and the police authorities of different countries. Often scams and illegal acts are difficult to trace back to one particular country and therefore the question of who has the responsibility to arrest and convict these fraudsters is muddled. It is also a world where the development of new and appropriate legislation is lagging behind, which adds to the opportunities for large gangs to profit from high-tech internet crime.

Some people rise naturally to become leaders within gangs and subsequent power struggles sort out who will take the big decisions and lead the criminal empire into the future. Few gangs are very democratic by nature and the range of activities that a gang gets involved in can come down to the attitude of just one or two people. For many years most of the big Mafia families of New York tried to operate a no drugs policy. Younger mobsters on the make saw the opporunity and that stance was bound to change. There is no doubt that, in many parts of the world, the growing levels of affluence have led to increase of opportunities for organized criminals. Some crimes are responses to more obvious opportunities than others, while some are undoubtedly worse than others. For many years, the Sicilian Mafia used to tax young lovers throughout Italy. A man wanting to take a girl out would be required to guarantee their safety by paying a levy called 'the price of a candle'. The Mafia have also been known to take advantage of their religion by manufacturing large quantities of fake Catholic artefacts and selling them in the USA.

As recently as July 2006, there were allegations in the press that the online betting company Betonsports had had links to the Bonanno crime family. The company once shared the same address, the same technical support and the same legal representative as Safe Deposit Sports (SDS), a company linked to the New York crime family. SDS was part of an illegal gambling ring that generated millions of dollars of profit for the Bonanno family, according to US prosecutors. SDS was based in Costa Rica, the home of Betonsports' founder, Gary Kaplan. It is believed that the investigation into SDS and other companies using Costa Rica based firms to get around US laws may have brought about the prosecution of Betonsports. In May 2005, the US authorities charged thirty-six people linked with SDS with running an illegal gambling operation that had netted $360 million over more than two years.

It is at least conceivable that some gangs may be formed with good intentions – to fight against political corruption, or dishonest local civil servants who have diverted the course of justice, or untrustworthy landlords, or hostile groups attempting to extort money, or local officials who have absconded with large amounts of public cash. However, research seems to suggest that while some gangs may start off in this way, most of them are soon attempting to operate outside of the law. It is certainly true that years of political oppression or of living under foreign occupation can drive ordinary people to a life of crime in an attempt to right the wrong that they have experienced. Empires built by the British, Greeks, Romans, French and, more recently, the

Russians have certainly driven many people to perpetrate criminal acts, but much of this criminal behaviour is the result of attempts to survive rather than a desire to do wrong per se. One of the problems facing many police forces is that revenge, vendettas and restoring honour can drive young men to extreme acts and once one bad act has occurred it sets off a whole chain of others. These could certainly be seen as quite basic, primal emotions and reactions, untroubled by their implications. Gangsters often try to keep their acts secret, but it is not in the nature of all gangsters to behave in this way, which has certainly led to the downfall of a number of gangsters. It certainly seems possible for a tendency to gangsterism to be passed down from one generation to the next, with fathers inducting sons into the 'family business'.

The archetypal gangster is probably the image established in the USA in the 1920s and 1930s: a man wearing a pin-striped suit with wide lapels, spats and a trilby, and carrying a smoking machine gun, much the way Hollywood has encouraged us to remember them, in fact. Today's gangsters look different, they act differently and are, in many cases, in very different businesses: no longer bootlegging moonshine in the face of Prohibition, but defrauding people and institutions in cyberspace. The global supply and demand for illegal substances of all kinds has overtaken all other criminal acts by its sheer scale. There will always be small-time hoods who run illicit gambling, human smuggling, counterfeiting, prostitution, robbery, extortion and other scams but police forces have improved immeasurably in detecting these kinds of crimes and laws now offer better support for arresting and imprisoning such gangsters. The real threat today comes from large multinational gangs who have the cash reserves to take on whole governments and who are able to benefit from global markets for many of their goods and services. These gangs are usually more violent and often more ruthless in the pursuit of their aims. Although gangsters have changed appearances over the last hundred years, the opportunities to amass vast new wealth and to wield power on the streets of the world's cities has arguably never been greater. For these reasons alone it is unlikely that we will see a substantial reduction in gang-related crime in the foreseeable future.

Further Reading

Ambrose, Stephen E. and Immerman, Richard H., *Ike's Spies*

Balsamo, William and Carpozi Jr, George, *Crime, Inc: The Inside Story of the Mafia's First 100 Years*

Barnoze, Joseph R., with Messick, Hank, *Barboza*

Barrow Marie with Steele, Phillip, *The Family Story of Bonnie and Clyde*

Bergreen, Laurence, *Capone: The Man and the Era*

Blum, Howard, *Gangland: How the FBI Broke the Mob*

Blum, Howard, *The Reluctant Don*

Blumenthal, Ralph (foreword), *The Gotti Tapes*

Campbell, John, *The Underworld*

Campbell, Rodney, *The Luciano Project: The Secret Wartime Collaboration of the Mafia and the US Navy*

Cepeci, Jerry and Mustain, Gene, *Gotti: Rise and Fall*

Carpozi Jr, George, *Bugsy*

Dentry, Brian, *A Brief Look at the Japanese Yakuza*

Edmonds, Andy, *Bugsy's Baby: The Secret Life of Mob Queen Virginia Hill*

Eisenberg, Dennis, Dan, Uri and Landau, Eli, *Meyer Lansky: Mogul of the Mob*

Eppolito, Louise, *Mafia Cop*

Franceshini, Remo, *A Matter of Honor*

Fry, Colin, *The Kray Files*

Hill, Peter B. E., *The Japanese Mafia: Yakuza, Law and the State*

Hinton, Ted, *Ambush*

Jennings, Dean, *We Only Kill Each Other: The Life and Bad Times of Bugsy Siegel*

Johnson, Adam, *Yakuza: Past and Present*

Johnson, David T., *The Japanese Way of Justice: Prosecuting Crime in Japan*

Kray, Ron, *Born Fighter*

Lacey, Robert, *Little Man: Meyer Lansky and the Gangster Life*

Lehr, Dick and O'Neill, Gerard, *The Underboss: The Rise and Fall of a Mafia Family*

Maas, Peter, *Underboss: Sammy 'The Bull' Gravano's Story of Life in the Mafia*

Morton, James, *Gangland*

Morton, James, *Gangland International*

Philips, John Neal, *Running with Bonnie and Clyde*

Ranali, Ralph, *Deadly Alliance*

Saga, Junichi, *The Gambler's Tale: A Life in Japan's Underworld*

Schott, Ian, *World Famous Gangsters*

Seymour, Christopher, *Yakuza Diary: Doing Time in the Japanese Underworld*

Sterling, Claire, *Thieves' World*

Teresa, Vincent with Renner, Thomas C., *My Life in the Mafia*

Teresa, Vincent with Renner, Thomas C., *Vinnie Teresa's Mafia*

Webb, Billy, *Running with the Krays*